Solstice Wood

Ace Books by Patricia A. McKillip

THE FORGOTTEN BEASTS OF ELD
THE SORCERESS AND THE CYGNET
THE CYGNET AND THE FIREBIRD
THE BOOK OF THE ATRIX WOLFE
WINTER ROSE
SONG FOR THE BASILISK
RIDDLE-MASTER: THE COMPLETE TRILOGY
THE TOWER AT STONY WOOD
OMBRIA IN SHADOW
IN THE FORESTS OF SERRE
ALPHABET OF THORN
OD MAGIC
SOLSTICE WOOD

Solstice Wood

PATRICIA A. McKILLIP

ACE BOOKS, NEW YORK

THE BERKLEY PUBLISHING GROUP
Published by the Penguin Group
Penguin Group (USA) Inc.
375 Hudson Street, New York, New York 10014, USA
Penguin Group (Canada), 90 Eglinton Avenue, Suite 700, Toronto, Ontario M4P 2Y3, Canada
(a division of Pearson Penguin Canada Inc.)
Penguin Books Ltd., 80 Strand, London WC2R 0RL, England
Penguin Group Ireland, 25 St. Stephen's Green, Dublin 2, Ireland (a division of Penguin Books Ltd.)
Penguin Group (Australia) 250 Camberwell Road, Camberwell, Victoria 3124, Australia
(a division of Pearson Australia Group Pty. Ltd.)
Penguin Books India Pvt. Ltd., 11 Community Centre, Panchsheel Park, New Delhi—110 017, India
Penguin Group (NZ), Cnr. Airborne and Rosedale Roads, Albany, Auckland 1310, New Zealand
(a division of Pearson New Zealand Ltd.)
Penguin Books (South Africa) (Pty.) Ltd., 24 Sturdee Avenue, Rosebank, Johannesburg 2196, South Africa

Penguin Books Ltd., Registered Offices: 80 Strand, London WC2R 0RL, England

This book is an original publication of The Berkley Publishing Group.

Copyright © 2006 by Patricia A. McKillip.
Text by Kristin del Rosario.

ACE is an imprint of The Berkley Publishing Group.
ACE and the "A" design are trademarks belonging to Penguin Group (USA) Inc.

First edition: February 2006

Library of Congress Cataloging-in-Publication Data

McKillip, Patricia A.
    Solstice wood / Patricia A. McKillip.— 1st ed.
        p. cm.
    ISBN 0-441-01366-X
        1. Young women—Fiction. 2. Grandmothers—Fiction. 3. Women—Societies and clubs—
    Fiction. I. Title.

PS3563.C38S65 2006
813'.54—dc22

                                                                                        2005054719

PRINTED IN THE UNITED STATES OF AMERICA

10   9   8   7   6   5   4   3   2

For Kate,
my other sister

And every turn led us here.
Back into these small rooms.

—*Winter Rose*

· 1 ·

Sylvia

Gram called at five in the morning. She never remembered the time difference. I was already up, sitting at the table in my bathrobe, about to take my first sip of coffee. The phone rang; my hands jerked. Coffee shot into the air, rained down on my hair and the cat, who yowled indignantly and fled. I stared at the phone as it rang again, not wanting to pick up, not wanting to know whatever it was Gram wanted me to know.

At the second ring, I heard Madison stir on my couch-bed.

"Syl?"

"I'm not answering that."

He unburied his face, squinted at me. "Why not? You having a clandestine affair?"

"It's Gram."

His head hit the pillow again on the third ring. "Is not," he mumbled. "Tell him to leave a message and come back to bed."

"I can't," I said firmly, though his naked body was exerting some serious magnetic pull. "I have to go to the store and unpack a dozen boxes of books."

"Come back for five minutes. Please? She'll leave a message."

"She won't." It rang again. "Only the weak-minded babble their business to inanimate objects."

"Hah?"

"She says."

It rang for the fifth time; I glowered at it, still not moving. I could have shown her any number of fairy tales in which important secrets imparted to a stone, to the moon, to a hole in the ground, had rescued the runaway princess, or the youngest brother, or the children lost in the wood. But Gram believed in fairies, not fairy tales, and in her world magic and machines were equally suspect.

I picked up at the sixth ring. She would have hung up at the seventh, before the machine started talking. So, in those strange moments, thousands of miles apart, we had been locked in silent argument, counting rings together.

"Sylvia," she said, before I could say hello. "I need you to come home."

She had needed me to come home for seven years. But I heard an odd hollowness, a fragility in her foghorn voice that kept me from offering her whatever was the most likely on my list of excuses: can't leave my bookstore now, everyone on vacation, am apartment-sitting, dog-sitting, fish-sitting, too busy this week, am leaving the country this month, just signed a lease for another year, I'm sorry, Gram, I'm not coming back.

"What is it? Gram?"

"It's your grandfather," she said, with that unfamiliar wobble in her deep, husky, imperious voice. "He's dead, Sylvia."

My throat closed. I had to push to get a word out. "How?"

"He wandered out in the middle of the night and fell asleep under the pear tree. I always knew he had a streak of Melior in him—roaming through hill and dale and whatnot at any hour of day or night. He didn't wake up. Hurley found him this morning lying on the grass in his nightshirt."

"I'm sorry, Gram," I whispered. I heard Madison shift again, pull himself upright to listen.

"So you'll come home."

Even then, I knew to bargain. "Of course I'll come for the funeral, but—"

"Good," she interrupted with a more familiar briskness, having heard as much as she wanted to hear.

"I won't be able to stay much longer."

"Just come." She'd figure out the rest of my life later. "As soon as you can. Today. I'll expect you for supper."

"I'll make my arrangements, Gram, and let you know when—"

But she had already hung up.

I sat there, staring numbly at the phone again, feeling that slow, painful prickling begin behind my eyes, the swell of tears that never fell. Memories swept like leaves through my head: Lynn Hall, the low, ancient mountains I'd grown up in, the fields and small villages, the endless woods. Grandpa Liam was all I knew, all I ever had, of a father. He had taught me how to tie my shoes, how to bait a hook; he knew the names of every tree and wildflower and weed in the woods. He alone knew how to change Gram's expression from determined to uncertain. His gentle voice, his calm strength, had grown around me like a vine, bindweed, still with me after all the years away.

"Syl?" Madison said behind me. I felt his long fingers on my shoulders; he bent to peer at my flushed face. "What's wrong?"

"Dry fire," I whispered.

"What?"

"Grandpa Liam died. This is as close as I could ever get to crying."

He drew me to him; I sat still another moment as he rocked me, feeling his bones against my face under the sweet, taut skin. Then I pulled away, stood up restively.

"I have to pack. Find a flight. Will you feed my cat while I'm gone?"

"Syl, I can come with you," he said steadily, reminding me, despite his long black hair, the violet stone in his ear matching his eyes, of Grandpa Liam.

"No."

"I'd like to meet your mysterious grandmother."

"No, you wouldn't."

"Yes, I would. I'd like to see where you grew up."

I felt like throwing something, then; I wished I could burst into tears. I went to the closet instead, picked my black suit off the hanger, and pulled a wheeled bag off the shelf to pack it in. He followed me to the closet, and then to the antique steamer trunk I used as a dresser.

"Syl—"

"I'll be back as soon as I can," I told him, pulling clothes out of the fabric-covered drawers, piling them efficiently into the bag: jeans, two sweaters, underwear. Socks. "I have to call the bookstore. Jo will cover for me; she went on vacation just down the coast, with an armload of mysteries. I'll give her an extra week off for this." I thought a moment, then took off my bathrobe, wrinkle-free polyester, folded that and a pajama top into the bag.

"Can I at least take you to the airport?"

Madison taught music fundamentals at the community college; his summer course hadn't started yet. It was like Grandpa Liam to die sleeping out under the stars, I thought; he'd probably been waiting for the summer solstice.

"Okay. What else do I need?"

"Toothbrush. All that."

"Got it." I showed him the little airline bag of bathroom supplies I'd acquired once when my luggage spent the night somewhere. "Oh." I went to the refrigerator, examined my collection of nail polish I kept in the egg bin to prevent streaking. Black? White? Plum? My mind went blank. Then I saw Grandpa Liam again, his rangy body hunkered down over a patch of tiny wildflowers growing along a stream bank. They were as lightly blue as his eyes. Sun fell on his hair, turning it into smooth ivory. He smiled at me, and said,

"Forget-me-not." I felt the blotchy swelling under my eyes again. I grabbed a bottle without seeing it, zipped it into a side-pocket along with my travel alarm.

"What else? Oh. I need to book a flight."

"Syl." Madison put his arms around me again. Over his shoulder, I saw the sky lightening, revealing, out of my high, uncurtained window, block upon block, mile upon mile of stone and cement and winding tarmac, flowing everywhere around me, hills covered with buildings instead of trees, everything blocked, gridded, measured, planned, the earth so buried that nothing could bloom in secret, unseen in the light of day.

"What have I forgotten?" I asked him, soothed by the sight. I would come back to those predictable streets as soon as possible; not even Gram could stop me.

"You could get dressed," Madison suggested gently. I pulled away from him, looking bewilderedly down at my naked self. He kissed my ear. "I'll find you a flight while you shower."

So I made my arrangements with almost annoying ease, until there I was, just where Gram wanted me, driving a Popsicle-red rental car from the airport at twilight through the village where I was born, and hungry on top of it.

The ancient village I'd left for good seven years earlier hadn't changed much. A pizza parlor had opened up where Andie Blair had had her diner for fifty-two years. The new owners had kept the thick, bottle-blue windows and the stone shed in the back for storing bodies in winter when, a couple of centuries before, the place had been the village apothecary shop. The creaky inn with its meandering halls and narrow stairways had a new ramp for the handicapped zigzagging from the slate steps. It was a bed-and-breakfast in this century, owned by the Starr sisters and their dead brother's widow. I saw the twins' heads in the lounge window as I drove past, both covered with the same tight gray snail-shell curls, their pleated faces tinted purple in the reflected light from the VACANCY sign.

Time had slowed in the fields along the road between the village and Lynn Hall. So little had changed, I might have been driving back into my own past. A barn roof that had been sagging for years had finally dropped a beam. The crusty old harrow still decorated the Thorntons' cornfield like a piece of sculpture. Lynn Hall, a solid rectangle of pale stone looming unexpectedly over the fields, looked oddly bigger than I remembered. It should have been smaller, I thought uneasily. Things grow in memory, in the dark; they shrink, lose their power, in reality. As I pulled into the drive, I saw the wood behind the hall, which had dwindled, as I had grown, from a boundless, tangled mystery into a tranquil patch of trees. Now it seemed to dwarf Lynn Hall, an immense, dark, frozen wave about to break over it. I nearly hit the brakes, backed out in a flurry of gravel to head for the airport again. Some of the dark, I realized slowly, was just that: the night I wasn't used to any longer, flowing over hill and field, no city lights to push it back, only stars, and the rising moon, and the occasional porch light in the crook of a mountain road to tell me where I was.

I parked at the end of the drive near the carport, where Gram's burgundy sedan the size of a cruise ship, and my great-uncle Hurley's pickup, so old it was held together by duct tape and rust, spent their declining years. As I picked my way across the grass, a luna moth went ahead of me, a fluttering wisp of moonlight. The front door was locked, and the doorbell made no sound when I pushed it. By which I could have concluded, if I wasn't sure, that Hurley, who liked to tinker with things, was still alive and kicking.

The thick door groaned as I tried the doorbell again. I pushed; someone pulled. The door squealed against its warped, swollen posts and sprang open. A lanky, twiggy troll and I stared at each other across the threshold. Then the troll touched his glasses into place, and I recognized those green eyes. They belonged to my aunt Kathryn's son Tyler, who had barely cleared my shoulder the last I saw of him.

"Syl?" he said uncertainly, and I remembered that I'd changed, too.

I reached up, saved by my thick-soled boots from having to stand on tiptoe. "Me," I agreed, breathing a kiss on his cheek. "Hi, cuz."

"What—where's the rest of your hair? And your glasses? How'd you get so—so grown-up?"

"City living, I guess."

"I guess," he echoed, still staring. This Tyler had a volcanic complexion, a ring in his left eyebrow, and spiky hair with mossy green highlights in it. His brows were still black.

Thirteen years separated us, along with the distance I had to look up to see his face. "Is there, like, a name for the color of your hair?"

I had to think. "Sahara Sunrise this month. Yours?"

He smiled, showing a dimple I remembered. "Mom calls it Froggy Bottom."

"Where's Gram?"

"She's in the kitchen with my mom. I was watching TV with Grunc. I saw your car lights on my way to the bathroom."

"Grunc?"

The dimple reappeared. "Great-uncle Hurley. Gram and Grandpa and Grunc." It faded; he stood blinking at the floor, then amended softly, "Gram and Grunc."

I nodded tiredly, feeling the painful heat fan briefly beneath my eyes. "When is the funeral?"

"I don't know. Gram and my mom have been on the phone all afternoon, making arrangements. Where's your stuff?"

"In the car."

He wandered out with me, picked my bag out of the trunk, and wheeled it over the threshold in front of him like an antique plow. I planted a boot on the ponderous door to shut it. Chandeliers tinkled above us, but nothing fell. The long hallway was dusty; shadows flickered as bulbs buzzed and sputtered in their sockets. All the doors along the hallway were closed, as though Gram no longer used the rooms. Dust balls drifted; paint blistered on the sills; cobwebs trailed down from the dusty prisms. It looked as though everyone had gone to sleep for a hundred years. I wondered idly who needed rescuing.

Tyler, maybe. His shadow stretching down the worn flag-stones seemed to take on a life of its own; there were too many arms under the crosshatch of lights, another head, other Tylers trying to emerge from the gangling, awkward sprite. His thin, dirty feet slapped the stones, the threadbare carpets. He cast a forlorn glance at me, looking even more otherworldly, a changeling child patched together out of this and that, trying to pretend that its cobbled face belonged to the stolen human child.

I pulled my eyes off Tyler's shadow, my thoughts back across the ambiguous boundaries they had crossed. Aunt Kathryn lived well out of those time-warped mountains, but only by a couple of hours' drive, and Gram, refusing to let me forget my past, plied me relentlessly with gossip.

I tried to be tactful, gave up, and asked baldly, "Did Aunt Kathryn's boyfriend come up with you?"

Tyler hesitated, pushed his thumb against the bridge of his glasses, and mumbled to the floor, "Stepfather."

I stopped dead. "No."

"Yeah. They got married last week."

"What did Gram say?"

His shoulders hunched a little. "I don't know. I've spent most of the time watching TV with Grunc. It seemed safest." I nodded wordlessly. Tyler's father, my uncle Ned, whom we had all loved, had spun across a patch of black ice into a tree a couple of years before. "Anyway," Tyler continued, "he didn't come with us. My mom was planning to leave me here anyway, while they go sailing around some islands." He scratched his brow, near the silver ring, then sighed. "At least

Grandpa Liam died in his sleep under the stars. Gram keeps saying he's a throwback to the Melior side of the family. Who were they?"

"Rois Melior. Your great-great-great-grandmother. Maybe another great or two. According to family lore, she used to wander around in the woods rain or shine until she lost her heart and finally her wits. She managed to find them both again and married the heir to Lynn Hall. Which is why we're here."

Tyler grunted. "Sounds like Grandpa Liam. Except for losing his wits." He was silent; I heard him draw a breath, then swallow. He was leading me toward the kitchen and the rooms clustered around it. His steps slowed to a crawl while he searched for words. "Do you," he said finally, without looking at me, "still miss your mom?"

"Oh, yeah." That was one thing in the world I was certain of. "I was your age when she died. But I never stop thinking about her."

His eyes slid to my face, then. "I still miss my dad. They keep telling me I'll get over it. I guess my mom got over it okay."

"I doubt that. I don't think that's the way love works."

"How does it work, then?"

I didn't have a clue; I could only tell him what I had been told. "Nobody can tell you how to feel, or how long you're supposed to feel that way."

He nodded, swallowing again. He turned down the shorter hallway at the end of the house, and I heard Gram's voice coming out of the room across from the kitchen. That was the old breakfast room, where the windows faced the rising sun and the rose garden that had been there as long as the hall. Grandpa Liam and Hurley had turned it into a sort of den, where they could shut away Gram's world and read their papers, watch football. Hurley, Gram's older brother, had been invited to live in Lynn Hall as its handyman after his wife died, a quarter of a century earlier. To judge from the state of the hall, he wasn't very handy anymore. But at least now he would be company for Gram.

The door opened abruptly before we reached it. Gram had sensed me, I guessed, or sensed something moving along the trembling threads of her awareness.

"Sylvia!"

Seven years had done nothing to diminish the force and energy of her voice, which could have cut short a brawl between sea lions. But either I had grown, or she had shrunk. Once a tall, beautiful woman with bones to die for, she used to tower over me. Now we stood nearly eye to eye. She felt feathery when I put my arms around her, as though she would fall over at a shout. Her white hair, a dandelion gone to seed, would float away with her if somebody sneezed. But the elegant bones of her face, and her birds' eyes, dark and piercing, hadn't changed. She still seemed able to see through me, check out my tidy white skeleton if she wanted. "You've come home," she declaimed tearily, as though I were a runaway pet.

On the couch behind her, Hurley was struggling, making vague noises. "Ah?" he demanded. "What? Sylvie, is that you?"

I went to hug him before he got all the way up. He was confused, expecting to see what he remembered. "Where's all those long, dark curls?" he asked, touching my smooth, gilded helmet. "Is it really you? You look so—What have you done to yourself?"

I grew away, I thought. He had been a big man when he came to live at Lynn Hall, hale and burly; he carried me easily on his shoulders, then. Now I felt hollows and crooks in my arms, memories of where his body had been. My eyes burned. I had left my past, but I hadn't expected it to change: what I loved should have stayed exactly the same.

"How are you, Uncle Hurley? Still stargazing up in the attic?"

"When I can. On the days when there aren't so many stairs. And I've been working on things around the house, for Iris and Liam."

He stopped, looking confused again. So was I. Someone was missing; my eyes kept searching for the tall, gentle, good-humored man with his ivory hair, and his eyes as clear as a child's, smiling contentedly at me. Aunt Kathryn swept into the room instead, laughing and weeping a little.

"Syl," she said, hugging me hard. "Look at you! You've gotten so beautiful."

So had she, I thought, amazed, and tried to remember the name of the man I assumed was responsible. She looked, with her red-gold hair and gray eyes, so much like my mother. But my mother had let her hair grow wild, and her eyes, fierce and impatient, seemed to see, even before she knew, that she hadn't long to live.

Still holding me, Aunt Kathryn appealed to Gram. "She's every bit as beautiful as Morgana was, but she never looked at all like her. You know everyone in the county, Mother; you must see a resemblance to someone."

I had been born there in Lynn Hall during a nasty blizzard, in an immense old bed, under the glacial eyes of a portrait of Liam's fastidious mother, Meredith. My mother hadn't bothered to marry; my father was Anybody's Guess. And guess everybody did, for years; but not even Gram, who could sort out the genealogies of families for miles around, including barn cats and a few flocks of geese, could put a name to him.

Gram tried again, holding me in another dark, unnerving scrutiny for a moment; my thoughts fled like mice, scattered among my bones to hide. She shook her head finally and loosed me. "Not a clue," she said briskly. "Sylvia, you must be hungry."

It sounded like a command, but I was. I said meekly, "I remember some kind of bag lunch on a flight."

"Come into the kitchen. We made roast chicken, and slaw, and fresh oatmeal bread. You stay here with Tyler," she told Hurley, and Tyler, who had been hugging a doorpost and watching us, dropped down beside Hurley on the couch. "We'll feed her and bring her back."

"Show her what I did in the pantry," Hurley said. "The folding shelves for all your jars."

"I haven't canned in ten years," Gram murmured as she closed the door behind us. "And if you look at those shelves cross-eyed, they fall down."

I went down the hall to the bathroom. Uncle Hurley had been playing in there, too: a towel rack as spiky as a porcupine took up half the floor. Gram was filling a plate for me when I came back. Aunt Kathryn had poured us each a glass of wine she must have brought, since there were no cobwebs on the bottle.

The kitchen was a vast square cavern that had been thoroughly modernized sometime before my mother was born. The pineapple wallpaper above the wainscoting, big prickly ovals of yellow on blue, had been there since before Gram was born. I sat down beside Kathryn at the sturdy oak table, with its familiar history of scars, cuts, water rings, the place where I had banged it with a tack hammer trying to imitate my mother's carpentry, the burn I had made smoking my first and last cigar with Grandpa Liam. Gram sliced bread, piled coleslaw on a plate, plucked a fork out of a cobalt-blue tumbler filled with them, country-fashion.

"Your old bedroom is ready for you," she announced, putting my plate down. I swallowed a laugh; it had probably been ready for the last seven years.

"So was mine," Kathryn murmured to me; Gram, fussing at the stove, ignored us.

"This is good, Gram," I said after a few bites; she could be right about some things. I put my fork down after a few more and raised my wineglass to Kathryn. "Tyler said you've remarried. Congratulations."

Kathryn turned bright pink. A deep snort came from the direction of the stove. "It would have been appropriate to have brought him," Gram remarked to a saucepan, "since I have never laid eyes on him."

"Oh, stop fussing, Mother," Aunt Kathryn pleaded. "You

never laid eyes on Syl's father, either." Gram banged a spoon against the pot, speechless for once. "Patrick and I had planned to come up together when we brought Tyler here," Kathryn explained to me. "But then this happened, and so we decided to keep things quiet for a while, not introduce my second husband to half the county at my father's funeral. Anyway, he's working until the end of the week. So I came up alone. With Tyler," she amended hastily. "How long are you staying?"

"Just a few days," I said clearly; Gram's spoon had stopped stirring, as though it listened.

"No longer?"

"I own a bookstore. It can't just run itself. When is the funeral?" I asked, to get off the subject.

"The day after tomorrow." She paused, her eyes reddening, making my eyes hurt, too. At the stove, Gram was still quiet. "Tomorrow, he'll be—"

"On view," Gram said harshly.

"At the funeral home."

"Ridiculous custom."

"I know," Aunt Kathryn sighed. "But he is Liam Lynn, of the village of Lynnwood, and Lynn Hall. Everyone knew him; people will want to say good-bye. He'll be buried in the village cemetery the next day at noon."

I took a tasteless bite, remembering my mother's funeral. "People eat afterward. Don't they?"

"Yes. They'll come here afterward."

"Do we cook?"

"Something," Aunt Kathryn said vaguely. She took a hefty

gulp of wine, then reached for a napkin and dabbed at the tears on her mascara. "But by tomorrow evening, we'll be up to the rafters in food. Someone dies around here, people cook. I don't know why."

"It's comforting?" I guessed.

"He wanted to be cremated," Gram, her back to us still, said abruptly. "He told me a dozen times to burn him and scatter his ashes in the rose garden."

"Mother," Kathryn said, her voice trembling. "That's a thoroughly disquieting idea. How could you stand to dig in the dirt, knowing he was all over the place?"

"I know," Gram said. She turned finally; her own eyes were red-rimmed. "I couldn't do it. It was that streak of Melior in him—wanting to turn into a rosebush when he died. I didn't want him blown all over the county by any passing wind. Or into the wood. I want, for once in my life, to be certain where he is. Do you think he'll forgive me?"

"I don't know," Aunt Kathryn said, wiping at tears and getting up to hug Gram. "I suppose if he doesn't, he'll let you know."

I got up, too. We put our arms around each other, and our heads together, and rocked each other in the middle of the kitchen. Aunt Kathryn shared her tears with me, but Gram's face, pale and fragile as ancient porcelain, remained dry. She could cry, but never easily, not even when my mother died. She swallowed her tears, I guessed, held on to them, fashioned them into something other, rather than letting them fall uselessly all over the place like more careless mortals did.

The phone rang then. Aunt Kathryn reached for it with a

grim efficiency that told me she had been fielding calls most of the day. Tomorrow, at Jenkins Funeral Home in the village. Noon to two. The day after, in the morning at eleven. Yes. Yes. Thank you. She's bearing up well, thanks. I'll let her know you called. She put the receiver down and told Gram, "Penelope Starr. She and the twins will drop off a smoked ham and half a dozen jars of Penelope's spiced pears before the funeral." She pulled a drawer open under the phone, which was so old you had to put your finger into a circle with holes in it above the numbers to dial. "I'd better make a list. So you can thank people later."

She was talking to Gram, but she glanced at me when she said that. I drew breath, held it a moment. It was going to be a tough fight getting out of there.

I had no idea.

We sat a long time in the kitchen, reminiscing, since Gram showed no signs of ever wanting to sleep again. Aunt Kathryn opened another bottle of wine; Gram actually had a sip or three. Tyler and Hurley drifted in and out. Hurley pulled a bag of chocolate cookies out of the cupboard to share with us. Near midnight, Aunt Kathryn made tea, and Tyler, squirreling around for a snack, found a jar of mixed nuts. Later, we could hear Hurley snoring in the breakfast room. The TV was still on, but very soft. Tyler drifted in and out again, with a bowl of nuts and cookies, to sit with Hurley.

"He stays up all night," Aunt Kathryn sighed. "He'll play computer games and watch videos until dawn, even on school nights, if he can get away with it."

The phone rang. We all blinked at it: it was one-twenty in

the morning. Then Gram put a hand on Kathryn's shoulder before she could move, and said briefly, "That will be Owen."

I stared at the cigar burn on the table, suddenly wide awake, remembering again what complexities, what mysteries, I had ventured back to. Both Kathryn and I were silent, listening, while Gram said, "Yes, she's here. Yes, I did. No, I didn't. We'll see. No, I don't expect you. Yes. No. Yes."

She hung up, as usual without saying good-bye. She stood silently, looking vaguely bemused, missing something, forgetting what she was missing, why we were there instead, and then remembering again.

Aunt Kathryn said gently, "Let's go to bed. Mother?" Gram nodded, still without speaking. "You get Syl settled; I'll take Tyler up."

Gram nodded again. Then she said with an effort, "Throw a blanket over Hurley; he'll be fine on the couch. I put some soap and towels out for everybody in the upstairs bathrooms. The well's brimming; no need to keep your showers short."

Aunt Kathryn smiled wryly. "I think Tyler's version of a shower is standing as far as he can away from it and turning the water on and off."

Gram carried the teacups to the sink, checked the stove settings, pushed a drawer closed, an old witch putting her lair in order. How much did Aunt Kathryn know? I wondered suddenly. How much had Gram told her of what went on in the shadows, the corners, behind and beneath what people expected to see?

We filed out. Gram shut off the light. Aunt Kathryn disappeared into the den; I collected my bag and purse in the hallway.

"You don't have to come upstairs," I told Gram. "I know my way."

She smiled suddenly and took my face in her soft, wrinkled hands. "Do you?" she asked me. Her crows' eyes looked dusky, weary, but hopeful. She dropped a kiss on my cheek. "Sleep well. If you can't, I left something by your bed. I know how you love to read."

I kissed her back. "Thanks, Gram. I'll see you in the morning. Good night."

Upstairs, I wandered restively around the room Gram had refused to let me outgrow. The wallpaper was sprigged with violets; the curtains over the windows facing the wood were eyelet lace. The rug she had hooked for me in violet and ivory to match the wallpaper lay beside the bed. The same worn candlewick spread covered the bed. From somewhere on the other side of innocence, she had unearthed an old ballerina lamp, pink toe poised on what looked like a water lily, hands uplifted to hold the light.

I stared at it, wanting to laugh and flee at the same time. For no reason, lines from a rhyme Gram had taught me echoed out of the past: *Three with eyes to see, Four to shut the door* . . . I went to the windows, pushed them open to get at the cool night air. The waxing moon, dipping over the trees, cast a silvery glow above the wood. I remembered watching the wood on early-summer nights when I was young, feeling restless and curious, impatient with my ignorance, yet not even sure what it was I wanted so badly to know. I would wait breathlessly for the moment when something shifted among the trees. In that moment, just before I recognized what I saw, anything might be moving toward me through the wood, anything or anyone at all.

I turned my head, gazed at myself in the mirror above the fireplace to see if I had left any trace in it of that young girl with her books and her ballerina lamp and her uncertain vision. Gram had finally gotten me glasses, and then I saw clearly what she saw, what she didn't see.

I tripped over what Gram had left me to read when I finally tried to crawl into bed. It was a box full of old papers. I crouched beside it, too tired, I thought, to do more than lift the first page, decipher the delicate, even lines of what looked like copperplate: handwriting so old it was faded, on paper that crumbled at the edges, and smelled vaguely of mice.

Then I recognized it. I had found it in the attic years before, read it there in secret, one gray afternoon while the rain tapped softly, insistently on the roof, and in the wood the trees loosed bright leaves like messages on any passing wind.

The voice I heard in my head speaking the words seemed as familiar as family, which I knew, from the writer's name, it was.

"My name is Rois and I look nothing like a rose."

I hauled the box into bed with me and read it all over again: a message from Gram, though what, and why now, I had no idea.

· 2 ·

Tyler

It was a weird day. And it got weirder after everyone went to bed. Syl didn't look like Syl anymore, and my mom hardly saw me when she looked at me. She saw Patrick, who she just married, or Grandpa Liam, who had just died. She and Gram spent the afternoon answering the phone or making calls and talking about caskets and what Grandpa Liam should be buried in, and flowers, and food, about what to say, and should someone sing? Half the time it sounded like another wedding, except my mom didn't cry so much for that. Gram was pretty much the same though, except she would look at me, when I went into the kitchen to make a sandwich or get a drink, like she expected somebody else to be walking through the door. And then her eyes would see me and go blank. So mostly I just stayed with Hurley, who didn't cry, and only talked about his telescope in the attic, when he talked at all.

My mom made me turn off the TV and sent me upstairs when they all finally came out of the kitchen. I wasn't sleepy, so I sat on the window seat, which ran under the sill and opened like a chest to keep wood in for the fire. It was empty, a cool place to keep secrets in if I found any. The moon was this bright eye, nearly wide open, staring down into the wood, and that's how I saw her.

Everyone else seemed to be asleep. No light from Gram's door when I went down earlier to get a Pepsi from the fridge; no noises downstairs but Grunc snoring. He sounded like something that lived back with the dinosaurs. A saber-toothed tiger, napping after its kill. Or a twelve-foot polar bear hibernating in an ice-cave. But it was only Grunc, the oldest tortoise in the world, dreaming turtle dreams. By day, he seemed human. But you could tell what he really was by his reptile eyelids, and his skinny, wavering, crinkled neck. I'll be like that when I'm old. Maybe not a tortoise. But something ancient with lots of armor and no need anymore to move fast. If I get old. It's easier to imagine that than grown-up. Old and young are more alike than grown-up. Grown-up is a different planet.

He reminded me of a game I'd downloaded where you have to battle your way through a primeval landscape full of flowers with shooting killer seeds and vines like boa constrictors and enormous lumbering things like fire-breathing tortoises. So I sat at the window, and that's what I was playing.

The window was open; everything was dead still. Sometimes I smelled the killer flowers in Gram's garden, sometimes the gigantic ferns that were as tall as the trees outside. I heard a rustling. At first I thought it was the game. But when I looked up, I heard it outside, and I thought for a moment that I had accidentally fallen into the game.

Then I saw her.

She looked unreal, floating in and out of moon and shadow. A thought somebody had forgotten to put away. A memory. The way her white dress seemed to drift around her, and her hair melted into dark, then light, then dark. A ghost. I shifted, turning my head to see her more clearly, and she saw me. I knew that because she stopped in a patch of moonlight, with her face turned up toward me. So she wasn't a thought or a ghost. She was somebody real, a villager, wandering around Gram's wood in the middle of the night.

I put the laptop aside and pushed my head out the window. She didn't run. She didn't move. She just looked up at me, her face the color of moonlight and her hair like a curly tangle of spiderweb. She stood like a statue; I couldn't even see her breathe.

And then she raised one hand and told me with her fingers to come down.

I forgot my shoes, I went out so fast, but I had socks on, and I was careful going through the roses. Some of those old bushes had tentacles like giant squids; they should have been in the game with the killer flower-seeds. I missed them all though. She waited at the edge of the trees, where the lawn ends and the wood begins. Close-up, I could see the freckles on her white skin. And the dirt and pulled threads and fraying lace on her dress. She wore sandals, not much more than a sole and a couple of plastic straps. Her feet were dirty. She wore rings on her toes and most of her fingers and on the rims of her ears. They were all silver; they flashed little stars all around her in the moonlight. Close-up, her milky hair was matted with leaf-bits and twigs, as though she had been lying on the ground. Her face was small and secret; her eyes were big and shadowy. I couldn't tell their color. Close-up, she smiled at me, and she was the most beautiful girl I'd ever seen.

"I'm Undine," she whispered, and took my hand.

She led me through the trees until I stepped on a bramble and let out a yell that probably brought Grunc straight up off his couch. Undine waddled in circles around me and laughed so hard her nose ran; she had to wipe it on her skirt. By then I was beginning to laugh, though I was limping on one heel. She pulled me over to a shadow under a tree and we sat down. My cousin's light was still on, but she hadn't come to her window; she must have had better things to do. The rest of the house was dark.

"You're Tyler," Undine said then, keeping her voice soft.

"How did you know?"

"Everyone knows everything around here. Anyway, I remember seeing you around the village before, when you came to visit with your parents."

I looked at the ground between us. "My dad's dead. Car crash, two years ago. My mom's going on her second honeymoon after Grandpa Liam's funeral."

She didn't say what I expected about my grandpa; she just nodded and asked, "Where are they going?"

"Sailing, somewhere. I'm staying here with Gram."

"Do you like him?"

"Patrick?" I shrugged. "I don't know. He's just some stranger who likes my mom. Seems all right. He doesn't tell me what to do, doesn't expect me to call him 'Dad' or anything gross like that." I touched my glasses straight. "He thinks I'm weird. I see it in his eyes. Like he doesn't really think I'm human."

She leaned a little closer to me, over her crossed knees. "Maybe you're not."

"He was probably a jock at my age. White teeth, just enough brains, basketball and soccer, girlfriends since kindergarten . . . He never paid attention to the cave-dwellers, the geeks in glasses. If he has a son, it won't be like me. That's what his eyes say."

"You don't like him."

I shrugged again. "It's not that. I just don't care."

"What was your dad like?"

That made me smile, almost. "More like me." Then it was like a door trying to open inside of me, and me shoving against it, trying to keep out all kinds of things I didn't want to look at, not yet anyway. I won this time. I swallowed what felt like a bramble. "Anyway. That's why I'm staying for a while with Gram and Hurley."

"And who else?" she asked. "There's a red car spending the night in the driveway."

"Oh. That's my cousin Syl. She flew out for the funeral."

"Do you like her?"

I thought about that, how she used to have long, curly, dark hair, and glasses like me, and she wore jeans all the time. When we came to visit, she would hug me and let me follow her around, show her bugs and old nests, stuff. Now she wore tight skirts and cool boots. Her hair was like a golden bell; I could see her face. She wore contacts; I could see her eyes. She had grown out of herself into someone else, who drove and carried a cell phone, who had a job in a big city on the other side of the country.

But she still wanted to hug me; her eyes told me that. She was still Syl, my cuz, and I could still show her weird bugs if I wanted. So I said, "Yeah. I like her."

"Your grandmother is scary," Undine said. "She sees things."

I looked at her, wondering what she meant. "Does she know you run around in her woods at night? Does she see you do that?"

"I don't know. Your grandfather saw me sometimes, but he didn't care. He showed me things—where the underground stream runs, and where a squirrel buried its seeds for the winter, and where the first violets grow when the ground thaws." She paused, picking a leaf off the ground and frowning at it. "I'm sorry he's gone," she said finally, what I expected to hear, but now I knew it was true.

I asked her curiously, "What are you doing in my Gram's wood in the dark?"

She looked back at me without blinking; I saw tiny moons in her eyes. "I'm searching for the magic." She was whispering again, so softly not even wind could have heard. "I want to be a witch."

I rubbed the sore spot on my foot where the bramble had bit me. "Don't you need a book or something? Or a coven? Candles and chants and stuff?"

"No. Not that kind of a witch. I want to be a wood-witch. They know everything there is to know about plants and animals. They can hear trees talk, and they always know where the moon will rise. Toads are their familiars. Birds bring them messages. If I were a true witch, the bramble would have moved out of our path before you stepped on it. True witches know all the secret places that open to the other world."

I felt my mouth struggling with that one, before I could say it. "What other world?"

"The world beyond this one. They come and go—"

"Who? Witches?"

"No. Them. They. They've been doing it for centuries around here. They have their places of passage. Mostly by water, because water goes wherever it wants. Sometimes they pass between worlds through trees, but there aren't many old enough, not in this wood. Most of the old ones got chopped down ages ago. You can tame a forest. But no one ever really knows what water will do. Even here. You wake up one morning, and there's a lake in your basement. Or the shallow stream across the road got huge and carried away a house. Or your well is dry; the water has gone elsewhere. It has its secret ways. So do they."

I was breathing through my mouth; it had gone dry. "Who?"

"You should know. You're related to them."

I didn't understand a word she was saying. But it didn't matter. It was like watching a movie, I decided. Part of you gets caught up in it; the other part of you knows it's not real. I watched the little silver stars wink on her ears and smelled the fruit-candy whiffs of her shampoo and watched her body shift under the white dress when she scratched herself or yawned.

"Who?" I asked now and then. "Who?"

But it was dangerous to say; nobody really called them anything, or spoke of them much; people just knew they existed. Some people. "They're ancient," she said dreamily. "They lived here before people ever came."

She was telling me fairy tales, I realized. About people who only pretended they were human, who lured true humans into their strange world with their great, eerie powers. I couldn't tell if this was good or bad. According to Undine, their world was maybe very beautiful, maybe deadly, maybe both. Being in it could change you. You never saw your own world the same way after you'd seen theirs. If they let you go, once they caught you.

"It's in your blood," Undine told me. "Because you're a Lynn. Your heritage. Part of you belongs to the world within the wood."

I was getting sleepy. I stretched out while Undine tried to explain magic to me. I put my hands under my head and watched the stars above the trees. At home, in the city night, I only saw a handful at a time, and half of them were airplanes. Here, they swarmed, they flowed, they glittered like sequins. They actually made the shapes on the star map Syl had sent me for my eighth birthday. The Hunter, the Bears, the Seven Sisters. I closed my eyes for just a moment, trying to remember how to find the north star. I thought Undine was still talking when I opened my eyes again.

But I was alone.

I got off the ground, feeling stiff and clammy. The moon was disappearing; the wood had grown darker. Something scuttled under a bush, made me jump. I could see the hall by the fading moonlight reflected in the upper windows. Syl must have fallen asleep with her lamp on. I wondered if I was the only person awake in the world.

Then I saw Undine again, a faint scrap of white on the other side of a field, just about to disappear into the same dark wall of mountain that was swallowing the moon. Before she vanished completely, I saw spangles of white fire blaze all around her, as though the entire constellation of her rings, ears and fingers and toes, had caught moonlight at once. I wanted to shout, it was so amazing. Magic, I thought. That's what she meant by magic. It made my heart float. I watched for a long time, but she and the moon had both melted away.

So I took the long walk home through the lurking brambles in my socks.

·3·

Syl

I didn't remember falling asleep. I remembered putting down the last page of Rois Melior's tale. And then I was fighting my way out of some strange underground passage guarded with thorns and enormous roses. I could see light in the distance, the end of the tunnel, but it seemed impossibly far away, and I kept getting grabbed by thorns and blinded and smothered and confused by huge blooms looming in my face.

Then I woke abruptly and thought: I forgot to call Madison.

It was very early; morning sunlight hadn't reached the wood yet. I listened, heard water run in the pipes, something clank in the kitchen. Gram, probably, making coffee. No using the phone in the kitchen, then. I didn't feel like explaining Madison to Gram; I didn't want my separate worlds to touch.

I'd met him a year earlier in the bookstore, browsing the music section during our Third Birthday party. A year later, we were closer than ever. I knew he was content with me. I had thought he was just as content in his musical universe with his students and his weekend folk band, his disorderly apartment full of vinyls, books, old sheet music, and peculiar instruments, his shaggy dog who howled when he played the nose harp, or the saw, or the didgeridoo.

"You must live in here like a ghost," he commented, awed, when he first saw my spotless studio apartment. "If you jumped with both feet into a puddle, you wouldn't leave a footprint on your carpet."

It was true that I vacuumed up cat hair twice a day and didn't keep much in my fridge besides coffee beans and nail polish. "I like knowing where things are," I told him.

"No surprises."

"It's not that. Maybe I just like to be prepared for anything."

And I truly didn't mind vacuuming the stray dog hair that came in on his jeans, or storing the odd jars of spices, capers, olives, whiskey marmalade he liked to cook with. Or the things falling on my head in his apartment when I opened a closet to hang my clothes, or the phone that was always buried under something. I loved his music; he loved my books. But I thought the differences between us pretty much marked the boundaries of our friendship. Venturing past them, we would find pitfalls, chasms, dragons.

I thought that was plain to him, too. So I was astonished when he brought up the idea of change.

It wasn't that I didn't love him, I explained. It was just obvious that we already had irreconcilable differences; living in our opposite worlds, we had already gone as far as we could safely go.

"Why? Because I have dog hairs and you have cat hairs? Because you can never find a hanger in my closet? I leave toothpaste open on the bathroom sink? You'll get over it. You love me."

I loved a thousand things about him. His long black hair and placid temper, his big hands that could play a penny-whistle, open any jar, his cooking, his deep voice, his music.

"I love a thousand things about you," I told him firmly. "But not enough to marry them."

"Think about it," he suggested. "That's all I'm asking now."

"No."

"You will anyway," he said calmly, "now that I put the thought into your head."

But I didn't want to think about it, let alone bring his name up in Gram's kitchen. Whatever else, he was my good friend; I missed his voice; I had promised to call him when I got myself safely to Lynn Hall. Since I'd asked him not to call me here, he couldn't do much besides wonder.

I got up, showered quickly, and put on black jeans, a gray sweater, boots. Early mornings in the mountains, even on the threshold of summer, could be chilly. But that was the price of privacy, since I couldn't find reception for my cell phone in the bedroom, and I didn't want to roam around the house searching for it.

So I went to roam the woods instead, sneaking past the kitchen to the back door, which opened without the fuss and drama of the main door. I cut through the rosebushes into the wood and started dialing. Nothing. I wandered through the trees, hearing squirrels scold and birds flit among the leaves, nameless things scurry through the bracken, everything but the sound of Madison's phone ringing.

That's when I saw her.

I stared mindlessly at her, lost in that little, enchanted moment when you recognize something unexpectedly, overwhelmingly beautiful. She seemed another expression of the wood, as natural and astonishing as an oak full of owls, or a perfect ring of scarlet mushrooms. Like a figure hidden in a painting, she seemed visible only because I had seen her. My eyes could just as easily have told me that her hair was light, her eyes leaf, her skin the tender white of birch, her garments tree bark, root, earth.

Then I realized she was looking back at me.

Time shifted abruptly. I wasn't in her timeless moment any longer; she had melted into mine, and that was when I felt my heartbeat. In my walks with Grandpa Liam, he had shown me the fawn hidden in the underbrush, the rare wild orchid, the eagle's nest, but he had never shown me this bit of wildness and put a name to it. I knew her, though. Who wouldn't? She was as old as words, and she might have just stepped out of Rois Melior's story to find me.

I had run to the other side of a continent, surrounded

myself with stone, so that we would never meet. She recognized me, too; her eyes darkened to that deep, late-summer green with its hint of shadow. She took a step toward me; I took a step back, stumbled against a root. She stopped, raised her hand to stop me, and I heard her voice, a murmur of wind, a lilt of water in it.

"Stay," she pleaded. "Talk to me. Tell me your name."

I pointed my cell phone at her like a weapon and dialed 911. It was all I could think of, and of course nothing happened. Why would she fear my little handful of technology when there were telephone poles and pylons everywhere in the woods? And even if I'd gotten through, what would I have said? The Queen of Faery was standing in front of me, wanting to chat?

"I know your father," she said.

I felt the blood slide out of my face, leaving it icy. The cell phone slipped through my fingers.

"I don't—" My voice came only in a harsh, raw whisper. "I don't want to know." I took another step back, felt brambles snag my jeans. "Leave me alone."

"How can I? Your heart's blood calls to me." She came closer to me, then, without seeming to move, as though she had drifted on a passing breeze. "You are mortal, you are faery, you are the bridge across our boundaries."

I glanced quickly behind me, as though Gram in her kitchen could hear. "How dared you show yourself in this wood?" I demanded. "How can you?"

"Death opens doors not even the witch of Lynn Hall can see. She will never listen to me; she has stopped her ears with her own stitches. But if you tell her, maybe she will begin to listen."

"Tell her what?"

She seemed very close, something strange and beautiful and extremely dangerous in Gram's wood, like the pale and lovely Destroying Angel that Grandpa Liam would sometimes show me, growing in its solitary splendor under a tree.

"What you are."

I turned and ran, scrabbling for my cell phone and jerking free of the thorns in my first ragged step. I didn't want to face Gram; I was shaking, my skin still cold. I pulled off my boots at the porch, snuck back upstairs for my purse and car keys, and drove away to clear my head before I called Madison. I would never go into the wood again, I decided. I would stay around people. I'd leave as soon as possible after the funeral. Nobody could tell me what to do, force me to stay, not Gram, not even the Queen of the Wood. I'd fly back to my city of stone and stay there forever.

I was pulling up beside field walls, stopping in the middle of bridges and old railroad crossings, still trying to call Madison while I pieced my thoughts together again. I found myself in the village before I realized how far I'd gone.

I finally stopped at the bed-and-breakfast; even that early, the Starr sisters would be up supervising breakfast. By then I had stopped trembling. Any other signs of disturbance, I knew, could be laid at Grandpa Liam's door.

A couple of young guys whose bicycles were chained to the porch railing were already checking out when I opened the door. Lacey Starr gave me a narrow, speculative stare as she ran a charge plate over a card. Her light blue-gray eyes widened. Her sister Miranda blinked at me, then pitched her deep, throaty voice to bring their sister-in-law Penelope out of the kitchen.

"Sylvia! Is that you under that hair?" They both came out from behind the desk to give me twin, lavender-scented hugs.

"We're so glad you were able to come out to be with Iris," Lacey murmured. She had the gentler voice, and only wore pearls for jewelry. Miranda wore only gold; they were like sisters in a fairy tale.

"Well, at least we found out what it takes to get you home," Miranda grumbled, but without bite, so I could ignore it. "What are you doing up so early?"

"Trying to make a phone call," I said tersely, and had to jerk my wayward memories out of the wood again. I turned to hug Penelope, who came up from the kitchen drying her hands on the dish towel tucked into her jeans.

"You look so grown-up," she said, amazed. "I wouldn't have recognized you." Plump and freckled, she changed her own hair color, it was said, more often than some changed their socks. She was honey-haired and pink-cheeked that day, like a Golden Delicious apple.

The two young men, in beards and microfibers, watched patiently, smiling. Miranda finally rescued their slip from the plate.

She inquired innocently as the owner signed, "Iris's phone out of order?"

"No," I answered, remembering then how gossip hitched

a ride through the village on any aimless breeze. "I just wondered if there was any hope at all of getting a call out on my cell phone."

"I found a great spot near the bank," one of the guys told me. "The back of the parking lot where those big flower bushes are."

"Hydrangeas," Lacey murmured.

He nodded. "Clearest reception around."

"That's what it was," Penelope exclaimed. "Angie stopped by in her patrol car the other night to chat and got a dispatch about a suspicious stranger in the bank lot, sitting under a bush and yelling to himself."

"Tourist with a cell phone," the other bicyclist guessed. They were grinning, proud of sharing a local detail the locals didn't know. I sighed noiselessly. The bank. I might as well make my private call standing under the only traffic light at noon.

The sisters waited until the strangers left before bringing up family matters. Lacey took one of my hands, held it in her long, ringed fingers, while Miranda said, "Of course we'll be in to say good-bye to Liam today, between lunch and check-in. And we'll have a chance to visit with you tomorrow, after the funeral. If there's anything Iris needs—besides you, that is—you let us know."

Penelope patted my shoulder; Lacey hugged me again. Surrounded by sisters, sympathy, and scent, I remembered the bizarre image of menacing roses in my dream.

"I will," I promised, and eased my way out of there.

I parked in the far corner of the bank lot and hunkered down behind a huge hydrangea. The river ran below, shallow and quick; across it woodland opened into farmland. I dialed Madison's number. While the phone rang, I watched a tractor lumbering along the river road, trailing a line of cars behind it. One lost patience, darted out on a curve. I held my breath, seeing the truck it didn't rounding the hill toward it in the same lane. The car ducked back into safety; the truck passed with a grumble of air brakes, and Madison picked up the phone.

"'Lo?" he said sleepily. I looked at my watch.

"Oops. Sorry."

"Syl!" I heard bed noises as he struggled up. "Where are you?"

"Under a hydrangea."

"Country living," he commented through a yawn. "Did you have a good trip? Everything okay there?"

"Yes," I said steadily. "The flight was fine and Gram is okay. My aunt Kathryn was with her when I got there; they pretty much had everything arranged. The funeral is tomorrow. I'll be home as soon as possible afterward. One minor detail is I can't call you unless I happen to be squatting in the bank lot."

"Syl—"

"Under a bush."

He was silent a moment, breathing at me over the phone. "You sound funny."

"No, I don't."

"What's wrong?"

"Nothing's wrong. Except for Grandpa Liam, of course. I just called to tell you I'm here, and I'll be back before you miss me."

"I do already," he said. "Syl, let me call you at your grandmother's house."

"No."

"That way you won't have to sit in a parking lot."

"No." I heard him draw breath, hold it. I added, trying to ease the tension out of my voice, "I'll be back so soon you won't need to call."

"What if you're not? What if she wants you to stay?"

"She can't. I'm a working girl. She'll have to bear up without me. Anyway, she has half the county to look after her. And anyway, it's no use you calling me there. She's too deaf to hear the phone ring, and Uncle Hurley always answers the door instead."

"Liar," he said. "Listen. If you don't come back right away—"

"I will. I have to."

"You sound scared."

My lips pinched together. I opened them finally, said stubbornly, "Sad. I'm just sad."

"I'm sorry, Syl. I wish I were there with you." I pushed the phone closer to my ear, wishing he were, too, but enormously relieved that he wasn't. "I miss you," he said again. "I was thinking, if you end up staying out there longer, I could join you for a long weekend, do some hiking—"

"I'm flying home after the funeral," I said adamantly. "Bye, Madison."

"I love you."

I tried to say it; I didn't know suddenly what it meant to someone like me. "See you soon," I murmured finally. "Bye."

I sat gazing thoughtlessly across the tranquil fields to where the wood began again, trees covering the gentle mountains so thickly you couldn't separate one shadow from another; you'd never see what was going on among them until you were already there. What had happened to my mother in the wood? I couldn't imagine, judging from Rois Melior's tale, that love had anything to do with it. Passion? Maybe. For a moment. Her fairy lover might have caught her eye, come and gone as quickly as sunlight on a cloudy day. What she felt about it, she never said. All I knew for certain was that she had loved her halfling child, but I had no idea why.

A throat cleared itself above my head, and I jumped. I looked up through the hydrangea heads and found a human face.

I started again, recognizing it.

"Owen." I stared at him, horrified, wondering if he'd read my thoughts and would tell Gram. Then I scrambled out from behind the bush, feeling briefly like a kid again, vaguely guilty of something, while an adult waited, exuding a dampening cloud of patience and gloom.

"It's the community phone bush," he explained in the even, sinewy voice I remembered. His dark gaze remained politely blank while I got myself upright, and I breathed more easily. He didn't recognize me, I realized, his daughter's best friend through twelve years in the village school. Owen Avery had been one of those adults who always seemed to be around Lynn Hall, waiting at the door for Dorian to find her jacket, in the den talking to Grandpa Liam, at the kitchen table with Gram, sipping something out of a teacup that didn't smell like tea. He had been remote and ageless to me while Dorian and I were growing up: an alien being of incomprehensible whims who barely spoke our language. Now, in my adult eyes, he became suddenly human: timeworn, a bit silvery, but still lean and dark, and younger than he had seemed during all those years when I had no idea what old was.

I heard the odd silence between us; he was gazing at me curiously from some distant place. Then he blinked and gave a faint laugh. I smiled, relieved.

"Sylvia."

"Hey, Mr. Avery."

"You look so much like one of them, I couldn't imagine how you knew my name."

"One of—Oh." Tourist, he meant. Outsider. "My hair."

"It's more than your hair," he murmured, giving me another bleak, disconcerting gaze. "You've been away for years, and then you magically pop up from under a hydrangea bush."

His comments, I remembered, thrown at random like stones pitched in water, could come eerily close to smacking whatever lurked beneath the surface. "Gram told me to come as soon as I could," I said evasively.

His face tightened; he looked away a moment, at a memory. "I'll miss your grandfather more than I can say," he breathed. "He didn't have to ramble so far away that he couldn't find his way back."

I swallowed. "That's pretty much what Gram thinks."

"The Melior in him."

I was silent at that, wondering suddenly how much he knew of Rois Melior's story. How much had Gram told him? He had a hand in this and that around the county—banking, real estate; he also owned a tree farm and a nursery on the hill behind Gram's property. His wife had vanished out of his life before Dorian started school; as far as I knew, he'd never re-married. I got used to seeing him in my grandparents' company; perhaps he was the son they never had. Or that they wanted to have, I guessed, remembering the two beautiful daughters they did have. But nothing had come of that. As far as I knew. Which wasn't very far, I realized, when I thought about Owen Avery.

"Is there anything I can do for Iris?" he asked.

"I don't know," I said tightly. "She's—she always seems so strong."

"Yes."

"But she won't—she doesn't want to see my grandfather all laid out in a suit and a tie. She's having trouble with that."

"So am I," Owen admitted dourly.

"Maybe you could stop by and talk to her about it. See what she wants to do; take her if she wants to go. You know her as well as anyone, I think."

"Of course I will. What about you?"

I shrugged. "I can go with Tyler and Aunt Kathryn. Whatever's lying there isn't him, so it doesn't matter what he's wearing, does it? They should have just left him in his nightshirt."

"Spoken like your grandmother," Owen said, making me stare at him again.

"I'm not," I blurted. "I'm not like her at all."

He only gave me a bittersweet smile that mystified me completely and didn't argue the point.

"How's Dorian?" I asked quickly, to change the subject.

"She's fine. She's around here somewhere, shopping. She's been teaching kindergarten, this past year. During the summer she takes care of the nursery for me. Come and visit us, before you leave?"

"She's still living with you?"

"The apple didn't fall far . . ."

"I thought she'd be married by now. It's what people do around here. And boys have trailed after her since she was two."

"They still do," her father said a trifle fretfully. "One in particular."

But his cell phone chose that interesting moment to ring, startling us both, before he could tell me who.

"I'll see her soon," I said quickly. "Tell her that?"

He nodded, waving the phone apologetically as he raised it, and I took myself out of earshot.

The stores were all open by then. On impulse I went across the street to the feed and hardware store to buy a couple dozen chandelier bulbs. It would give me something to do in the stray hours before the funeral.

The smells of the place—organic, mealy, redolent of barns mingling with the tangy whiffs of metal and leather tack—led me straight back to childhood again. I heard my mother's voice, always on the edge of impatience or laughter, sprung taut with her effort to outrun her future. Drill bits, we searched for together, tenpenny nails, duct tape, dowels. Like Hurley, she loved to tinker with things; toward the end she was replacing drawer pulls all over the house. My eyes flooded with memories. I turned, blind, and bumped into somebody. Muttering an apology, I heard my name.

"Syl? Is that you?"

I blinked away the past, found Dorian's face on the other side of them.

She'd hardly changed in seven years, still slender, taller than I by a head, still with those straight shoulders and that nutmeg hair, a long tangle of knots and curls. She wore the uniform I remembered: faded jeans, scuffed clogs, a handkerchief of a top that clung closely around her long waist and showed off her tanned, muscular arms. She balanced a forty-pound bag of fish fertilizer against her calf and had her arms around me before I could speak.

"I knew you'd come back! Oh, Syl, it's so good to see you! I've wanted to talk to you a thousand times." She loosed me to gaze at me reproachfully, her eyes, an odd pale gray flecked with colors, covered with a sheen of tears. "Why did it have to take something like this to bring you back?"

"I'm sorry," I breathed, shaken. "Maybe because it's easier to stay away than to keep saying good-bye?"

"Tell me you're staying all summer."

"I can't."

"Oh, Syl—" She reached out, touched my unfamiliar hair

lightly, swallowing. I saw in her agate eyes the shadows of worry, trouble.

"We'll talk," I said abruptly. "We'll make time. Midnight beside the creek where we used to smoke to keep the mosquitoes away and gossip about boys—you remember?"

"Of course," she said, half-laughing. "I remember everything."

"I just saw your father in line for the phone bush, speaking of boys. He told me you're seeing someone. He had that look in his eyes."

The worry in her own eyes spilled into her face. She gave her hair a sudden flick, curls hiding her expression. "I have a lot to tell you," she only said. "And a lot to ask you. Gossip from the far side of the world doesn't travel well across these mountains." Then she was smiling again, giving someone behind me the peaceful, trusting kind of look that love inspires before it gets broadsided by life. "And speaking of boys, here he is. Do you remember each other? Leith? Syl?"

A young man was at her side so suddenly and quietly he seemed to have sprung up out of the floorboards. We looked at each other wordlessly. I remembered his eyes, still and very dark, until at a shift of light you saw the midnight blue in them. I hadn't known him well; he had been a couple of grades ahead of us. But even in the schoolyard I'd been aware of that silence, that reserve in him, as though he'd been raised by foxes and language was his second language.

"Leith Rowan," I said slowly.

He smiled; he'd gotten that civilized. "Hello, Syl. You've changed."

"Not really."

Neither had he: still tall and spare, with lank red hair and level brows the color of fire, and the mysterious scar under one cheekbone that had brought a taller tale out of him every time he was asked. A bar brawl at the age of eight, a slash from a bear, a dropped rifle that miraculously just missed blowing his head off, ditto a bow-hunter's arrow, an owl that had mistaken him for a snack as he wandered through the hills at night: those were a few that came to mind from ancient schoolyard gossip.

The Rowan family, old as the hills and scattered all over them, had probably named every Hardscrabble Road in the county. So Gram said of them when I mentioned Leith and his tales. Fishers, hunters, farmers, they made do with what they had, and had just enough of that to make do. Self-sufficient and solitary, they lived in hollows, down back roads, along the banks of creeks. Leith, Gram had told me during one of her detailed attempts to keep me connected to my roots, was the first of them to leave the hills to go to college. He owned books, she'd heard, and sat studying them on his cabin porch with his rifle across his knees.

"I hear you own a bookstore on the other side of the world," he said. He had a gentle, quiet voice that always caught my ear in the rowdy playground when we were growing up.

I nodded. "I haven't heard yet what you do."

"I work for Dr. Caddis," he answered, which didn't surprise me: Dr. Caddis was the local veterinarian.

"When can we get together?" Dorian asked abruptly, her fingers closing around my arm. "We'll be at the funeral, of course, along with a hundred other people who haven't seen you for—Oh." She paused, thinking. "And I'll be at the guild meeting, unless Iris cancels it. But I've heard she hasn't missed a meeting in fifty years."

"Guild meeting?"

"The Fiber Guild. Iris called the meeting at the hall this month, on the third Friday."

"The day after the funeral," I said doubtfully. Then I asked, "What's a Fiber Guild?"

Dorian stared at me, a disconcerting sight because I hadn't a clue why. "Iris never told you?"

"No."

"I wonder—Oh," she said again, illumined, while I was still in the dark. "It must be your—" She glanced at Leith then, and finished delicately, "your complete lack of interest in anything to do with a needle and thread." I was silent, mystified; Dorian had never hidden things from me before. Maybe, I realized, she was hiding them from Leith. But that only made me more uneasy: he and I in the dark together. "We sit around and sew, weave, crochet, whatever," Dorian explained. "Darn socks and exchange yarns."

No wonder Gram never mentioned it to me. I could thread a needle, maybe, if my life depended on it. "It might be comforting for Gram to have all her friends around her then," I said. "But how did she keep the guild secret all my life? And why?"

Dorian reached down for the fertilizer; Leith got it first. She smiled at him and hugged me again. "Let her tell you," she whispered, sounding oddly fierce about a sewing circle. "If she doesn't, I will." She let me go. "I'll see you soon."

Over her shoulder, Leith gave me a slight, barely perceptible nod.

"So will I."

I saw those Rowan eyes at the edge of my thoughts as though they watched me drive back to the hall.

There, I found Gram at the kitchen table, chopping vegetables. A bone simmered in a pot on the stove. Aunt Kathryn sat at the table in her bathrobe, clutching a mug of coffee, her face still smudgy with sleep. Gram, fully dressed, gave me one of her crow-glances, black and expressionless, as I came in.

"You were out early!" Aunt Kathryn exclaimed.

"I couldn't sleep. I took a drive to the village." Being among people had blurred the memory of the disturbing vision in the wood; I had caught my balance again in the human world. I cut a slice of oatmeal bread, dropped it into the toaster, and raised a brow at her.

She shook her head. "I can't eat breakfast. I woke up early, too, so I called Patrick before he went to work."

"I saw Dorian in the hardware store," I told Gram. "She said something about a Fiber Guild meeting here the day after tomorrow."

"What's a Fiber Guild?" Aunt Kathryn asked, yawning. So Gram had never told her either. I wondered if even my mother, who lived here all her life, had known about the guild.

"Just a fancy name for a sewing circle," Gram said vaguely, lifting the bone out of her pot and letting it fall into the lid.

"What are you making?"

"Vegetable soup for lunch."

Aunt Kathryn took a swallow of coffee, looking more awake. "The day after the funeral you're going to throw a quilting bee?"

"I don't know," Gram said firmly. "I haven't thought that far ahead yet."

"You'll be exhausted!"

"Then I'll cancel it." She inspected the bone, let it slide off the pot lid into the garbage; then she carried the cutting board to the stove, pushed chunks of carrot, onion, potato, celery, into the broth. We watched her wordlessly: the old woman with her knife and her bone, transforming things. She gave me another, more human glance. "If I'd known you were going to the village, I would have given you a grocery list."

"I don't mind going back." My toast popped up; I rummaged for a plate. "It's such a short drive."

"That would be a help. Oh, when you're finished with your breakfast, will you check on Hurley? I heard him climb up to the attic earlier."

"Sure, Gram." The phone rang. I was closest, so I dropped the toast on my plate and picked up. "Lynn Hall," I said efficiently. "Sylvia Lynn speaking. How can I help you?"

"Sylvia!" a sharp, dour voice exclaimed. "It's about time! Seven years without a visit, and it takes your grandfather dying—"

I placed the voice and held the receiver out to Gram,

while it was still scolding me. "Jane Sloan." She was the only woman around who knew more local history than Gram and who might be able to take her in a shouting match.

I took toast and coffee to the table and sat down next to Aunt Kathryn. She patted my hand while she sipped coffee; I ate with my other one. Gram was saying adamantly, "I'm not going, Jane. I don't see the point of seeing Liam all dressed up with rouge on his cheeks, or whatever they do—Yes, Kathryn took his suit down yesterday. Of course we remembered a tie. He hasn't worn a tie since Kathryn got married the first time." Kathryn's hand clamped down suddenly on mine; it sounded like the telephone barked. Gram, evidently feeling vibes, covered the lower end of the receiver and hissed at Kathryn, "Well, she was bound to know sooner or later. Nothing stays secret long around here."

"Evidently," Kathryn said tightly. "Jane will have it spread around the county by dusk, how I barely got one husband buried before I married the next."

I had a sudden image of Jane Sloan in her suit and gloves, standing next to the body at the mortuary and transfixing each mourner like the Ancient Mariner with her glittering eye and the news of Aunt Kathryn's latest marriage. I swallowed most of my toast in a bite and took my coffee with me to the attic.

I found Hurley near the top of the stairs, aiming his telescope out a skylight inset in the lower part of the slanted roof. The attic ran the length of the hall, brick and fieldstone chimneys thrusting through it and out the roof from the rooms below. I wondered how many old swallows' nests were clinging to the stones. Half the attic had once been servants' quarters. The rest of it, a huge open space interrupted here and there by the chimneys on their way up, was full of what looked like the shipwrecked salvage of centuries: traveling trunks, heavy, cobwebby furniture, boxes of fabric, antique clothes, vast portraits of dusty ancestors, dishes, knickknacks, whatnots, and what-have-yous. I closed my eyes, opened them again; it was all still there. It made me think of those fairy tales where the princess, trapped in the tower by her husband, the evil retainer, or her mother-in-law, has to move a mountain of something by dawn to get free.

Hurley murmured something. His telescope was slanted down toward the wood.

"Anything exciting?" I asked.

"Come and see."

I waded through boxes of old crockery to squint into his eyepiece. I saw a very pretty young face among the trees, masses of pale, curly hair, wide-set eyes sliding toward some sound. I blinked; the face turned into a foot in a rubber flip-flop. In the next moment even that was gone.

"The great horned owl," Hurley intoned solemnly. "Asleep on its roost."

"Looked like a girl to me."

"Really?" He swung the telescope toward the sky. "Where?"

"Well, she's not on the moon."

"No?"

"Look down," I suggested. "In the wood."

He did, letting the telescope roam for a bit. He said lucidly, "Ah. That would be Judith Coyle."

"What's she doing in Gram's wood?"

"She likes it."

I grunted, hoping she didn't smoke in there and set the trees on fire. My cup was empty; I went back downstairs, detouring along the way to my bedroom to hang some clothes to wear later to the funeral home. The box of papers sat where I had left it, papers facedown now, endpaper on top. I looked at it, not wanting to think about it, then nudged it under the bed with my foot. All gone.

Passing Tyler's room on the way to the kitchen, I saw him sitting cross-legged on his bed in a vortex of sheets and blankets, tapping at a laptop. His room smelled dank, like old socks. He had apparently slept in his jeans; his hair stuck up and his eyes were still rheumy with sleep. I could have counted the ribs in his bare, skinny torso. His green eyes swam toward me behind his glasses; he grinned sleepily.

"Hi, cuz."

I wended my way through an archipelago of clothes flung out of his backpack, CDs, and empty Pepsi cans, to push his window up. "Making ourself at home, are we?"

He nodded absently, still typing, then studied the screen. I looked over his shoulder, but light from the window washed over the screen, and I couldn't see what he was doing. He made an impatient noise and hit a key; whatever it was vanished.

"What are you doing?"

He mumbled, then made an effort. "Trying to find something." He hesitated. "You know water?"

"What?"

"Water. You drink it, you wash in it—"

"Yeah," I said, bemused. "It's coming back to me."

"I ran a search and got three hundred and seventy-one million different things I could look up about it, and I can't find a single one that tells me what I want to know."

"What do you want to know? Are you looking up where your parents are going for the honeymoon?"

He waved that away; nothing so fatuous. But he couldn't just say it, either. He took a breath and stuck, his eyes going wide and still behind his glasses. I waited; he tried again, his skinny fingers twitching. I glimpsed something then, a vision in my great-great-great-grandmother's strange manuscript: secret waters running deeply into shadows and earth, and then out again. Out the other side. Into another world. I felt a word fill my mouth; Tyler turned his head slowly, stared at me out of his elongated eyes.

The word came out of me. "Poetry."

He blinked; his lips echoed the word soundlessly. I put my hand on his shoulder, felt the narrow bones, light and vulnerable as bird-bones, where in a universe next door he might have wings. He tensed suddenly under my hand, peering at something out the window.

"There's Undine." He slithered his long bones out of bed, trailing sheets, and shouted out the window, "Hey, Undine!"

I joined him, and saw again the tangled ivory hair, the small, wary face looking up at us from the edge of the wood. I glanced, amused, at Tyler: he'd just gotten there and already young nymphs were emerging from the trees.

"Uncle Hurley says her name is Judith," I told him. "Judith Coyle."

"Huh," Tyler grunted. "She calls herself Undine." He waved; she beckoned, and he glanced around hastily, pulled a T-shirt off the floor, and sniffed it. "Guess this'll do. Tell my mom—" He caught my eye then, and amended sheepishly, "I'll tell her."

"Why does she call herself Undine?"

"She says it's magic." His face vanished into the shirt; he pulled and popped out again, glasses askew. "She's trying to be a witch."

"How do you—"

But he had picked up his shoes and vanished out the door, the gangling troll trailing after the beguiling Undine.

I went back downstairs, met Tyler again, talking with his mouth full of buttered oatmeal bread while he bumped backward out the kitchen doorway.

"We'll just be in the wood."

"Please stay close to the house," Aunt Kathryn said. "We're going to the funeral home after lunch. And after that I want you to help us straighten the house for company."

"I will—Bye—"

"Be back for—"

"Lunch, okay, Mom, bye."

He danced around me and out the door through the rose trees. Aunt Kathryn got up, rubbing her eyes.

"Hormones," she murmured. Gram shot her a glance but refrained from comment. "I'm going to shower."

Gram was mixing dried cherries and toasted walnuts into a chocolate dough. I scooped a fingerful and nibbled it, wanting to stay close to her, wanting to hide from her, challenging her to see me truly, terrified she might.

"What are you making now?"

"I hardly know. Something for the funeral. It helps to keep busy."

"Are you really not going to the mortuary?"

"Funeral home," she amended dourly. "Around here, it's a home. As though you just left your own and passed through into somebody else's. I haven't made up my mind, yet."

I picked another cherry out of her bowl and changed the subject. "Why would Judith Coyle call herself Undine?"

"Undine is a water nymph."

I nearly bit my finger. "And you let him go?"

"Not all of them are dangerous. Anyway, Judith isn't."

"Isn't dangerous?"

"I don't know about that. But she isn't a water nymph."

"Tyler says she wants to be a witch. Why is she doing that in your wood?"

She gave the dough in the bowl a hefty swirl with her spoon. "Did you read Rois Melior's story?"

"Yes," I said tersely.

"All of it?"

"All."

She was silent a moment, studying me, hearing the uneasiness in my voice, I was sure. What frightened me was not knowing why she had given it to me to read in the first place.

"What did you see in it?"

"Imaginary worlds," I answered carefully. "A lot of maybe–maybe nots." I paused, drawn into the tale again, feeling hot summer light, hearing secret water. I smelled roses fully opened, hanging heavily under the sun, and started as though the scent had wafted out of the tale. Then I realized the back door was open; I was smelling real roses from the garden. Or was I? What was past? What was present? What was true? A young woman fell in love on a summer's day with a man who had returned home to put his estate in order. My great-great-great-grandmother had looked at my great-great-great-grandfather in the wood behind the hall and seen the fairy blood in him. Or had she?

What was true?

I drew breath; better to know than not, I thought.

"Gram. What did you want me to see in her story?"

She was silent again, stirring, stirring, like an old witch in a tale. Then she lifted her head and gave me that black, still gaze that saw into my bones, and made thoughts in my head scurry for cover.

"From the sound of it," she answered finally, "what you saw. Not yes, not no, but maybe–maybe not." She stirred again, holding me with unspoken words, the endless turn of her spoon. "You might as well know now, so you can think about it: your grandfather left Lynn Hall to you in his will. I want you to have it, too." My mouth opened; she raised the spoon between us, stopped me. "There are other things you must know, but they can wait until the Fiber Guild meeting."

"Gram," I whispered. "Don't do this."

"It's done," she said, and put down the spoon. "Hand me that pan."

I drove to the village for the second time that morning, with Gram's grocery list and my cell phone. I sat under the hydrangea bush again, before I went to the store. It was mid-morning by then; the harrowed fields were awash with gold, and the pale green stubble of whatever was coming up. The drone of machinery rumbled from across the river, where they were mowing the long early-summer grasses for the cows. The river glittered like fake money, like a fairy-tale river, winding gently through the fields. Along a curve, tiny figures cannonballed into it off the high bank; their shouts, faint as hawk-cries, twined into the mowers.

I had to dial twice; my fingers kept hitting wrong numbers. I wasn't even sure why I was calling. I would know when I heard Madison's voice; he would ask me, and I would tell him.

But I only got his voice on the answering machine, brisk and cheerful, telling me to leave a message.

I almost hung up. Instead, I said shakily, "Madison. I've changed my mind. Call me at Gram's house if you need me. Okay?"

I gave him the number, then held the phone to my ear until the machine clicked off, but nobody answered.

· 4 ·

Iris

I went with Owen to the funeral home. Parlor, they called it back when Milton Jenkins bought the old Ayers house in the village and turned it to a profit. Funeral parlor. That had gone the way of girdles and pillbox hats. I didn't go to see Liam. I didn't know him anymore; he didn't know me. I went along to have five minutes alone with Owen.

"Does she know?" he asked, turning the car out of the drive onto the road toward the village.

"Yes," I said.

"Did she read—"

"Yes."

"What about—"

"No. But there's the Fiber Guild meeting. Kathryn will be

gone by then, and for once Sylvia will be exactly where we need her. We can explain things then."

He didn't have to ask what we were talking about; neither did I. So it had always been. I had known his father and his father's father. Protectors of Lynn Hall, they'd always been, the whole line of Averys, who came from the outside world on Corbett Lynn's wedding day, and never went back. An Avery had married Corbett and Rois's youngest daughter; an Avery had been at every Lynn funeral since Corbett's death. An Avery, or some relative of one, had been with the Fiber Guild since it was started over a hundred years earlier by Liam's grandmother Sarah Lynn, who worked her knitting into knots one day and dried up a stream running through Tye Gett's cow pasture.

"I'll stay in the car," I added, as the passing fields gave way to houses. "I saw Liam's face after he died. It was about as peaceful as it ever got. That's enough for me."

But it wasn't; I tasted the lie even as I said it. Nothing would be enough, except Liam's tranquil eyes opening and his mouth under its white brush smiling at me. I felt my eyes burn. But I sent the tears back in a hot wave toward my heart, where love and grief and anger tangled so tightly you couldn't even separate a single thread to begin to unravel them.

Owen gave me one of those heavy, brooding glances that seemed to take a sounding of everything but words. He didn't care; he didn't bother to say. He only murmured succinctly, "Nothing," which pretty much said everything. Nothing left of Liam; nothing would come of seeing him lying meekly in his satin box with a tie on; nothing would ever be the same. Even Owen wasn't wearing a tie, just jeans and a dark linen jacket. He hadn't shaved either. I could see the stubble coming out, silvery gray and black, along his lean jaw.

"I saw Sylvia in the village this morning," he said, turning around the square. Both sides of the street were lined with cars in front of the funeral home. "She asked me to bring you here if you wanted."

"Don't park here," I said, more sharply than I meant to. He didn't comment, just drove to the other side of the square and stopped there. He sat a moment before he got out, watching Bethany Hines and her daughter go in, Rafe Hagarty holding the screen door open for them as he came out. The home, painted the color of vegetables you have to be taught to like, mushroom with eggplant trim, the dark, neatly trimmed junipers lining the porch and the walk, made me impatient again. What did all that decorousness matter to Liam? What could anything matter again?

Owen looked at me quizzically. I shook my head. He put his hand on my shoulder gently, then got out of the car. I watched him cross the green, and realized what he had said. He had already seen my disguised granddaughter; she had recognized him for what he was; she had asked him to watch over me. That made me smile. She knew what she needed to know; she just didn't know she knew. At least that much was going well. Then I felt the emptiness where Liam usually sat, the breeze blowing aimlessly through the open car window, sun falling on the motionless wheel. For no reason at all, I remembered our wedding day at Lynn Hall, my white lace and pearls, the great bunch of orange roses Liam had chosen for me from the garden, his mother Meredith's wince when she saw them, as though I carried a bridal bouquet of cow parsley. Then the years slid past, swift and bright, like cards flowing between a magician's outstretched hands, and, watching them, I took a little nap.

The rest of the day and the next morning blurred together that same way. I blinked and heard someone vacuuming the hallway. The phone rang; someone spoke; I spoke. Things got cooked, eaten; the phone kept ringing. I sat down in my rocking chair, closed my eyes for a moment, opened them again, and it was dark. Then it was morning, and Kathryn was frying eggs, while the handsome stranger beside her buttered toast. Clothes appeared on my bed. I looked up and saw Hurley in the hallway, wearing a suit. I nearly asked him why: he looked so dark and tidy, unfamiliar. Who died? I wanted to say, and then remembered.

I put on the lavender crepe suit that Kathryn had chosen. Pretty, I thought it was, before memory overtook me again. I had bought it for Meredith's funeral, then put it on again for Morgana's. And now for Liam. Might as well be buried in it, I thought. It's what I wear when somebody dies.

Then I was sitting in a car. Then walking across graves in the cemetery. Then sitting again beside a hole in the ground. Men from the oldest families around—John Travers, who ran the village clinic, Millford Turl, who owned a riding stable, Jay Gett, whose farm was as old as the village—carried the coffin, along with Owen, and Tyler, blinking nervously, and the blond stranger who had been making toast in my kitchen. Patrick, I remembered finally. Kathryn's new husband Patrick Lawson, who'd arrived unexpectedly sometime during the night. He wore a solemn expression for the occasion, his sculpted face a tad fatuous. But on the whole, good-hearted.

Kathryn sat on one side of me, dressed in shades of gray, weeping into a crumpled ball of lace in one hand, and squeezing my hand with the other. Sylvia, in a short, tight black suit, black fingerless gloves, and heels so high they must have aerated a few graves, didn't move or make a sound. I could smell the lilac bushes along the graveyard fence. In the little grass beds marked with stone headboards, the dead idled under a sky so blue and full of light you wanted to open your mouth and drink it in. Liam would have been long gone on a day like this, prowling the woods, maybe, on the hill above the cemetery, where the trees clustered so thickly together anyone could be watching within the shadows, and we'd never know.

People were speaking, reading things over the grave, poems, memories; some dropped wildflowers or a handful of dirt into it. I didn't listen. The one poem that crept past my thoughts was so dreadful it made me snort with laughter. Kathryn gave a quick sob to cover it; Sylvia bowed her head, stared rigidly at her tightly folded hands. Then I heard Owen's sonorous voice, quoting Tennyson—*From the great deep to the great deep he goes*—and I wanted to wail like a winter wind and sit by myself in a blizzard until I was covered with snow and no one could find me again. Instead, I stared stonily down at Sylvia's long, lovely fingers and made my thoughts as harsh as snow. You didn't wait for me, I told Liam coldly. You could have just once invited me to come along.

Finally, everyone was quiet; only the wind spoke, and a hawk circling high above us. Somebody whispered to me. I started to stand, but it wasn't as easy as it should have been. Then Owen was at my side, and Sylvia, both holding me, and I could breathe again, and walk. People started talking softly, trailing after us. I took step after step away from Liam, except when I stopped suddenly, remembering what he had wished.

I asked Owen abruptly, "Will he forgive me?"

As always, he knew what I was thinking. "Yes," he said firmly. "We couldn't have Liam Lynn blowing all over the county. Plant a rosebush on his grave and stop worrying about it."

But I looked back anyway, suddenly uncertain. Liam was the only one who could make me feel that way. As though I might be—well, simply wrong about something. I stared at his open grave, half-expecting him to sit up and give me that bemused, vulnerable expression he got when I said something cruel or made an inconsiderate decision. Should I have burned you up and scattered you? I asked him. How much did it matter to you?

On the hill where the graves ended and the wood began, a group lingered within the trees, watching. I saw only blurs for faces, shadowy green, maybe leaves, maybe clothes. Owen made a faint sound. I turned after a moment, went on toward the cars.

Owen, whose eyes were better than mine, said, "Rowans, I think. Too shy to come down among the villagers."

Then we were in the car, driving slowly back to the hall, with half the village snaking along the road behind us, a few hapless tourists caught up in our wake.

Kathryn put me into a chair on the back porch, told me

to stay there. Somehow tables, chairs, a yellow pavilion had appeared on the lawn on the other side of the rose garden, around the old pear tree where Liam had fallen asleep. Offerings crowded the tables in every kind of bowl, platter, casserole dish. I watched Penelope Starr and Kathryn and Dorian Avery working methodically, taking off lids and foil, raiding my kitchen for knives and serving spoons and ice, making punches out of liquids so garishly colored they looked lethal. People crowded up the porch to speak to me before they ate. "He was so wonderful," they told me in lowered, husky voices. "We'll miss him so much. You're so fortunate he went quickly, peacefully, so like him not to cause a fuss, just go when it was time." They patted my hands, wiped away a tear or two, then turned away, and their normal voices came back as they went down the steps.

Kathryn brought me a cup of tea.

"It looks like a circus," I commented, "with that pavilion."

"The Rotary Club donated it."

"Liam was never—"

"It doesn't matter. He was Liam Lynn, of Lynn Hall. They're paying respect."

Patrick came up to join her. He kissed my cheek; I smelled cologne. "I'm sorry to meet you this way, Iris," he said. He had one of those sincere, manly voices that sounds vaguely foolish. But there he was, causing that smile on Kathryn's face, so I was polite. Nothing else to do about it.

"You were brave to come."

He nodded, looking a trifle wide-eyed. "That's some extended family you've got."

"I've been here in this small world a long time. We've all grown together, and believe me, when a stranger appears in our midst we pay attention."

"I noticed." He hesitated. "Kathryn will be following me back tonight, so that she can pack while I work tomorrow. I hope you don't mind Tyler staying with you."

"Not at all."

He brightened. "He's a good kid. He can help you around the house. It's only for a couple of weeks. Unless you decide you want him longer, of course. He'd be company for Hurley; they can go fishing together, or—"

Kathryn put a hand on his arm. "I don't know if I want to be without him too long."

"Oh."

I sipped more tea, feeling tired, though it was early in the afternoon. "Patrick, why don't you get something to eat. I need to talk to Kathryn a little." I watched him bound lithely down the steps, then turned to Kathryn, who was looking wary. "You didn't want Lynn Hall, did you? Because it's not going to you."

"No," she said instantly, looking relieved instead. "I don't want to live here. You have to drive forty miles just to find a shoe store."

"Half the family money will go to you and Tyler, a quarter to me, and a quarter to Sylvia, along with Lynn Hall. She'd need every penny, I know, to fix this old hulk up."

"Syl," Kathryn echoed, bewildered. "What would Syl want with it?"

"She doesn't."

"But—"

"But it's hers. Arthur Manning will read the will after everyone goes home this afternoon. There are other bequests. But this is the gist of it."

"Mother," Kathryn said softly, "you can't force Syl to stay here that way."

"That's not my intention. She'll most likely want to leave me in it until I die, and then sell it."

"That's putting it a bit harshly," Kathryn complained. "After all, she was born here."

"I'm suggesting that's what she'll want to do. Not what she will do. She might find a reason to stay."

Kathryn drew a breath, held it. "Mother," she said again, in that voice of sweet reason I never found any reason to pay attention to, "she's a grown woman. She has her own life. Let her be."

"It was Liam's wish, as well as mine. What do you want me to do about it? I can't change the will."

"You could have changed his mind."

"Then you or Tyler would have had to deal with it," I reminded her. I saw Sylvia then, leaning like a shadow against the pear tree in her black suit, talking to Owen and his daughter. Owen was frowning, intent as he listened; he said something when Sylvia finished, and I knew that she had told him about the will. He was dressed as usual like a rumpled squire, in an old tweed jacket with a belt across the back and an elegant gray silk tie. Dorian glanced at me then, a quick, fluttering look that let her see without being seen. She walked away to join Leith Rowan at a table, her pretty skirt sprigged with tiny roses blowing up around her cowboy boots.

Sylvia came to me, then. I took a look at her stiff, mutinous face and got to my feet. "Let's take it inside," I suggested, before she could speak.

"Gram—"

I shook my head, led her into the house. I heard the television going behind the closed door of the den. A male voice gave a sudden whoop. Patrick must have bonded with Hurley already. Nobody was in the kitchen, so we went in there. Sylvia shut the door behind us.

"Gram," she said again; her voice shook. Her wide eyes, her pale skin, and sharply tapered jaw reminded me suddenly of Morgana. How could I have thought they didn't look alike? But maybe it was only the familiar, stubborn expression that verged oddly on desperation. "I don't want this place. I don't want to live here. I'm happy where I am. If I inherit Lynn Hall, I'll sell it when you die. It will pass out of the family. If you don't want that to happen, you should think about what you want done with it."

"I want you to have it," I said simply.

"I'll give it to you. Put the papers in your name. You can will it to Tyler, or Owen, or something—"

"It will come right back to you, when I die."

"Then I'll sell it."

It went pretty much as I expected; she couldn't know how comforting her objections were. The door opened abruptly; Penelope came in with a couple of empty platters.

"Oh, sorry, Iris," she said quickly and left, knowing that women hold their councils of war in kitchens: the knives are there, and the cups of coffee, and the towels to dry the tears.

"You can do whatever you want," I told Sylvia. "You can leave, and never come back, you can sell this place, you can tear it down—"

"For what?" she interrupted, her nut-gold eyes narrowed, knowing me as well as I knew her. "In exchange for what?"

"Tomorrow night. Stay for the Fiber Guild meeting."

She blinked, wordless for a moment. "Gram," she said, uncertain now, but still adamant, "a quaint country sewing circle is not going to persuade me to change my mind."

"Then you'll stay," I said briskly. "Good."

"I might take the first plane back the morning after," she warned.

"If you choose." I looked around then, suddenly tired again and wanting something. Food? Tea? Something stronger? It was Liam I wanted, I realized helplessly, and the rigid expression on Syl's face melted.

"Oh, Gram," she whispered, putting her arms around me. "Let's not fight now. Come back outside and sit down. Of course I'll stay tomorrow. After that, we can talk again."

We walked out together. I saw faces at the long tables turning toward us: the Starr sisters, Bet Harvey, Jenny Crane, Genevieve MacIntosh, Hillary Cross, Charlotte Henley, Jane and Agatha Sloan, Dorian. All silently questioning. I smiled, sat down again, and their attention went back to ordinary things.

So, later, after everyone had gone home, and Arthur

Manning read the will in Liam's study, with its untidy shelves of nature books, seedpods, fossils, and agates scattered everywhere, there were no surprises and no explosions. The pavilion had been taken down, chairs and tables carted away; many invisible hands had left the kitchen tidier than I had seen it in months. We gathered at the front door to wave Kathryn and Patrick off to their honeymoon. The four of us, suddenly alone, looked at one another blankly, wondering at the silence.

"I'm going to take a walk," Sylvia said. "Dorian said she'd meet me at our secret place; we have seven missing years to share."

"Oh, that secret place in the middle of the stream where the rocks are flat and you can lie and watch the fireflies and smoke?"

Her eyes widened. "Gram! How did you—"

"Liam," I reminded her. "The night-prowler. He liked to sit there himself, when you two gave him the chance."

Tyler said incomprehensibly, "C'mon, Grunc. I'll teach you how to play Space Scavengers."

"Ah?" Hurley said, and followed him obligingly.

"Gram?" Sylvia queried, and I patted her shoulder.

"Go on. I'm going to sit on the back porch for a while and watch the stars come out."

So we went our separate ways. I watched the sky darken and thought of Liam. Owen came, finally, as I wanted him to. We talked for a long time, mostly about Liam, a little about Sylvia and Lynn Hall, and what we knew we needed to do, what always needed to be done when the passing of Lynn

Hall from one heir to the next disturbed our work, and the opening of the earth threatened to open invisible doors everywhere.

The moon began its arc over the wood, and Owen left me alone. I lingered, waiting for Sylvia, but always it was Liam's step I listened for.

· 5 ·

Owen

I heard them on my walk home down the road that ran along the stream between the Lynn fields and Tom Trask's north pasture: the disguised Sylvia, with her hair like a sleek brass bell and her cool hazelnut eyes full of the secrets of an unfamiliar world, and my unchanging daughter, with her wild curls and the potting soil under her nails, whose eyes had seen no farther than the next hollow, where generations of Rowans lived without benefit of street address or mailbox, sharing a post office box and a few ancient trucks among them. The young women's voices, slightly deeper now but still light and sweet, tumbled over one another, discussing Leith, no doubt, Liam, me, Iris, and whoever it was that kept

Sylvia so far away from us. Invisible as naiads they were, on their stones in midstream behind a spinning, flashing galaxy of fireflies.

The moon, drifting overhead, illumined a gray blur of tarmac between the black wall of trees along the water, and the ditch at the foot of the field wall on the other side. I didn't need the flashlight I carried out of habit. Liam had never used one. He could tell where he was by the sound of the windblown leaves in the wood: he could hear the difference between the chatter of maple leaves, and birch, and oak.

He could smell where he was by the scent of wild grapes, violets, wild thyme. He could smell water: mud, wet slate, frog-spawn, fresh springwater, the damp stones above underground streams. Rambling along the mountain roads under the stars, he could smell the little hard apples in trees abandoned to the wild and know where we were. Water spoke to him: he knew the local flows in their changing seasons; the swift rush of early-spring snowmelt; the slow, languid, late-summer shallows. A whiff of smoke from someone's fire, the night smell of a planted field, a sudden breath of hemlock or cow pasture would tell him as clearly as the light of day where we were in the dark.

He taught me many things as we skirted the boundaries between sun and moon, between seeing and not seeing, the wood he saw, the wood he didn't see. If he saw what that streak of Melior in him might have shown him, he never said. He only showed me what he loved. It was Iris who kept an eye on the secret wood within the wood.

The lore was handed down through generations: my own

mother had learned it; my daughter had been taught. How to guard the passages between worlds. How to recognize them: the underground stream that feeds a hidden well, the lightning-blasted oak whose dark hollow, formed by fire, runs deeper into the earth than the passing eye would notice, the pond with the spring that feeds it springing from another world entirely. The great door between worlds, Lynn Hall itself, and all the places where water, or wind, or moonlight enter. How to seal those openings, confuse paths, lock doors, make fast the wall between the worlds.

Between all we love and all we fear.

So I was taught, by my uncle, since the gifts for seeing and protecting tend to leapfrog through the Avery line. A taciturn man, better at showing than explaining, he introduced me to Liam when I was very young. I followed Liam everywhere, even then. He taught me the names of wildflowers, mushrooms, beetles. Iris told me stories, real and fay; I hardly knew the difference for years. I would go home thinking that my grandfather, Marsden Avery, had fiddled at a fairy wedding in Lynn Hall, or that Liam's father had been stolen for a time when he was a baby, and a changeling made of twigs had been found in his cradle. Gradually, I sorted out the difference between what the world considered true and what Iris did. Years later, I chanced across my own version of the truth. Or truth found me, on a moonlit night, like the one I was walking through, and changed the face of my world.

She was waiting for me when I got home.

I saw the glimmer beside the pond, which was the reflection of her in the other world. It startled me, how fluid the boundaries were that night. Opening one passage in the earth for Liam, we had opened another. She didn't even have to hear my music to thread her way into my world. Death had unpicked locks, found its way under our guard, illumined all our illusions. The master of Lynn Hall had died; the heir had not yet accepted her place. Anything might happen, Iris had said. Imagining anything but this.

She sat among the reeds so quietly the frogs were singing their love song around her. I heard them plop into the water as I walked along the bank. I hadn't realized how much I wanted her until I saw her. And then I didn't care that I was middle-aged and dour, and she was fay. I wanted to kick off my boots, fill my hands with wildflowers, find a toad with a jewel in its eye, and scatter my gifts into her lap.

She grew more substantial under the moonlight as she recognized me. She smiled up at me. I knelt beside her, took her hand, brought it to my mouth, so moved that she'd come to me that I couldn't find words. I couldn't grieve, it seemed, until she laid her hand upon my heart. Then I felt it crack open like an egg. Then I felt the pain and love and sorrow kindle and sear; then I felt the tears. Inhuman as she was, she was the lifeline I needed to cling to while I admitted grief.

"What are these?" she murmured, taking one on her finger. "Owen?"

I loved to hear her say my name; it sounded ancient, when she spoke it, as though I heard it echo through countless centuries.

"Tears," I said, closing her hand around it. "Treasure it. I don't make them often, and look, they're almost already gone."

She kissed my eyes, tasting delicately. "Salt," she murmured. "Water. I have kin, I'm told, who live in one enormous tear."

I smiled, and was instantly grateful again, that I could laugh and weep in the same moment while I was with her. "Ocean, we call it," I told her. "And it does taste like tears."

She had me pick a flower name for her, so I called her Rue, for her yellow hair. And for the day I would rue when she faded from my life, or we were discovered. In over a decade, neither of those things happened. She would never tell me her true name. If I said it aloud in the wrong place or time in the wood, someone might hear; she would be in trouble, and I would be in danger. Ten years to her were nothing; only her expressions had changed in all that time, growing wise and more complex. Her eyes were dark as sloe berries, her smile ancient and eternally bewitching. Her long, light bones and silky skin seemed to change constantly, sometimes as strong and tensile as a sapling tree, sometimes melting like a dream in my hold, as though, like the name I gave her, even what I saw was false.

Maybe. I didn't care. Who would?

"What makes the tears?" she asked.

"Grief. When someone whom we love has died."

"Ah," she said softly. "We felt that. Wind from your world has been blowing into ours; water runs backward. It was easy for me to come to you; you opened the earth today, and passages stood open everywhere, unguarded. Even a few that have been closed so long we had forgotten them."

"Where?" I asked her immediately, but she only gave me her sidelong smile.

"So you can tell?" she asked me. "And have the witch in the great hall guard them more closely?"

"Of course. That is my solemn duty."

She touched my lips with the flowering end of a stalk of wild grass. "You do it so well," she murmured, and I felt her hair brush across my lips, and then I felt her lips. I sank back on the bank, amid the reeds and wildflowers, the dark water and the frogs. She opened my shirt, slid her slender hands into my sleeves, along my naked arms, held them out wide, and stretched herself over me. Heedless and exposed as any animal, me grunting with the frogs while she sang like a katydid, and the fireflies swarmed around us like an enchanted mist. At those times I couldn't think about who might wander by, even at high noon, while she stopped time with her body and drew my soul out between my teeth. But she hid us somehow; no one ever saw.

Afterward, I was alone. What I thought was the blur of her face turned into the moon, angled curiously toward me. I lay for a while without a thought in my head, until I heard a distant door open and close. A light went on in the house: another eye. It didn't touch me, but I felt exposed again, and slightly foolish, lying there with my clothes open like a teenager gaffed by hormones.

But the light went out almost immediately; doors opened and closed again. I heard Dorian's truck start, and knew, by the direction she turned out of the driveway, that she had gone in search of her own consolation.

And then I felt the touch of Rue again, and smiled.

"You're still here."

"I heard her coming. I thought you might want to leave me."

I shook my head, shifting to a slightly more dignified position and closing a couple of buttons. "She's gone to find her own love." I felt my voice tighten in spite of myself; then I had to laugh again. "Listen to me. I fret about Leith Rowan, and here I am with you."

"Here you are," she echoed contentedly, leaning against me, her hair green-gold in the moonlight. Then she murmured, "Leith Rowan."

"Do you know him?" I asked abruptly, feeling a sudden, raw pang of worry.

"We know some Rowans. I don't know which."

They might have been long dead, I knew; some Rowan a century or two ago had met a woman in the wood with her hair the color of flowering rue. Memory didn't fade in her world, nor did she really understand our habit of dying. It seemed more a matter of choice to her; she wouldn't assume that a two-hundred-year-old Rowan wouldn't find his way eventually back into her company.

Still, I asked with anxious precision, "What do you mean 'know'?"

She laughed at my finicky need for detail, and answered lightly, taking my breath away, "Rowans don't guard their boundaries. They have never been afraid of us. The ones who know of us."

"Some don't?" My voice sounded harsh to me, but she only shook her head tranquilly.

"Seeing is believing. Isn't that what you say? The Rowans

who can see us, or who are aware of us, don't fear us. Those who can't, don't believe in us. Either way, we live along our boundaries in peace."

"And Leith—"

She took my face in her hands then, looked into my eyes. "I don't know their names," she said again, gently. "Only that Rowan name, which is as old as any around here. It was old when Lynn Hall was a cottage in a clearing surrounded by the wood."

I had to be content with that. My daughter's lover had, after all, been to college and held a day job; a certain taciturnity and disinclination for noise and crowds didn't necessarily mark him kin to the Fair Folk. His interest in the wild life of the mountains might. But Liam Lynn had rambled all his life among the wild things and never wandered farther than he should have.

Until now, I remembered numbly, and reached out again, to close the little distance there was between our hearts.

"How strange," I breathed, "how strange . . . that day so long ago . . . I went into the wood, looking for Liam Lynn and I found you instead."

"Beside the honeysuckle growing up the old elm tree. But it wasn't so long ago. Was it?"

"A dozen years? Thirteen?"

"That's nothing."

"To you, a year is a day—"

"And a day is forever."

She smelled of wild grasses, sunlight, violets. When I closed my eyes, I wondered what I truly held in my arms: a fairy lover, or the life-giving earth itself, taking a shape I could touch and love, even if I couldn't understand it.

"Come tomorrow," I whispered. "And the next night. Every night. The moon finds a way; why shouldn't you?"

"I will try . . . It's not always easy. Your Iris twists the paths; it's like finding my way through bindweed and bramble. Or through water between our worlds that has stopped flowing; it takes me nowhere." She hesitated a breath; I stirred to look at her.

"What is it?"

"She would take you, if she could. If she knew."

"She—"

"Sh." She laid a finger on my lips. A face flashed across my thoughts, an imaginary vision left from one of Iris's tales when I was young, or from Rois Melior's papers: the winter queen with her heart of ice and in her face the haunting beauty of every season. "Don't speak of her. Just be careful. Never look for me; your heart may summon her instead. Always let me come to you."

I didn't tell her that of course I had wandered in search of her, many times. How could I not, especially in the early years? I had never found her by looking for her, but no one else had found me, either. Perhaps I had Iris to thank for that, though she'd hardly be grateful to me if she knew what I hid from her.

I saw her face then: strong, delicate with age, her shrewd, fearless, vulnerable eyes that watched over our world, and held that peculiar blind spot only when she looked at me. Then I saw both their faces: ancient sorcerers guarding their realms, putting up warning signs everywhere along their marches: Do Not Trespass.

And my gentle Rue, slipping past them both to come to me on a night when I needed her to take my mind off dying.

"I do not know what you are," I heard myself murmur, or think, or my heart tell her, "but I love you."

I sat with her for a long time until my arms held only moonlight, and even the frogs were still.

·6·

Iris

The circle was complete by eight-fifteen the next night; everyone came promptly to have a closer look at Sylvia. Dorian was last as always, flurried and windblown, though there was no wind, just the private little whirlwind she always travels in.

"Sorry, sorry," she said, though there was no need. She put a tray of stuffed mushrooms on the sideboard and gave me a hug, leaving a crochet hook dangling in my hair from the sewing bag in her hand. "Oh—sorry!" She looked preoccupied; I wondered grimly if she had decided to marry the Rowan boy. She turned to give Sylvia a bear hug, which made everyone smile: they had been running in and out of one another's lives since they were born.

A baker's dozen turned out, counting Sylvia. The Starr twins and Penelope had come at a quarter to eight on the dot, Lacey and Miranda in pastel crepe and their usual pearls and gold, as though they were going to a wedding or a funeral. These days it's hard to tell, with everyone wearing black to both, until they bring the bride or the body out. The twins sat on the velveteen couch together and took out their work, while Penelope added a huge rhubarb pie to my plate of cherry-chocolate cookies on the sideboard. Penelope wore jeans and high-top sneakers with glitter all over them. Her hair glittered oddly, too, in the lamplight; so did her eyelids. Well, even at her age, she was still a child compared to me at my age, and with her round sweet face she could get away with a lot more than most. She sat down, the quilt she was stitching by hand tumbling out of the bag at her feet.

Genevieve MacIntosh and Hillary Cross had come down the mountain together; they took turns driving each month. Hillary, with her big fierce eyes and short spiky hair, looked like an owl. She hated to cook; she brought a big bottle of white or red that always got emptied by the end of the evening. That night, most likely considering the occasion, she brought both. She wore holey jeans and muddy garden clogs that she kicked off at the door. She unrolled one of what she called her fabric paintings: a concoction of scraps and buttons, beads and trim she pieced together until for some reason she declared it done and framed it. They were pretty things, made of velvet and brocade, satin, watered silk, fabric she wouldn't be caught dead wearing.

Genevieve tended bar at the Village Grill, though she

didn't look old enough to drink, which she didn't anyway, except for herbal teas. She was very tall and willowy, the way they grow these days, with long straight blond hair and calm, gray eyes. She wore boots and a cowboy hat, a sweater that almost hid the garnet stud in her navel, but not quite. She put a mountain of peanut butter–chocolate chip cookies on the sideboard and pulled out the booties she was knitting for her sister's baby.

The principal's wife, Charlotte Henley, brought wool from her own sheep; she was crocheting an afghan for her teenage daughter. As always, she had made her cocktail meatballs, which never tasted the same twice. She made the sauce out of whatever she had in the back of the refrigerator—marmalade one month, peach jam the next—along with a healthy dollop of soy sauce and enough garlic to stun a vampire. A slight woman with a no-nonsense jaw and manner, she wore her platinum hair cut just so to her chin and parted on the right. In the nine years she'd been coming to the meetings, I never saw a hair's worth of change in it.

Jane Sloan, the village historian, came in with her embroidery bag dangling from her walker. She had seen as much local history as I had, and kept track of it for the historical society over in Highland. She had published a history of Lynnwood years earlier, and was working on another, secret history, about which she consulted me to niggle over points of memory. We had known one another since before the invention of the diaper pin. She moved slowly across the room with her walker, dressed to the nines in a suit and a hat with a couple of pheasant feathers curling down the brim. She reminded me of Liam's mother Meredith: the same beady magpie eyes looking for the chip in the cup, the dust on the whatnot shelf, the same pursed mouth, out of which dropped lemons and sour grapes more often than not. But there wasn't much those sharp eyes missed, and what Jane spoke stayed spoken.

She took her usual place beside me on the tapestry couch, leaving her daughter Agatha, with her big eyes and big, placid body, turning vaguely in the middle of the room, looking for a place to sit. Sylvia waved her over to an empty chair beside her, and Agatha's face brightened. She seemed bovine, even at third glance, the ox-boned, slow-moving country woman living behind her uncertain girl's face most of her life. But she worked magic with her hands. Her quilts hung in craft museums; her spiced pears made you want to lead a better life. She was kind to her difficult mother; she understood without being told what monsters lurked in an old woman's bedroom in the dark of the night. She put a plate of her savory mushroom turnovers on the sideboard before she sat, causing a moment of respectful silence as we acknowledged them.

"You probably don't remember me," I heard her say to Sylvia. "Your mama and I were in and out of each other's houses all the time when we were growing up."

I saw Sylvia's eyes widen; she said something that I missed under Jane's grumble.

"It's too bad what young women think they have to do with their hair these days." She was staring at Hillary's pale, choppy hair. Her voice wavered suddenly. "Is that a tattoo on her scalp?"

I inhaled a laugh; it came out as a snort. Jane's cold eyes swiveled toward me. "Something caught in your throat, Iris?"

"Nothing I can't swallow. Who's missing?"

"The farmers' wives," Jane said, pulling out her embroidery. "They're always late. And Dorian."

Bet Harvey and Jenny Crane came in as she spoke: two sisters who drove together from the next valley. The older, Bet, was tall and rangy, with long black hair in a clip; Jenny, shorter, stouter, kept her short gingerbread hair in the pin curls fashionable half a century ago. They had been born on a farm; they married local farmers, raised children and crops indiscriminately, it seemed. They drove big old station wagons that disgorged endless quantities of dogs, bedding plants, soccer teams, balls, bats, rackets, groceries, canning pots, school play decorations, and slumber parties on their way to or from wherever. They both carried overstuffed knitting bags; they were always halfway through a ski sweater or a baby afghan for somebody. Bet put a veggie tray with dip onto the sideboard; Jenny added a fruit tray with dip. Then they turned simultaneously, smiled at me, turned again, and had a hard look at Sylvia. Then they sat in a couple of high-backed oak chairs, unpacking their knitting and whispering together.

And at last Dorian came. Jane cleared her throat; it was a signal to me to get things going.

"Welcome," I said. "For those who didn't introduce themselves at the funeral, this is my granddaughter Sylvia, Morgana's child, the heir to Lynn Hall. She has done a little bit of required reading, but of more than that, she is as ignorant as a barn owl. And from what I can tell, she couldn't string two stitches together with any kind of needle to save her life. But her heart is good, and her instincts are every bit as sound as Morgana's. I propose her for initiation and education." I glanced at Sylvia. She was bolt upright in her chair now, gripping the arms and staring at me out of those golden hazelnut eyes. "You can stay or leave now," I told her. "Will you stay?"

Her instincts, as I said, were sound. She didn't throw up a flurry of protests and questions; she realized she already had the information she needed. She just swallowed, then said tautly, "I'll stay."

"We each get one question," I went on. "That's your initiation. I've already asked mine. You don't have to answer. We consider what you conceal as significant as what you reveal. You might consider it none of our business."

I glanced around the circle. Everyone had their projects out by now: yarn, embroidery, sewing and quilting threads, fine gold thread for Hilary, needles of all kinds. Sylvia was looking at us as though she'd fallen into the bear pit at the zoo, and she didn't know whether or not we'd been fed.

Jane took up the questioning, after spearing a nice little French knot into the middle of the violet she was embroidering on a linen napkin. "Did you ever find out who your father was?" she asked.

I saw Sylvia's slender throat shift in another swallow. She answered simply, "No."

"Pity."

Jane went back to work; Bet looked up from another of her endless knitted sweaters, this one lime-pie green out of what looked like angora. Bet had startling eyes you seldom saw; they usually focused on canning, or uprooting bulbs for winter storage, or any of a hundred daily chores. A gray like the sheen on a gun barrel. "Do you have any idea what this gathering does?"

Sylvia hesitated. Sew, she might have answered two minutes ago; now she just said again, "No."

Jenny, putting an edging on a baby blanket with hearts and rainbows stitched all over it, took up the thread of questions. "What have you read?"

Most of a bookstore, Sylvia might have said. But she knew what Jenny was asking, which was why she was there.

"My great—Rois Melior's account of how she met Corbett Lynn. Gram asked me to read it." Her eyes flickered to me as she said that; she realized that I had set her up for this. I first read those pages myself decades ago, when my eyesight was so clear I could see where one world ended and the Other began.

Across from her, Hillary raised her cropped head. Sometimes our words flowed around in a circle; other times we passed words back and forth, making patterns of angles and stars between us. She asked in her blunt way, as she fastened tiny crystal beads onto her pattern, "Did you believe it?"

"I'm here," Sylvia answered tersely, reminding me vividly of Morgana, getting to the meat of something so cleanly that it was only when the skin fell whole to the ground that you saw the knife. Her hands still clenched on the arms of her chair; her whole body was tense, as though she were on some wild carousel ride. Dorian, who had curled up in a chair on the other side of the lamp they shared, touched her hand lightly. Sylvia turned toward her, still set like an unsprung trap, and gave her an intense, wide-eyed stare, as though she were trying to recognize her oldest friend.

On the other side of her, Agatha asked placidly, as she threaded a needle, "Your mother never mentioned these things?"

Sylvia shook her head once. "Not to me. Never."

"You left this place where you were born just about as soon as you could," Lacey said. She was hooking the ugliest throw rug I had ever seen, all browns and grays and yellows, maybe to keep under her composter. "Why?"

"I—" She hesitated for some reason, and touched a strand of gilded hair. "I left to go to college, and then I moved across country to finish my degree. I used the money my mother left me to open my bookstore. I intended to stay there. I still do," she added stubbornly, just like her mother. "I only came back because of Grandpa Liam. And to help Gram."

"Do you plan to sell this place?" Miranda asked, crocheting a doily the silvery gray of her hair.

Sylvia's feet shifted, wanting her out from under the question. But she answered it honestly. "Yes. When Gram doesn't need it any longer." She looked at me. "I've already made that clear."

I couldn't say anything; she had no idea what had really drawn her back. I just nodded, and Genevieve picked up the thread, pulling stitches out of her baby booty, looking for the one she had dropped.

"If you chose a needle, which would it be?"

A practical question. Sylvia looked vaguely surprised. "I could thread a needle, maybe. Sew a simple stitch. Nothing more complicated."

"Needle and thread," Penelope murmured, and picked out both from her quilting basket. She sent it down the circle along with a square of linen. "Do you know how to tie a knot?"

"I think so."

"Yes?"

"Yes," Sylvia said, after a moment or two, doing the basic wrap-around-the-finger and snarl at the end of the thread.

"That was two questions," the principal's wife murmured.

"It was the same one twice," I said firmly. "Go ahead, Charlotte."

"Do you recognize what we're making?" she asked Sylvia, who was gazing bemusedly down at the needle and cloth in her hands. She raised her head, glanced around at us, opening her mouth to answer. But she didn't. Sweater, her eyes told her. Rug, baby bootie, quilt, doily, pillow slip . . . Then I felt her catch our thoughts, like the first tremble of a moth-step onto a web. Threads, she saw. Stitches. Patterns. Stitches to hold fast. Patterns to make boundaries, to cover, to shape. To mimic. Bindings to hold them there. Threads to create. Knots to bind.

She whispered, "Three for eyes to see. Four to shut the door."

Charlotte came as close to smiling as she ever did.

"Good enough," she said. A web was growing out of her hands, out of the soft ivory wools of her sheep. An afghan, anyone would have seen, a pretty, lacy thing for an early-fall day. But try to walk her patterns, and you'd find yourself in a perpetual twilight between here and there, and no telling which was where.

Dorian was last. She was making a patchwork scarf out of rich, bright squares and triangles of satin and black velvet. Pinning gold rickrack into place around one triangle, she asked Sylvia gently, "Do you have any questions for us?"

Sylvia eased back into her chair finally, giving us a haunted look. As well as could be expected, when the local sewing circle turns into a coven around you. I gave her back a smile, but her eyes just skittered off it nervously. She nodded finally, and lifted the square of linen, from which the needle was dangling ineffectually. "Could somebody show me what to do next?"

· 7 ·

Sylvia

Dorian taught me how to stitch a hem. For a while I couldn't talk; I didn't dare. I slid the needle in and out of my little square, pulled thread taut, pushed the needle through again, wishing with every bone in me that I had caught the next flight out after the funeral instead of staying to be trapped there like a fly in a web, hardly daring to think. The eerie stillness of the gathering had broken; women chattered easily as they took up their threads and fabrics. I couldn't look at anyone, not even Dorian, above all, not Gram. What if they recognized something less than human in my eyes? What if they found the last thing they expected among them? I just kept my head down, tucked the edges of my cloth down with uneven stitches and tried to keep my fingers out of the way while Dorian watched me and murmured encouragement.

I risked a look at her finally, when I stopped feeling curious eyes staring my way, and the volume in the room had ratcheted up a notch. "How long has this been going on?"

"Oh, forever," she answered calmly. "Iris said that she was a child when her own mother brought her into the circle, at the Sloans' farmhouse in Crabapple Hollow."

"My mother never told me about this. I don't even know if she could sew. Was she part of the circle, too?" If she had been, if she could lie to them about my father and her halfling child, and still sit here and sew, then maybe they wouldn't see me, either, hiding inside myself.

Dorian glanced at Gram, her brows crooking. She lowered her voice as though we were children again and Gram might hear us under the din. "I don't know. Your mother died long before I was told about this. Iris might have kept the guild secret from her because of your father."

"What about my father?" I asked sharply, alarmed. "Do you know something else I don't?"

"That's the point. Nobody knew who—or what—he was."

I closed my eyes tightly, opened them again, trying to believe I had heard what I had. "You mean, whether or not he was—"

"Fay." She said the word as though she were discussing the state of his finances, and I drove my needle into my thumb.

"Ouch!"

She tutted sympathetically, then caught my eyes, held

them in a clear, disconcerting gaze. "You never wondered that?" she asked.

"No," I answered tersely. I'd never had to wonder. I gathered courage, raised my head a little to eye the busy, vociferous group. "They don't seem worried tonight."

"Oh, you don't show any signs of it, Syl. You're hardly haunting these hills, and you've never wanted Lynn Hall. According to Rois Melior's tale, the hall itself is one of the most powerful passages between worlds. But you left it as soon as you could," she reminded me ruefully. "You couldn't wait to get out of the woods into civilization. Besides, you and I talked about everything while we were growing up. You wouldn't have kept something like that from me."

I was silent, trying to miter a corner. I had done exactly that, kept something like that secret from her. Getting out of here as quickly as possible had seemed the only way to keep it secret. I took a couple of pins from Dorian's pincushion, stabbed the folds into submission, then dropped the linen into my lap and looked across the room at Gram. She was listening absently to Jane and counting stitches as she chained them off her crochet hook. I wondered uneasily what she was making.

"And you," I asked Dorian softly, "how long did you know about this and not tell me?"

She shook her head, ducking for some reason into her hair. "Not as long as you might think. After you left for college. It was easier for me to keep quiet about it, with you away so much." She pieced a triangle of tangerine satin onto her scarf and pinned it, then added, "They weren't sure of me because of my mother."

"What?"

"The way she vanished like that, when I was so little. Some thought she might have been taken, or was part fay herself, or something."

"But she was born here. Everyone knew her parents."

Dorian nodded. "And everyone knew my father: how close he's always been to Iris and Liam. He's an Avery, born to serve and protect Lynn Hall and the family." My brows went up at that disquieting detail. "No one could seriously believe he would have been so blind as to fall in love with one of Them."

Now her eyes were hidden behind her hair; there was an edge to her voice I couldn't interpret. I opened my mouth to ask. But Gram was standing over us suddenly, studying my handiwork: an uneven shirttail hem on two sides of a square of linen held in place by stitches like the tracks of a drunken bug. She picked it up, looked more closely.

"There's blood on it."

"Does it matter?" I asked incredulously.

"It does in fairy tales." She dropped it back into my lap. "You'll have to be more careful."

"Okay," I said unsteadily, and tried to think where I would begin, what I would ask, if I thought she had all the answers. "What are you making, Gram?"

"A sweater-vest for Liam." She closed her eyes briefly. "For Hurley, now. That's what I would say, and he would see, if he asked me. Since you asked, it's a binding spell to protect the attic. I started it when Hurley began finding odd things in the wood with his telescope."

I sorted through this: Hurley seeing apparitions, Gram combating magical forces invading the hall with a crochet hook . . . At some moment the entire Fiber Guild had moved across an unseen boundary between not knowing and knowing, though I wasn't entirely sure yet what it was they knew. I smoothed the linen on my knee, touched my stitches. Unskillful as they were, they formed a pattern, I realized; they bound one thing to another; they changed the shape of a tiny piece of the world.

"What can this do? It's so simple."

"You'd be surprised," Gram answered. "Your great-aunt Maggie could set a binding around an entire field, every stream and gate along its boundaries, just by hemming a handkerchief. Some wood-folk were probably lost for years in the lace edgings she used to crochet around them."

"Wood-folk."

"They're called different things. No one speaks of them directly; you never know who might be listening." She reached down to stroke the velvet in Dorian's scarf. "Pretty. Look at that edging." She traced the zigzag path of the gold rickrack between the bright and dark patches. "Not easy to find your way out of that. Or so we hope. As I said, you never know . . . The Others, they're sometimes called in old writings. Them."

"There are other writings? Besides Rois Melior's?"

"You should see what Jane has dug up in letters, diaries, even account books. Payments to what were put down as dowsers, looking for underground water. Not everybody wanted to tap those springs. Some wanted to cap them. That's where the Fiber Guild comes in. Jane tracks down every reference to the guild in old papers. That way we can keep track of places that were suspect, watched."

"This house."

She nodded, her dark eyes distant, narrowed, as though she were looking through the walls of the house for suspect behavior. "Always this house. Every water-bearing pipe, every door, every window and chimney. The first thing I did when I married Liam and moved here was to make a quilt with a different wheel of crocheted stitches—like a web—fastened over every square. Each web makes a pattern guarding a different room in the hall. I put it away somewhere safe. Remind me to show it to you."

"Iris," Jane, the historian, called. She had a wizened, walnut face, and a body that looked frailer than the feathers in her hat. But her voice went through the din like a twang from an amped guitar. "Is she ready to continue?"

"Are you?" Gram asked, turning her remote, appraising look on me.

"How should I know?"

"Well, you're still here, aren't you?" She patted my hand. "Now we'll show you how to connect your stitches with ours. Don't worry."

I was beyond worry.

The room went silent again. Heads bowed over work. Sewing needles and crochet hooks flashed and dove; knitting needles clicked gently. No one said a word. Lowered eyes focused on threads, yarns, fabrics. So I did, too, sneaking a glance now and then between stitches to see what would happen next.

Nothing happened. We stitched in silence. At least we stitched without words. Having nothing else to listen to, I began to hear needle points puncturing cloth, threads drawn through, again and again, as rhythmically as breathing. Our breaths mingled with the sound, as though breath became thread, air became fabric. I stitched another corner carefully, thinking of other corners: in doorways, at field gates, walls joining at the edges of a house. My stitches pulling them together, reinforcing them . . . knowing how it was done, whatever it was they were doing, would be knowing how it could be undone . . .

I heard water.

It was very faint, a distant stream, an underground rill hidden by moss and stones, water trickling between, around, over things in its path. A stitch to stop it here would send it angling over there, or maybe drive it into earth. I tracked it with my stitches, dammed it, made a knot out of its flow so that it ran perpetually around itself. It whispered to itself, searching for freedom. I lifted it out of its bed, threaded my needle with it, stitched water in and out of earth, made it follow my pattern instead of its own wild, unpredictable path. Here, and here, I told it. Stitch and stitch. I bound the little rill, working it in and out of earth until it slowed and slowed and, as I joined my last stitch with my first, it scarcely moved, standing sullen in the moonlight, a powerless seam of water that had nowhere left to go.

I stopped, studied my hemmed square, my guarded field.

I heard our silence again, the creak of a rocker, the busy click of needles. I looked up, found Gram's eye on me. I didn't look away; I challenged her to see me. For a moment, I heard the sounds of other secret places in the world: the trembling waters of hidden springs, leaves chattering at the sudden passing of wind on a windless night, the heartbeat of steps across an empty meadow. Walls of stitches rose against the wind; labyrinths of stitches trapped the footsteps.

So they kept their worlds separate, themselves safe. I sat within Gram's threads at every door and window, guarding against fears as old as night. Her eyes, beginning to question me, found their answer as I understood what was done, how it was done. Our gazes joined like stitches across the dreaming silence; she only saw enough to smile at me.

Dorian dropped one of her bright triangles into my lap. I changed the color of my thread to saffron and began again.

Slowly time began again. Someone leaned back and sighed. Somewhere a stitch dropped. Genevieve dug a tissue out of her tight jeans and blew her nose. On the other side of Dorian, Agatha cleared her throat. I heard a yawn. Then a clock chimed, and all over the room women knotted threads, brought a row to a finish, cut their yarns, folded their fabrics.

Jane spoke first. She caught my attention with a hard, insistent gaze. When I met her eyes, she said simply, in her nasal boom, "Good, Sylvia." She turned to Gram. "She takes after you, no matter who she came from."

I heard Dorian snort. Gram shot Jane a narrow, dark glance. But Jane just snipped her embroidery thread with the beak of a strange little pair of scissors that looked like a stork's head and said imperviously, "Agatha, put this away and bring me a cup of tea. Just a couple of dips; you know how weak I have to take it this time of night."

Agatha got up. Everyone moved then, stretching, milling toward the bathrooms, the feast on the long oak sideboard. In her chair, Dorian curled her legs up and leaned toward me, the way she used to do when we were young, sharing secrets while the grown-ups partied.

"Be sure to snag one of Charlotte's meatballs," she said. "They're awesome."

Suddenly curious, I asked her, "Does Leith know what happens here?"

She shook her head quickly. "Why would he?" Then she was looking straight at me with her flecked-agate eyes, and I saw the trouble in them. "My father does."

"Well, Gram tells him everything, doesn't she?"

"Yes, but—" She stopped, holding her secret on a breath. I thought bewilderedly of Owen Avery, who had been like everyone else's father when we were growing up: a sort of random force in the world, with no clear set of motivations, able to take us places when he chose, granting or withholding time, money, patience, permission. He hadn't seemed any more or less predictable than other adults. He wore ties more than most around here, but he went to turkey shoots and took Dorian and me fishing now and then; in memory at least he behaved like an ordinary adult.

"But?"

Dorian let out her breath. I saw Jane watching us, then,

and Charlotte, her eyes cold and pale as fog. Dorian shifted. "Not here," she murmured, and stood up.

"When, then?"

"Tomorrow." She leaned down to bundle her patchwork into her bag. "I'll be working in the greenhouse, repotting seedlings to sell. Come there."

"Okay," I said, completely mystified, and drifted after her toward the table. I felt an arm slide around me, and looked into Gram's smiling eyes.

"You did well, Sylvia."

"I'm not sure exactly what I did."

"You were working around our field on the other side of the wood. I recognized the path of water. I hope you're not upset with me. It was easier this way than trying to explain."

"Do you always do it this way?" My voice shook a little. "What would have happened if I'd thought you were all lunatics—including the principal's wife—and went out and told everyone about it?"

"No," Gram said calmly. "We wait and watch for a long time, usually, before we invite. And we are very certain about people before we let them in."

"Did you invite my mother?"

"No."

I felt my heart pound at the word. "Why not?"

"Because Morgana couldn't sit still to save her life, and she was happier nailing shingles to a roof than knitting. Even when you proved to us that it was safe to ask her, none of us suggested it."

"How?" I asked dazedly. "How did I prove that my father

wasn't—wasn't one of Them? How would you recognize Them if you saw one?"

"Some are better at recognizing than others. Your great-great-great-grandmother, Rois Melior, for instance. Others have written about encounters, glimpses, descriptions—that helps us know what we're dealing with. They run cold, in that Otherworld—cold-blooded, cold-hearted. They can be very cruel. At their best, they break your heart; at their worst, they kill. As teenagers, they usually don't wear glasses and chase after fireflies to catch one in a jar for their younger cousin. You were a kind child, Sylvia, and your heart was always in the right place. So we figured that's where Morgana's must have been, too, whomever she loved to get you."

She moved toward the table. I stared wordlessly after her, stunned by all she thought she knew, and all I didn't know she knew.

"Gram—" I caught up with her. "How did you keep this secret from me?"

"You were no more interested in needle and thread than your mother was. I said 'sewing circle,' and your eyes glazed over. The guild didn't meet here, the years we were unsure of you, and when we finally were, you were old enough to make sure you had somewhere else to be, those nights."

"Then why now? I still can't sew."

"We need you to know all there is to know about Lynn Hall before I die. Whatever you decide to do with it, you must take this into account."

She left me reeling again, got a couple of plates from the sideboard, and handed me one.

"Don't worry," Penelope Starr told me cheerfully. "Anything you can manage will be useful. You'll get better, the more you do. It's ongoing, you know; we can't just do it once a month when we meet. Things require attention constantly. Isn't that right, Genevieve?"

The bartender nodded, bending her willowy body as she bit into celery to keep veggie dip from skidding down her sweater. "For sure," she said, after she swallowed. "I'm working on my ninth pair of baby booties. My sister thinks I'm nuts." She grinned. "I crochet when the bar is slow. There's an underground lake under it that I keep an eye on. Still water is the most dangerous kind."

"Why?"

"It runs deep," Gram said simply, and dropped a mushroom turnover on my plate.

I added a few more goodies, wandered around dazedly, looking at various projects, making normal noises most of the time, until someone explained an edging in the context of a cow pasture, or a sequence of embroidery stitches as a bridge across the river. Then a world would superimpose itself over the one I knew: a nameless, vague, darkly powerful realm, rarely seen, but strangely recognizable when you came across it in a tale, between the lines of poetry, in your life.

Finally, plates and cups started making their way to the kitchen. Visiting platters were stowed; sewing bags closed. Car keys began to rattle. Cheeks touched; dates for meetings of various kinds were fixed. There was a tidal shift of noise and movement down the hall. Hurley appeared at the bottom of the attic stairs to watch us, smiling vaguely, as though we might be hallucinations, but then again maybe not.

The front door closed; the final car started. Gram and I went back down the hall to put the kitchen in order. Hurley followed us to snare the last of Charlotte's meatballs.

"She has absolutely no sense of humor," Gram said, piling plates beside the sink. "But she works magic with those." She turned the water on, then off again, to look at Hurley, who had spoken. "What, Hurley?"

"She's there in the wood again tonight," Hurley said, licking sauce off his thumb.

Gram and I consulted one another silently. "Judith Coyle?" I guessed.

"The older one." He took a chocolate chip cookie. "I thought you'd want to know. She comes out when your sewing circle gets together. I see her through the telescope when it's early enough, or the moon is full. Only way I've ever seen her." He bit into the cookie; we stared at him silently, waiting for him to swallow. "Look at her with my eyes: nothing. You have to look at her like a star you only see if you don't look straight . . . And the boy is with her."

"Tyler?" I said incredulously.

"The other one. Thought you'd want to know," he said again, and took a handful of cookies on his way out, leaving us spellbound behind him.

Gram went out the back door. I ran up to the attic, swung Hurley's telescopic eye all over the moonlit night. But all I saw was Tyler and the Coyle girl going separate directions very quickly when Gram called Tyler's name.

·8·

Tyler

I went out the back door when all the women started coming in. I could have stayed in my room with the laptop and all my CDs, or in the den, where I could sneak into the kitchen when I got hungry. But I saw Undine in the wood. She was watching the women get out of their cars, talking, waving at each other. She didn't let them see her. The sun was balanced on a hilltop, making long, long shadows across the shining grass. I was watching it, thinking: that must be what they mean by magic, because in that light, the end of daylight, it didn't look like the same world. That's when I saw Undine's shadow, stretching across the lawn.

So I went down.

She had her arm around one of those thin white trees;

their shadows merged, as if she was growing out of the tree, or turning into it. She smiled when she saw me. Her hand told me to hurry, hurry, so no one would see me and call me back. Uncle Hurley saw, though. I saw his telescope lens flash in the attic window when I turned back to see if anyone had noticed me. But that was okay; he wouldn't care.

She wasn't wearing her white dress, just ordinary jeans and a weird stained vest with all kinds of pockets in it that was way too big for her. There was something lace under that; I saw it through the armholes. She saw me looking and flipped open a pocket.

"My dad's old fishing vest. It's great for collecting things." She poked around, pulled out an acorn cap, a blue feather, a little red mushroom with white freckles on the cap. It looked like something out of a cartoon fairy tale.

"*Amanita muscaria*," she said mysteriously. "It's poisonous. I found a whole ring of them in Owen Avery's trees. He has a tree farm up the hill over there." She pointed across Gram's field. She added, putting her findings back in the vest, "His daughter Dorian comes to your Gram's meetings, too."

I grunted. "Sewing circle. That's what Gram said. Why are you watching them? You must have seen them all your life."

"Because they're witches."

I blinked at her. "Gram? Come on—"

She nodded. "All of them. I listen under the window. To the first part of the meeting, anyway; after that they stop talking and all they do is sew. Even the principal's wife, Mrs. Henley, is one of them. She's the one with the short blond hair."

She pointed again. I glanced toward the drive, not buying any of it. My eyes got pulled up short by a tall thin girl with long blond hair. Her jeans started at a pair of high-heeled clogs and went on forever; her sweater stopped just short of her belly button, which flashed red as she hoisted a bag over her shoulder. I blinked again.

"That's Genevieve MacIntosh. She's the bartender at the Village Grill." Undine was grinning at me. I felt my zits prickle and knew I was blushing. "The other blonde just getting out of her car—that's Mrs. Henley."

I could believe she was a witch; she looked like her face had been frozen in one expression since she was born. "She's scary."

"Yeah."

"But that doesn't mean she's a witch."

"They're all witches," Undine said calmly, watching them through the windows now. "Not the kind I want to be. But they know things. They're like guardians. They keep the Otherworld from spilling into this one."

"The Otherworld."

"You remember—I told you about it last time."

"Oh, yeah."

"They raise walls, keep doors shut, with their sewing—"

She lost me. I couldn't see it. I let her wander on without me. Syl was in there with them, my cuz from the city with her hot red car, and her shiny black boots, and her hair like pirates' gold. No way she'd sit around pretending to be a country witch.

"There's Dorian Avery," Undine said. I watched a tall,

pretty woman with long curly hair hurry out of her car. "She's always the last one." The sun finally lost its balance and went sliding down the other side of the hill from Owen Avery's tree farm. Inside, the noise was dying. The windows along the room were all open, thin white curtains drifting in and out of them like little ghosts. "I'm going to listen. Come with?"

"I'll wait," I said, and sat down under the tree. Undine snuck across the lawn, parked herself beneath a window. I poked around in the dead leaves, trying to find something special, magic-looking for her. All I scared up was a beer bottle cap, some ants, and a big black beetle that fell on its back trying to scramble out of the leaves away from me. It waved its legs helplessly while I stared at it, wondering if it would bite. Finally, I flipped it over with a twig, and it crawled away.

The sun disappeared. A star burned a hole in the deep blue above the hill where the sun had gone down. Planet, I remembered. Not star. I was trying to think which one it might be when Undine scuttled back across the grass, into the shadows.

"Your cousin's a witch now."

Oh, yeah.

She took my hand suddenly, tugged to make me get up. Her hands were small and warm; I felt my face tingle again. But she wasn't looking at me. Her eyes were on the darkening hill beneath the star.

"Come on. I want to show you something."

We ran across the broad field beside the wood that went

from the road near Gram's house all the way to the dirt road going past Owen Avery's farm and up around the hill. It was Gram's field; she grew grass on it to make hay that people bought for their cows. The long grass tangled in our steps and smelled the way I remembered the world smelling when I was little. The star danced as we ran. Other stars pushed out of the sky overhead; dark chased us across the field. But we could see the dirt road when we reached the end of the field. Across it, tiny pyramids of baby trees covered the hillside. Above it, overlooking them and the field and Gram's wood, was a big farmhouse. The porch ran all the way around it. Little curlicues and diddleybobs decorated the house under its peaks, above the windows and doors, along the porch posts. Even its roof was decorated with weather vanes and fat chimneys. A big barn stood on one side of it, a garage on the other. I could see greenhouses in the back, and a pond beyond them, with a rowboat floating on its dark reflection in the still water.

All the lights on the bottom floor of the house were on, and somebody was playing a fiddle.

"It's Owen," Undine whispered. "As long as we hear him play, we're safe."

We were close to his porch by now. Peering around a bush, we could see him standing in one of the big rooms downstairs, a chandelier made out of what looked like deer horns blazing over his head. I couldn't see his face clearly, but I remembered him from the funeral. He wore a plain white shirt with its sleeves rolled up; he was sawing away at the fiddle. I could see the muscles shift under his shirt. There was a music stand with some music on it in front of him, but nothing was open. I didn't know what he was playing. It sounded fierce and eerie; it made me wonder who he played it for.

"Witches," Undine whispered, giving me a double shock, because she had read my mind, and because her lips were so close to my ear I could feel her warm breath form every letter. I nearly fell in the bush.

But she was already on the move, heading toward the back of the house.

She ducked into one of the greenhouses, where she studied the little plants in their pots and read the labels. Now and then her voice pounced on one; she would read it to me— mandrake root, or hellebore—as if it proved something. I didn't know what. I could still hear the wild music from the house as the sky got darker. It went on and on without a break, as though Owen never got tired, never forgot the next note, or couldn't decide what to play next. The fiddle might have been playing itself.

"Vervain," Undine whispered, trailing her fingers across some pink clusters of small flowers. "It protects."

"From what?"

"Other witches." She sucked in her breath suddenly. "Look at this. *Circaea quadrisulcata*," she read carefully on the little plastic card tucked into the pot of what looked like a gangly weed. "Enchanter's Nightshade. Circe used it."

"Who?"

"The one who turned sailors into pigs. In *The Odyssey*."

I got lost again. "So?"

"Owen is a witch."

Everyone in the entire village was a witch, it seemed. "So who's not?" I asked; she ignored me.

"Only I'm not sure what kind he is. Look. Marigolds. You use them in a potion to see them."

"Who?"

She did that thing to my ear again, breathing into it, "Fairies."

"Undine—" My voice wobbled.

"Shh—" she said sharply, her head turned away. I heard it too then: the silence.

We made it out of one end of the greenhouse just as Owen came through the other. He didn't waste time going through the plants; he backed out the way he came in and charged outside, where he could see us. Or where he might have if we'd still been running. But Undine had jerked me toward the pond, her fingers locked around my wrist. The moon was just beginning to rise over the other side of Gram's field, so my eyes actually picked out a few lines of the rowboat on the black water before we tumbled into it, and I didn't yell.

We made a thump, maybe a little splash as the boat wallowed under us. It drifted to the end of its rope. I felt the tug. I couldn't hear Owen. Neither of us moved; I don't think we breathed.

My foot, trapped between Undine and an oar, went to sleep. The moon drifted up, a huge white balloon; anybody could have seen us then. I heard night noises: something creeping through the bushes, a bird complaining about the moonlight, some unidentified flying bug whirring past my cheek.

Then we heard the fiddle again, and Undine started to untangle herself from me. Her head popped up above the bow. I pulled myself into the stern, sat looking at all the stars in the black pond above our heads. I tried to see them in the water. Undine put her hand down in a trail of moonlight, stirred it up; needles of light darted like moon-minnows away from her fingers.

She whispered, "We'd better go before he hears us again."

"How could he have heard us? We weren't making any noise; he was in the house wailing on the fiddle and we were in the greenhouse whispering."

"He sensed us."

She stood up carefully, caught the rope, and pulled us to the bank. I got a breath of pond water then, all dank with mud and weeds, tadpoles, turtles. I didn't want to leave. I wanted to float there all night on the water, watch bats flit across the face of the moon, wonder what was creeping around us while we were safe between worlds. I felt the boat dip, then rise a little as Undine stepped out. She stood waiting for me, her face pale, her hair all frosty with moonlight, the snaps on the fishing vest pockets glittering, the rest of her gradually disappearing into her dark jeans and the weedy bank.

I started to pull myself up. Then the boat was moving, its bow turning away from Undine. I lost sight of her, saw the moon above the distant line of hills, huge, white as an ice

cube. The bow swung again, and I saw Gram's house, a scatter of lit windows beyond the wood. Then dark, and stars,
and the boat was floating toward them.

Somebody was pulling it. Undine, I thought, excited. She
must have changed her mind about leaving and slipped into
the water to tug the boat out farther. She would have taken
the fishing vest off, I thought. I'd see what that lacy thing under it was.

I saw her head rise out of the water in front of the boat,
her wild hair all smooth now, wet and glistening. She turned
in the water like a seal; I saw her pale, moon-blurred face, her
hands rising above water, the rope coiled around her fingers,
taut and dripping water as she pulled me after her.

Then I heard a deep voice shout behind me, "Tyler!"

I jumped. The sleek head in front of the boat went under.
I stared at where it disappeared, and felt the boat glide more
quickly, the bow dipping a little, as though she pulled the
rope from down deep.

"Row!" It sounded like Undine's voice behind me, and I
went stiff with surprise. "Tyler, row!"

Now I was confused—was Undine ahead of me in the
water, or behind me on the shore? I didn't know whether I
should row back into trouble, or jump over the side of the
boat and swim to the far shore with Undine. While I was trying to make up my mind, my hands were moving. They decided for me. They got the oars into the water without
dropping them, and paddled backward with more strength
than I thought I had. I heard a gurgle of water or a laugh.

Undine? Water splashed under my oar, rippled and coiled around the swimmer ahead of me as she surfaced again. I dipped into moonlight, tried to heave the boat backward. That's when I realized I was hearing familiar night noises— water, crickets, peepers—in the quiet night. No fiddle.

"Row!" Owen shouted. Well, it was his boat and his pond. I gave the oars another good pull toward his voice, wondering if he would get me into trouble with Gram over this.

The oars stuck upright in the water. They refused to move. I heard both Owen and Undine shouting behind me. And then I was shouting, too, at the oars, which seemed to have gotten stuck in cement, at the head in the water, telling her to go, get away, escape, even if I didn't know anymore who I was yelling at, Undine behind me on the shore, or Undine in the water, pulling me into the night.

The boat tilted suddenly, prow lowering down into the water and down until it broke the surface and all that dark and moonlight spilled in around my feet. I tried to scramble out; the boat was moving too fast. I couldn't go anywhere but down.

So down I went. I was never so surprised in my entire life.

·9·

Sylvia

I couldn't find my way out of the woods. There were trees everywhere, enormous, blocking the sky. Even in spiked heels, I could barely see over the gigantic ridges of their roots. An acorn as big as my head hit the ground near me with a ponderous thud. Its cap split off. Tyler's voice came out of it, calling: *Syl.* I picked it up, looked inside for him, but it was full of water. I dropped it and the water gushed out, a silvery stream that surged between the trees to pour down a dark opening within the rootwork of an immense oak. Water flowed without stopping, bright as moonlight, swift and strong, so strong that it seemed to pull taut as it ran, thin and quivering with movement, like a thread somebody was tightening into a stitch between worlds.

Gram! I shouted in my dream, suddenly terrified that she was sewing a boundary through the wood, and that she would trap me without knowing on the wrong side of her seam. I tried to leap over the narrow stream. One heel caught in the fierce current; I lost my balance and fell in.

As the water pulled me under I woke up.

I lay tangled in sheets, hot morning light pouring mercilessly over me. I heard Gram's kitchen noises and turned my face into my pillow. I didn't want to face her. I just wanted to get dressed, pack, and drive away as fast as possible. Scraps of memory from the previous evening mingled with images from my dream: women in a circle, intent on their work, water flowing like thread, Tyler and Judith running away from each other in the moonlight, the secret in Dorian's voice.

I rolled onto my back then, blinking in the light. Something she wouldn't talk about in front of Gram, something about Owen. I saw his face again, shadowed and unsmiling, through the nodding hydrangea heads. I lay there looking at it a moment, this face out of my childhood, trying to remember if he had always exuded that mysterious darkness, as though he ate secrets for breakfast.

I could give him another secret . . .

I sat up abruptly, feeling the prickle of inspiration. I could tell him, I thought dazedly. What was it Dorian had said? He was supposed to serve and protect Lynn Hall, its heirs. I could tell him that I was half-fay, and he could tell me what I should do. He could make Gram believe that I couldn't possibly stay, and that the safest place for me was as far away as I could get from Lynn Hall. I had promised to visit Dorian that day; I would find Owen while I was there, give him my oldest secret.

As I went down the hall to take a shower, I saw Tyler through his open door, bundled in sheets with a pillow over his head. Earphones to his pocket CD player trailed out from under the pillow. He could inherit Lynn Hall, I decided with relief. The only thing fay about him was his age. He could marry someone who belonged to the Fiber Guild, the way Grandpa Liam had; she could take Gram's place as the resident witch. Nothing would change, fall apart, or come to an end if I left. Lynn Hall would continue as always, and I would become just one more bit of weird family lore.

I could face Gram now. I found her after I dressed, in the kitchen, washing plates and cups from the gathering. I watched her a moment before she saw me. Standing at the sink, waving a scrub brush at cookie crumbs and veggie dip, she didn't look like someone who believed you could trap a fairy within a baby bootie. It was only when she turned, and I saw her eyes, remote and black as the eyes of an old raven going its way, that I could believe she held woods and fields and entire rivers in her head beneath her milkweed hair.

"Where's Tyler?" she asked abruptly, without even saying good morning.

"Asleep."

"You're sure?"

I nodded, pouring coffee. "Unless there's somebody else in his bed." I sat down at the table, pulling the morning paper under my nose out of habit. A picture of someone named Tarrant Coyle, grinning fatuously under a hard hat at some ritual groundbreaking, made me push it away again. "Gram," I said, and stuck, remembering my dream, she drawing the thread between us, separating us without realizing it. In the dream, in the Otherworld, she hadn't heard me call. I didn't know what words to use that would find their way past her thread.

But she mistook my silence, put her own words into it. "It's all right, Sylvia. Things found by moonlight always look different in the light of day. Don't decide yet what's true, what's not; just wait and watch, and keep an open mind, until the next gathering. Meanwhile, it would help if you got started making something." I wouldn't be staying even long enough to start, but I didn't bother to get into it, then. "Anybody can sew a few scraps together," she added. "There's all kinds of fabric around. Your old clothes, since when you were a baby. Make a patchwork quilt out of them."

I stared at her. "You kept all my clothes?"

She turned back to the dishes abruptly. "I never could bear to throw anything away that belonged to you or Morgana," she said, and changed the subject. "Are you going into the village today?"

"I could. What do you need?"

"This and that."

She made a list while I ate cereal and finished my coffee. Sudden pounding made us both glance at the ceiling. "Hurley's probably up there putting a skyhook through the skylight," Gram said dryly. I thought that would get Tyler out of bed, but he was still motionless in a cocoon of sheets when I passed his room later to get my purse.

Instead of driving straight to the village, I took the turn in the road just beyond the hall that ran between fields toward Owen Avery's house.

I knew that place like I knew Lynn Hall, attic to cellar. I had run across those fields from one house to the other, and to all the secret places in between, as many times as there were stars on a midsummer night above the open fields. Dorian and I would sneak out on those nights, meet in Gram's wood, or at the stream that bordered the fields to listen to peepers and watch the fireflies, and, later, to practice smoking, and gossip about who was going with whom. By moonlight, we swam in her father's pond, followed the glinting path of the old train tracks, wandered down dirt roads that had No Trespassing signs nailed to every seventh tree.

I thought we had told each other then as much as could be told.

I found her in the long greenhouse between the house and the pond. The familiar smells—damp humus, sundrenched leaves, water dripping onto the floor—made me forget for an instant that we had ever grown up and away. Dorian, barefoot and wearing a sundress so old it might have seen life in a settler's wagon, was shifting plants with plumes of lavender flowers from small pots into bigger ones.

I hazarded a guess. "Lavender?"

"Heather, city girl." She put down her trowel and gave me

a quizzical glance out of her odd, speckled eyes. "So. How does it look today?"

I didn't have to ask what she meant. I shrugged slightly. "I'm willing to go along with it for now. Until it gets too kinky."

She smiled. But I saw the shadow in her eyes, just before she looked away. She turned a pot upside down, gave it a couple of taps with the trowel; the plant slid out into her hand. She started to speak, stopped.

I said, "I need to talk your father." Her brows went up questioningly; I added vaguely, "Something to do with Gram. Is he around?"

She nodded. "He's out inspecting the baby trees, should be easy to spot . . ." Her voice trailed, and I remembered what she'd hinted the previous evening.

"You were going to tell me something about him."

"It's kinky," she warned me.

"Really?" I turned over a wooden planter box, sat down on it. " And you never told me?"

"I didn't know until you went to the city. Then I found out things—about my father—" She paused; I watched her tuck the plant into its new pot, prod some dank-looking soil out of a bag around it. She sighed finally, brushed her forehead with her fingers, leaving a streak of dirt behind. "He's—he's in love with someone."

I waited. "Is that the kinky part?"

"One of Them."

"A Rowan?" I guessed, flailing. "So are you."

She sighed, said baldly, "Not human. Wood folk. He's

been meeting her secretly for years. It hasn't been easy for him. Iris keeps the boundaries sewed up so tight, guarding them, that almost nothing can cross into this world. My father makes a path for his lover with his music on nights when the boundaries are fluid, when the moon is full, when the owls speak in the wood, when water rises in its beds. Iris is always there, one stitch on either side of them, he says. But his music can be stronger than the guild's spells, and on those nights she comes to him. So they keep meeting, and the guild keeps sewing, and I'm beginning to wonder if he isn't spellbound by the Fairy Queen herself, because he can't seem to free himself from her grip and turn to human love instead." She turned another pot upside down and whacked it so hard the plant fell headfirst onto the potting table. "I don't know what to do for him. I've wanted to tell you this for years, but you weren't here and you wouldn't have understood before last night."

My mouth was hanging open, I realized, just like in novels. I waited for something to come out; nothing coherent did. "Dorian—" I started, and stuck again.

"I told you it was kinky."

"How could—how does—"

"Oh, Syl," she pleaded, "just pretend it's true. Just do that much for me, just this minute. Okay? You felt it last night—I know you did—when we all came together in the weave, when all our thoughts overlapped. What did you see when you sewed that hem? Tell me."

"I saw water," I said, piecing the memories together for her sake. "A stream flowing under my needle. I blocked it with my stitches. I slowed it until it wouldn't go anywhere, it had to stop."

"You see," Dorian whispered.

"Oh, yes." My voice shook. "I see."

She sighed, her shoulders slumping with relief. "My father has learned to hide so well. He's an Avery, bound by tradition to protect Lynn Hall in whatever ways he can. And he does. He doesn't see that this—possession—might interfere with his judgment. It doesn't seem terrible to him, dangerous or crazed. He says the guild doesn't see all that needs to be seen, that not everything fay is wicked. He's always very careful; I live with him, and I can only tell when he sees her by the way he plays. His life seems an open book around here. People just think he got so hurt and grew so bitter when my mother left him that he's incapable of falling in love again. He hoped for years that I would be invited into the guild. Just so that I could try, in whatever way I can, to undo what it does."

"Do you?" I asked, stunned.

She shook her head, reaching for another pot. "I have no idea," she answered grimly. "I really don't. The gathering is so . . . persuasive. I think I get as easily tangled in their thoughts as you did. But I try. He is under a spell. I want to free him. It makes us both feel less hopeless, for me to be part of the guild."

I shook my head, too, trying to rattle my thoughts into order. The world seemed to be turning itself inside out; boundaries were shifting everywhere. "What do you want me to do?"

She moved abruptly to crouch beside me, put her arms

around me. "Oh, Syl, I'm so glad you're here. I don't know how much either of us can do. But if you could help me instead of the guild, help me open a passage somewhere instead of closing it, just for a little while, just long enough to convince my father that he has a chance to see for himself that he's lost in a delusion of love."

He wouldn't be the first, I thought dazedly. "I'll see what I can do." I held her tightly a moment, then stood up, brushing potting soil off my jeans. "I'd better go talk to him. Gram's making a stew; she's waiting for a few things from the supermarket."

"You won't tell him I told you. He never told anyone but me, and only because I suspected he was in love. He can't hide everything from me."

"No. I won't."

She smiled at me crookedly. "When you walk out that door into the familiar world, you'll remember what I told you but you won't remember that you believed me."

"You'd be surprised how much willing suspension of disbelief my mind can hold. Have you told Leith any of this?"

"No," she said quickly. "I've never been able to tell anyone. I'd have to reveal the secrets of the Fiber Guild, and anyway, anyone else around here would think the local kindergarten teacher was inhaling too many paste fumes. Leith . . . I love him, Syl, but you know how Rowans are. They've been living in those mountains for forever, and they think there's nothing they don't know about them. If they haven't seen it, it isn't there. Leith just thinks—like everyone else—that my father never got over my mother disappearing like that. Three years and five months of marriage, one child, he plays the fiddle, she plays the flute, they love each other—and she vanishes one day off the face of the earth."

"Stolen away?" I suggested.

"Or—" Dorian hesitated. "She was one of them, all along. That's what Iris suspected at first. But my father got around her suspicions. She has always trusted him with everything. She must have decided that he would have more sense than to love a loveless dream out of the wood."

"He just loved a loveless human woman who ran off with another lover? Or who ran away to find her freedom? Is that what your father thinks? What do you think?"

"Oh, Syl, I don't know. It was so long ago, and I hardly knew her. I only know that this secret love of my father's, that he thinks is so vital to him, terrifies me. I want to help him. I'll do anything, believe anything I must to help him."

"Then I will, too," I said staunchly, completely confused. "It won't be the first time I've followed you into trouble."

"Thank you, Syl."

I heard the greenhouse door close behind me as I left. So I knew she didn't see what I saw: her father, standing at the edge of the pond, staring into the water. He turned his head, gestured to me. I wondered if he had already seen what I was and wanted to tell me that he knew. It would make things immeasurably easier. I joined him, hearing frogs plop into the water as I rounded the bank. I didn't see what he was looking at until I reached him. A little rowboat floated upside down in the middle of the pond, the oars drifting idly nearby.

He asked abruptly, "Have you seen Tyler this morning?"

I stammered, alarmed. "He was—I saw him asleep—Did he do this?"

"I hope so," Owen said heavily, and held my eyes in his heavy, brooding gaze that saw past boundaries, into other worlds. "I think you should wake him and ask."

I didn't know what Tyler had done to cause Owen's mysterious forebodings, but I decided that my own problem could wait an hour. I went through the supermarket in a dazed rush, greeting old friends as I tossed Gram's groceries into my cart, trying to get back as soon as possible to check on Tyler.

Someone followed me home. I had noticed the truck pulling out of the parking lot behind me only because of the ornate gold lettering on the door of an otherwise unremarkable black pickup. That and the hearty backfire that came out of it as it turned behind me. Then I forgot about it. Winding out of town, the road met the river, ran beside it for a little. Water glittered through the trees, flowed into my thoughts, transformed itself into Owen's pond, the empty, overturned boat. Then the river took a turn away from the road to cross the fields, lose itself in a distant wood.

I turned into the hall drive, and the black pickup followed me.

I parked. It pulled up beside me and I read the lettering on the door: Titus Quest Company. The man who got out was beefy and sweating. He pulled off a baseball cap with TQ stamped on it and tossed it on the seat. He wore slacks and a

tie; he looked as though he would have been far more com-
fortable in jeans belted low under his belly and a T-shirt that
said: GONE FISHING.

"Miz Lynn?" he said, puffing a little and running a hand
through his thick, graying hair. "I overheard your name in the
supermarket. I'm Tarrant Coyle."

"Titus Quest Company," I said, at a loss, and his face
brightened a little.

"Oh, you recognized me."

"No. That's what your truck says."

"Oh, yeah. Well." He stuck, glanced at the hall, then at
the wood, and lowered his voice for some reason. "Titus
Quest Company was very sorry to hear about Liam Lynn's
death. We sent that horseshoe of red roses, yesterday."

"Oh."

"Rumor has it that you're the heir to Lynn Hall."

I blinked. Rumor was getting awesomely efficient, even
for that forgotten part of the world. "What exactly does your
company do?"

"Development," he answered briskly. "A little of this and
that. We put together the Hartford Mall project up the road a
ways—you might have heard. Which is why I stopped. To
give you my card." He searched a couple of pockets, then finally pulled one out of his wallet. It said pretty much what his
pickup did. "In case you're interested."

"In what?"

"In selling."

I shook my head quickly and took the easiest way out.

"You should talk to my grandmother. She'll be living here as long as she wants."

"I have suggested it to her," he said carefully. "More than once."

"And she wouldn't bite?"

"Not even a nibble. So I took a chance, when I heard about you—you live so far away, maybe you wouldn't want to take on such a big place way out here."

I looked at the hall, sitting like a placid old tortoise in the sunlight, moss growing on its roof and the mortar cracking under the grip of ivy. "What do you want it for?" I asked be-musedly. "Another shopping mall?"

"No, no, Miz Lynn, we'd never do that to it. Titus Quest Company is committed to preserving the integrity and his-torical authenticity of these old villages. That includes grounds, of course. We'd want the entire property: gardens, and whatever fields still belong and the wood . . ."

"For what? A sort of museum?"

He nodded vigorously. "Exactly. A sort of museum." He paused, eyeing me hopefully. I gazed back at him, baffled. It would be an easy out for me; he seemed eager to have it as is. But why, exactly, still eluded me. Development companies made money from condos and malls, not village museums.

Maybe there was gold in Gram's wood.

I remembered the groceries still in the car, Gram waiting for them, the disturbing question of Tyler. "Well. Thank you, Mr. Coyle. I'll keep you in mind. Of course, I can't make any decision about the place at all, so soon after . . ."

He nodded, arranging his face suitably. "Of course. I understand. That's all Titus Quest Company asks now. That you keep us in mind."

He got into his truck and backed out the drive. I let his card fall into the grocery bag, totally perplexed. I heard the front door heave open and turned, nudging the car door shut behind me with my bootheel.

I nearly dropped the groceries, seeing what came out to meet me.

· 10 ·

Relyt

I woke up drenched. Water, I thought. Pond water. Wet and slimy as the frog in the tale; I must have just changed shape. But there was no one around to change me. Then I felt the light pouring in the window, heavy and hot, steaming me, stewing me, making a broth out of my sweat. I got my head out from under the pillow. There were things coming out of my ears. I was a bug with antennae in a cocoon. I had to unlayer myself from twists and tangles of damp cloth to find out what I had turned into.

Finally, everything else was on the floor. I looked and found some of the words: sheets, blankets, wires, pillow, little clam thing that opened when it hit the floor, popping out a perfect circle. Staring at it, I found its word in my head. CD.

Music. I sat on the empty bed, making more words as I looked around the room. Some I knew; some were new. But I found them all in my head, all the ones I needed.

I saw my face in the mirror across the room. Like still water, its surface, and clear, so clear you could dive into it, get to the other world inside it. The Otherworld. I smiled at my face, wondering if the mirror would crack at what it saw. But no. It didn't care. It just said what it saw, dank teeth and mossy hair and all. Skinny body, white as a fish. Feet that could grow mushrooms in the dirt on the soles.

Well, I go where she tells me.

I smelled something that wasn't me. Something that made me want to follow it. Want to eat it. I got out of bed, started to track it. Words caught my eye before I got out the door. Pants. Shirt. Hide this, hide that. Brush, comb, wash. File, scrub, deodorize. Rinse, spit. Some of the words were very faint. Others just lay on the bottom of my mind and nodded at me without bothering to get up. I shrugged back at them. How was I to know which? Teeth and feet gave me the broad picture. Shrug. But she said: Do what they do, my clever one.

So I did. All of it.

Then I followed the smell, which was smaller now, but still there in the air, sweet and warm and dense. I found it in the room called kitchen, where the witch Gram was stirring her cauldron.

She jumped when she saw me. What? I thought wildly. What did I do?

"What's that smell?" She sniffed, and her black witch eyes widened at me. "Tyler. Is that my old bubble bath?"

"Vanilla musk," I said, staring into her pot.

"You took a bath?"

I showed her the bottoms of my feet. And then my teeth. She scratched one eyebrow with her left thumb, making me shy again. I couldn't find a word for that magic.

She turned back to her stirring. "Are you hungry?" I nodded so hard I thought my head might fall off. "I just made Hurley a toasted cheese sandwich. How does that sound?"

"Like a toasted cheese sandwich."

She made a little toad-noise in the back of her throat, then shook her head a little. I waited for her to speak the words of the spell for the toasted cheese sandwich. But nothing happened. So I had to wait longer while she took out more words, bread and cheese, sliced and melted, turned and turned, while a hollow thing with wicked teeth tried to eat my insides, and I could see the colors the smells made in the air.

Finally, she put it on a plate and gave it to me. I bit into it, and it bit back. I whined like a dog, feeling cheesy strings hanging out of my mouth. She poured me cold milk, watched me drink it.

"No wonder you're gobbling your food. You missed supper and spent half the night running around in the wood. Well. At least you're out of bed by noon, today. Good. You can go upstairs and give Hurley a hand with whatever he's building in the attic."

Hurley. The Grunc. I nodded. He had a magic eye, she said. I must find it and tell her what form it took. If it was magic in itself, or if the power lay in the Grunc Hurley.

"Okay," I said. A strange word, but I liked saying it. OK. O. K. Oak. Hay. Oak. Aye. Eye.

"And keep an eye on him. Don't let him lift anything heavy or take a saw to anything that holds up the house."

"Okay," I said again.

"It's good to have you here, Tyler," she said. "I'm very glad you came to visit. It'll do us good to have some company now. Someone else to think about."

She touched my hair when she said that, stroked it like a cat. Then I felt her hand come away too fast, as though it felt something it didn't expect. Hair like a mirror. Or like twigs. I just ate my food. I felt her eyes on me. Her witch's gaze.

Then she heard her pot bubbling on the stove and turned away from me. But bubbles had a fat, rich, gamy scent, so I said, "I'll have some of that, too." More words came, just as I felt her eyes again. "Please, Gram?"

"It's stew I'm putting together for supper. You can have another sandwich if you want."

"Okay," I said. I smiled at her, and waggled my eyebrows up and down, which was another thing that my head told me to do. She made her toad-noise in her throat, but then she laughed after that, so I was safe.

When I finished the second one, I followed the pounding noise up and up into the top of the house. I found the Grunc in the hollow part under the roof. The attic. It had windows under the eaves. I could see the wood. So could his eye, which was pointed at it. His other eyes were busy seeing the wood in his hands, the hammer and nails, the saw and saw-horses, the little pile of dust the saw had chewed up and spat back out.

"Hey, Hurley," I said. His great cobwebby brows lifted; his eggy eyes with their blue cloudy yolks widened at me. His mouth stretched.

"Tyler. You came to visit me."

"Gram sent me up to help you."

I smelled mice and bats, ants, furry molds, and damps. There were words everywhere; most smelled old. Some I recognized from other times. That mantelpiece. That clock, that didn't say anything, though it must have recognized me. That old painting, with the face in it that might have belonged to one of us. I saw us in its foxy jaw, its great wild eyes, its hair like the night-wind blowing over the world. Those eyes seemed to watch me.

"I'm making a revolving platform for my telescope," the Grunc said. He stepped on a big, thick square of wood raised a few inches above the floor underneath a window in the roof. Skylight. The platform sagged a little, but didn't break. He put one foot on the floor and the platform revolved creakily as he walked it around. "This way I can keep the telescope in one spot and see out any of the windows—north, south, east, west—well, not north unless those doors are open."

"Wow," I said, another good word. Or was it whoa? Woe. "Brilliant, Grunc."

"Thank you, boy. Want to help me saw?"

He didn't see me out of the eyes in his head. In those eyes I was what he expected. The boy Tyler. Not the Other, the reflection. Sometimes they see. They see the shadow that doesn't quite match, so I stay where light doesn't fall. Or else on crooked surfaces, like stone and grass and old floors covered with forgotten things. Or they see our eyes reflecting moon or fire, so I stay in shadow at night. Or they feel, like Gram. They feel what they can't see. Maybe fingers longer than the eye sees, or hair not right for humans. Or they see the footprint on the ground with the wrong number of toes, or longer than the foot. Such things say that we don't belong here: we are Other.

But mostly, they just see what they expect.

I held the wood steady while he sawed. Molding, he called the long, thin stretch of wood. For a frame around the edge of the platform. To make it look nice. When he finished sawing, he glued the pieces into place. No nails, he said. Might crack the platform. So while he hunkered down, placing his pieces, I wandered over to his other eye, standing by itself and staring out a window. I looked into it.

I saw her in the trees, gazing back at me.

I started. And then, when I looked again, she faded; she went elsewhere. Maybe she was a tree; maybe she was the sleeping owl in the tree. I felt a hand reach out of me toward her, an invisible thing coming out of where they say we have no hearts. I was here; she was there. I was solid; she was air. I was shadow; she was light. No matter how close they lie, shadow and light, next to each other, so close there is no word for the place where they touch, they never enter one another's realm. So she seemed that far from me, even though I saw her fading like a dream in the Grunc Hurley's third eye.

But there are ways. Passages. Places to cross to and from, where even the witches' stitches haven't reached. So I came here, and he went there, where now he was with her, and I wasn't. I go where I am told. Nobody, not even she, told me not to have my own thoughts about it.

"There," Hurley said, pulling himself straight on his slow legs. "All glued and clamped down. We'll let it set and then we'll paint it. And then I'll mount the telescope. Did you have a look out there?" He came over next to me, put his eye to it. "What did you see in the wood?"

"Trees," I said. "Mostly." The wood that humans saw held a lot of words. But what they didn't see was an entire, ancient realm. Oh, they knew a few words, enough to say in their old tales and songs that it was there. But they had shut their eyes long ago; they didn't see anymore what was real. Now they only saw the words for it.

The Grunc made a sudden noise. I looked at him, wondering if he could see her. Then I saw what he saw: the red car on the gravel at the corner of the house, next to the black. Truck.

The Grunc made his grunting noise again. Doors thunked open, closed. I saw the cousin Syl's shadow, spilling over gravel and grass as she talked to someone standing on the other side of her car. Her hair was the color of fairy gold; her face could have belonged to us. No one knew about her, what her eyes saw. Find out, my clever one, I was told. See what she can see.

"There she is," Hurley murmured.

"Maybe she needs help," I said. I had to let her look at me, let her face tell me what her eyes saw. If her face said doubt, said wonder, or horror, or confusion, if it couldn't find the word for what it saw, then I would know what to do next.

"I don't think she needs help with anything," the Grunc said.

I saw where he was looking then: into the wood. The thing in me that wasn't a heart made a leap like a toad. I moved too fast; my hand blurred, reaching for the telescope. I saw my true hand, long and twiggy, skin like bark. I stopped myself before Hurley saw. He raised his head, blinked, both his eyes staring down at the wood.

"She's gone again."

"Who?" I asked him, my voice shaky like an owl's. "Who?"

But when he turned toward me he saw Syl in the window across from us. He forgot to answer me. "There's Sylvie," he said happily. The stranger and his truck had gone. "Looks like she could use some help with those groceries."

"Looks like," I said, and pulled my shadow out of the light on the floorboards before he saw my gnarly fingers, my bramble hair. "I'll go."

I shambled my barefoot, droopy-legged way downstairs. There were no animals in the house, at least nothing tame, that would wonder at me, scold or cringe when they saw me, or fluff out twice their size and yowl. I didn't think the cuz

Syl would do any of those things when she saw me coming out of the house. But her eyes did grow big; her hair might have straightened a little, for a moment.

"Tyler?"

Her arms were full of a bag. I took it, smelled more things to eat. "Hay, Syl," I said. "High."

"You're out of bed."

"It was too hot in there."

"What is that—" She bobbed her head at me and sniffed. Then she drew back, stared at me askew, her eyes puckered up. "What is that smell?"

"Vanilla bubbles."

"You took a bath? And you're helping me with the groceries?" Her eyes squinted at me some more. "Are you all right? Owen Avery said you had an accident with his rowboat last night."

I nodded. "I fell out."

"Well, what were you doing rowing in his pond in the middle of the night, anyway?" She closed her eyes, opened them again. "Listen to me. Of course I know why you were out on the water on a summer night. I did that often enough myself. But Owen was really worried. Are you—I mean besides the bath—"

"And I brushed my teeth."

"It's worse than I thought." Her eyes stared at me again, the pale golden brown of ripe hazelnuts. I didn't know what they saw. "Is that," she said slowly, "all you want to tell me about last night?"

Patricia A. McKillip

I shrugged. "Nothing to tell."

"You didn't see anything strange? You weren't—Nothing frightened you?"

"Nothing." I picked through words, found another one useful for dealing with humans. "I'm sorry about the boat. Did it sink?"

"No. It'll be fine. But, Tyler, be careful. You disappear into the woods at night; you are careless in water. You run around with a girl who calls herself Undine."

"Judith," I said, doing the Tyler amble back to the house. "She was there, too, and nothing happened to us. It's summer, and the dark smelled like frogs and trees. The fireflies were blinking messages back and forth. I was standing up in the boat trying to catch one and I lost my balance and we both fell in. Then Owen Avery saw us and we swam away in the dark. That's all. I guess he recognized me."

I wasn't sure she did, but I couldn't tell until after I put the grocery bag in the kitchen, and I went out again, stood in the hall so I could listen to what they said.

Gram said a lot first, words like clean and polite, helpful, breakfast with her instead of the TV. "He's a different boy," she said. "It's as though he turned into someone else overnight."

And then Syl spoke, and I knew she hadn't seen me with her hazelnut eyes; she didn't have a clue.

"I think he's just in love."

·11·

Iris

Tarrant Coyle's card came fluttering out of the paper grocery bag while I was folding it up. I took one look at it and tore it into confetti.

"Idiot!" I said so sharply that Sylvia, sitting quietly at the table and staring into her coffee, jumped. "Sylvia Lynn, if you let Titus Quest Company have this place, I'll haunt your marriage bed when I'm dead."

The startled expression on her face made my brows jump up. Then she hid behind a sip of coffee. "Okay, I won't. But why does he want it? He said something about a museum."

"Pah! That man wouldn't recognize a museum if he were hanging on a wall with a plaque under him."

"Well, then—"

"He knows something. Or he thinks he knows something. He thinks he can make money off of it."

Her eyes grew very wide. "You mean—about what you're warring with in the woods?"

"He hasn't a clue. It means Tinkerbell to him, little glowing lights at the far end of the garden, tiny winged creatures who wear acorn caps on their heads and ride black beetles for horses and feast on nectar and strawberries. He'd turn my wood into a kind of theme park."

Sylvia inhaled coffee on an incredulous laugh. "Gram," she said weakly when she stopped coughing. "You can't be serious."

"Try him. He'd open all the passages in Lynn Hall and wait to see what came through."

She sobered at the thought, told me, after a moment, what was on her mind. "I don't want to discuss anything yet. I mean about how long I'm staying."

"No," I answered equably, tossing a pinch of lavender in the stewpot to make the kitchen smell good. I'd seen her red car on that long road running between fields to the Avery place; whatever was talked about there had given her something to think about.

"I'll call the shop tomorrow if I decide to stay a little longer. But before I leave, I thought we might go through the hall, and I'll make a list of things that need to be done. Now, if you'd like."

"That would be helpful." I started cleaning the leeks she'd brought me. I really wanted to dance across the kitchen floor, cackling with glee, seize her in my hands and whirl her around a few times. But I controlled myself. "Very helpful. Just let me finish here."

I chopped the leeks, trying for once in my life to be tactful, not to say the thing that might force her to a hasty decision. Hurley was still playing in the attic; I wasn't sure where Tyler had gone. Back up to visit Hurley, or to his room, or out in the wood maybe, loitering in hope of his Undine. Syl had to be right about him, I thought. Love would make a growing boy brush his teeth and smell like a candy dish. I hadn't even seen then what he had done to his bedroom.

I added the leeks to the pot, along with a sprinkle of this and that. Then I put a lid on it and left it to simmer. I stood in the middle of the floor, my head empty, trying to remember what I had been about to do. Liam stepped into the emptiness; it spread suddenly through the rest of me, through the entire house, all the places where he wasn't, and never would be, ever.

"Gram?" I heard Sylvia say. I came back to life, untied my apron.

"All right," I told her. "I'm ready."

Rummaging in a drawer, we found an old spiral-bound notebook to record our findings. On the first page Sylvia wrote:

Kitchen: Replace pineapple wallpaper.
Paint window frames and moldings to match new wallpaper.
New linoleum?

I looked down at it. You could see bare floorboards in a couple of spots, but those were half-hidden under the refrigerator and under the bookcase where I kept my cookbooks and herbals and binders full of whatever local tidbits of history or family lore I had collected for Jane, or she had passed along to me.

"How old is it?" Sylvia asked.

I thought back. "Older than you are, younger than I am." It was covered with geometric shapes, half-circles, triangles, circles, in what had once been bright yellow, red, orange, green. "I think Liam and I laid it down ourselves in the fifties. It has that look."

She nodded. "It's not in terrible shape, and it can wait, if you can still live with it." She sounded doubtful.

"I think we bought it to match the pineapples. Yellow and green—"

She nodded again, pinching the bridge of her nose in a way that reminded me of her great-grandmother. "I can imagine."

"That's who you look like!" I exclaimed. "Those eyes, that pointy jaw—"

"Who?"

"Liam's mother, Meredith."

She slewed her eyes at me, just like Meredith used to. "Thanks, Gram. You never liked her."

"She was difficult," I admitted. "Persnickety as a cat, and so tart vinegar must have run in her veins. But she aged well; she always was a pretty woman. And she did dote on Morgana, from the day she was born. I remember once—" I stopped myself. "Don't let me get started on Meredith."

She smiled and turned to a new page. "What's next? What's bothering you the most?"

I went out into the hallway. "All those closed doors. I cleared most of the furniture out of them, over the years since you left and we stopped even thinking about using them. But I shut them up last fall; I've no idea what might have been going on in them during winter."

There were over a half dozen rooms down the long hallway, on either side of the warped and swollen front door. A formal dining room, I remembered vaguely. A library. A gun room. A couple of sitting rooms that opened into one another to make a ballroom. Meredith was the last of the Lynns to keep up every single room in the house, including the tiny servants' quarters in the attic and my laundry room, which in her day she referred to as the butler's pantry.

I looked at Sylvia, wondering if it was all too much; she looked so young and slight. But she didn't seem at all daunted by the thought of gun rooms and musty ballrooms. Maybe that came from dealing with business affairs and strangers and shipments on your doorstep from places halfway around the world. She just jotted down a couple of notes on the state of the paint on the wainscoting in the hallway, the faded paper and missing bulbs in the chandeliers. Then she turned to another page in the notebook, marched up to the first closed door, and opened it.

Something flew at us. We both ducked; Sylvia slammed the door. She stared at me wordlessly. I put my hand on my heart, panting. Then I said, trying to be firm, "We can't just—We should have more gumption than to be frightened away before we've even started."

She swallowed, then tilted her chin slightly, reminding me

of Meredith again. "Yes. This is your house. You have a right to know what's going on in it. Gram. Do you think it was a ghost?"

"Maybe it was Meredith," I said shakily. "She loved this old wreck."

Sylvia opened the door a crack, peeked in with one eye. Then she gave a snort of laughter and opened the door wide. She bent and picked up a long gauzy sheer that had frayed off its curtain rod and blown across the room at us. Somehow I'd managed to leave a window cracked all winter. We crossed the room to have a look at it. The sill and floorboards were pretty much worse for being snowed on. But other than curtains, the room was empty. No feathers or bird droppings in the hearth; no sign of small animals. Whatever might have come in out of the cold must have found cozier winter quarters.

Sylvia wandered, busily writing. I felt around under the mantelpiece, found the pattern I'd scratched into the paint with Liam's penknife.

"Come and draw this," I said.

"What is it?" she asked, ducking down to peer at it. "It looks like a web."

"It's a reminder of which pattern in my quilt guards which room. There's one in every room, under the mantels if there's a fireplace, or in a corner of molding behind the door if there's not. That's in case my threads fray; I'll know which room my stitches are guarding when I mend them. If you draw and label them in your notebook, I can refresh my memory. Or at least I can when I remember where I put the quilt."

Crouched down under the mantel, she got her pencil busy

again. I wandered, looking at memories in my head. This was one of the sitting rooms that turned into the ballroom; those wide double doors between the rooms would slide into the walls. There had been balls in her day, Meredith had told me when Liam brought me to meet her. The upper crust of three counties came to dance in Lynn Hall when she was young.

Well, that had been some time, and time again, ago. Liam and I had gotten married in those rooms; so had Kathryn and her first husband, Edward. After that, with Kathryn moving away, and Morgana pregnant and never bothering to marry, and then dying, I lost interest in those old rooms. I thought I had emptied them before I shut them up. But I had missed a few lingering memories.

"Replace windowsill," Sylvia read from her notebook. "Sand floor?" She tugged gently at another sheer; it came down off the rod. "Replace curtains." She walked back to the door, clicked the light switch. Only half the little bulbs in the chandelier and the wall sconces lit up. "Replace bulbs."

"Thank goodness I'll be dead and in my grave soon."

"You're not leaving me alone with all this," Sylvia protested, sliding open the doors into the next room. Dust fuzzies scampered along the floor ahead of her. The air had an odd smell of smoke and wax, as though someone had been dancing there by candlelight. Maybe smells haunted a room like ghosts do. Or maybe, considering all the doorways in the house, it hadn't been ghosts doing the dancing. I crossed the room to the fireplace, felt under the mantel for the pattern I'd left there.

"I'd better check these threads. Now where was it I put that quilt?"

Sylvia came over to copy the pattern. This time she tore a page out of the notebook, held it against the scratches in the paint, and ran her pencil lead back and forth over it. We studied the pattern it made.

"It looks like a snowflake," Sylvia said, and wrote on the top of the paper: Ballroom II. She turned, making more notes. Water stain under one window. Curtains. Wallpaper bubbling at seams. A curtain sighed, billowing outward over a closed window. For just a moment, music drifted through my head, like an echo from bygone years.

And then I knew it wasn't. It was no music I had ever heard played in those rooms. Sylvia had a quiet, distant look on her face; her pencil hovered, motionless above the paper.

I remembered finally where I had put the quilt.

"It's in the cedar chest that Meredith gave Liam and me for a wedding present."

Sylvia came back to earth. "The quilt? Gram, where are you going?" she asked, as I headed out the door. "We haven't finished in here."

"I have to find it."

"This minute?"

"I might forget in the next," I said tersely. She followed me to the attic. We had to go down the second-story hallway, past the bedrooms to get to the attic stairway the servants had used to climb to and from their little chambers. That's when I saw what Tyler had done to his room.

I stopped so suddenly that Sylvia bumped me. We both hovered in the doorway, staring. The bed was made. All the clothes that had been draped over the furniture and puddled on the floor had disappeared into closets and drawers. The CDs were stacked neatly on the desk. The backpack hung on a hook in the closet. Tyler's shoes, which evidently were for decorative purposes, stood toe to heel on the closet floor. His baseball cap, which I thought had taken up residence on the lampshade, sat on the shelf above his shoes.

Sylvia's face was so still it might have been a cameo.

"Do boys in love clean up their bedrooms?" I asked.

"Not in my experience. I mean, Madison—I mean some people are tidier than others. But—"

"Who is Madison?"

Her eyes flicked away from me; she didn't answer that. "It's usually consistent, this tidy business. I'm tidy, so I know. Maybe he wants to invite her up."

"The Coyle girl?"

"If that's who he's in love with today."

"He used my bubble bath."

"So that's what I smelled."

"I haven't used it for years. I thought it would be flat by now." I glanced up at the ceiling, trying to see through the floorboards. "I wonder if he's up there with Hurley. You could ask him."

"Me?"

"Well, you're his age, nearly."

"Gram, I've lived twice his lifetime." She was silent a moment, thinking, then added slowly, "I'll find a way to talk to him. Until then, we should just pretend he's normal. That way he won't think we've noticed anything."

"He won't feel self-conscious, you mean."

She gave a little nod, frowning for some reason, and still avoiding my eyes. Love, I guessed. This untidy Madison, whoever he was, might or might not be someone I would have to figure into my plans for Sylvia. But I did as she suggested, pretended not to notice. We went upstairs to the attic and found Hurley at the top, one eye glued to his telescope. His toys were scattered around him: hammer and nails, saw, sawhorses, wood glue, and metal measuring tape. Little piles of sawdust lay like anthills on the floor.

Hurley straightened, waved cheerfully. "I've been working on a moving platform for my telescope," he told us, and gave it a push with one foot. It turned ponderously. "I'm going to paint it sky-blue, before I mount the telescope on it. Then I can turn and watch Sylvia drive in, and then turn back and watch whatever is going on in the wood."

"What is going on in the wood?" I asked him. Wherever Tyler was, he wasn't in the attic; Hurley might have caught a glimpse of him among the trees.

"Crows, mostly," Hurley answered. "A couple of wild turkeys. Mourning doves." He applied his eye to the lens again, and added, "Tarrant Coyle."

"What?" Sylvia and I said at once. Sylvia glanced out the window overlooking the driveway.

"I don't see his truck."

"What's he doing in my wood?" I demanded. "Give me that."

I put my eye to the lens, saw what surely looked like the back of Tarrant Coyle, with his saggy jeans and his T-shirt that had the Titus Quest Company logo on the back. That man probably wore the company logo on his shorts.

"What's he doing?" Sylvia asked.

Not much, from what I could tell. Walking a little, looking here and there . . . I could feel my lips go thin, pushed tight against what I didn't want to say in front of Hurley. "Skulking," I said finally. "That's what it looks like."

Sylvia watched him, though he was barely visible to the naked eye, just a flick of blue and black among the shadows.

"Maybe," she murmured, "he's looking for his daughter."

"Maybe." But I doubted that. "I think I'll go down and ask."

"Wait, Gram," Sylvia pleaded. "Let's at least get what we came for. Is that the cedar chest?"

It was nearly hidden in a jumble of oddments in a corner, behind paintings and lamps; boxes were piled knee deep on the lid.

"Yes," I said, and Sylvia waded over, started to unbury it.

"Pretty," she commented, and it was: a simple varnished chest with a rounded lid that opened easily to give you a sweet breath of cedar. I helped her clear the boxes off, then opened the lid. As always, the smell made time turn for me, took me back through all the moments I had raised that lid to get a blanket on a cold winter night for a guest, for a child, for Liam.

The quilt lay on top. It was bulky, winter white. Onto each broad, pieced square of heavy cotton I had fastened a white, crocheted web of thread; each web guarded a different room, every window, doorway, chimney, every opening in it.

We were both quiet as we looked down at it. I heard Sylvia swallow. I closed my eyes, wanting to bang my head against a beam. Something had gotten into the trunk, nibbled away at the threads, fraying the crochet-work into tattered threads. I wondered if there was a complete pattern left anywhere on it.

Far away, I heard an engine start.

Sylvia rose to glance out. "He must have been parked on the road so that you wouldn't see him."

Hurley was still looking for him, shifting his telescope hither and yon as though he were following a flock of birds that couldn't make up their minds which way was south. Sylvia went over to him while I pulled the quilt out of the trunk to see if anything in our lives was still safe.

"What do you see?" she asked Hurley. Her voice sounded tight. "Is it Judith Coyle? If it is, I want to talk to her."

"Looks more like a Rowan," Hurley said after a moment.

"What?"

"Recognize that hair anywhere."

"Let me see," Sylvia said, and I raised my head at that tone: a Rowan was either the first or the last thing she wanted to see in Hurley's telescope. She put her eye to it, drew back as quickly, as though she had found herself being looked at.

"Who is it?" I asked.

"Leith Rowan," she said, and passed the telescope back to Hurley. She added on her way out, without meeting my eyes, "I'll be back in a moment, Gram."

But she wasn't.

· 12 ·
Sylvia

Leith led me a long way before he let me catch up with him. I walked fast, confused and desperate for answers, frightened for Gram and Hurley, whom I'd left alone with that unpredictable wood-creature, with its bright, false smile and its mysterious, inhuman motives. And frightened for myself, the changeling I'd made of myself that I couldn't protect anymore, and that seemed every bit as dangerous as the fay lurking in Lynn Hall.

But as quickly as I moved, Leith moved faster, somehow without disappearing entirely. I caught glimpses of his flaming hair ahead of me in the wood, and then halfway across a field, and then along the road between Gram's property and Owen Avery's hillside. I reached that road just in time to see

Leith turn down an ancient, rutted dirt road that ran along a brook to where a mill had been built, a couple of centuries before. That road ended, or at least the overgrown memory of it did, on a steep bank beside the only remaining wall of the mill. There, civilization ended; the woods ran wild. Rowans lived far back along the water. The land had been posted for decades against trespassing by a Rod and Gun Club that appeared to be mythical; I'd never known anyone who knew anyone who belonged to it.

I was slowed there by the ancient ruts of wagon wheels, by weathered stones and the roots of trees drawn up above the earth by pounding rains and shifting frosts. Maple, oak, and yew grew close to the water on both banks. The scene looked placid enough: the rocky, babbling country brook, pooling here and there just deep enough for a trout to linger in its shadows, buttercups and forget-me-not reflected in the water, flowering raspberries and honeysuckle tangled with wild phlox farther up the banks. But Gram had told me the shallow stream had flooded four times in her life, pulling up slabs of slate out of its own bed and carrying them away along with a cottage or two caught in its raging. Still waters ran deep; limpid shallows could be even more treacherous.

Leith was waiting for me at the mill. He was sitting on the stone wall, eight feet above the water, balanced in a broken hollow where the mill wheel must have turned on its axle. If I hadn't been looking for him, I wouldn't have noticed him; he could melt into stones and shadows until even his red hair seemed part of the placid landscape. Even if I hadn't been looking for him, I wouldn't have gone much farther. The road reached its abrupt end just beyond the mill; the massive, crumbling trunk of a fallen oak stretched across it like a boundary marker. Rowans had their ways of discouraging visitors; the rumor that any season was hunting season in that stretch of woods was one of them.

Leith shifted when I came up, turning his head to look at me instead of the water. He didn't speak. Neither did I. For a moment, I thought I didn't have words for what I needed to say; I had never said it before. His eyes were wide, wary; probably neither had he.

I said abruptly, "I wore glasses for the first time in the second grade. I remember how surprised I was when I could see the individual leaves on trees. Everything looked the same, but slightly changed. Clearer. I remember wandering around the schoolyard at recess, looking at the different world. I could see the way drops of water falling out of an old pipe caught fire in the light and turned to jewels. I could see expressions instead of blurs on faces across a distance. I could see bug-life going on around me, movement in the roots of things I'd never noticed before. I looked at you, and you looked back at me, and that's when I knew I must be wearing a pair of magic spectacles, because I recognized what you are. And in that moment, I saw you recognize me. It took me longer to realize that the magic wasn't in my glasses."

He gave a little nod, surprising me. "I remember," he said huskily, "you seeing me through those big lenses. I thought they were magic, too, for a moment. Then I realized I just had never noticed you before—you were one of the little kids. I didn't really look at you until that moment. After that,

I never forgot you." He paused, gazing down at me from the ledge, balanced to slide down and join me, but not yet. He added, "Must be something drastic going on at Lynn Hall to make you put all this into words. In this part of the wood anything could be listening."

"Well, what would they hear that they don't already know?" I demanded. My voice wobbled badly. "Gram, who thinks she knows everything, seems the only one who needs the magic spectacles."

He slid down then, landing like a cat, lithe and noiseless. "You never told her?"

"How could I? She hates what I am. That's why I live so far away from her, in the middle of a city, stones under my feet, over my head, and surrounded by books, so nobody is surprised by the odd things I know. Grandpa Liam made me heir to Lynn Hall, and Gram expects me to learn how to keep the doors and passageways protected against—against the likes of me—and the man she trusts more than anyone alive is in love with a wood-nymph, and there's a changeling living under her roof, and she can't see!"

Leith's lips pursed; he gave a slow, liquid whistle. A bird answered. He glanced at it sharply, then took a step closer to me, lowering his voice. "Who got taken?"

"My cousin Tyler. You must have seen him at the funeral; he helped carry the casket."

"The boy with the green hair." His brows crinkled; he asked hesitantly, "How can you tell for sure?"

I had to laugh. "He already looks like a changeling, I know. But the other—It shifts back and forth—I see fingers, then twigs, hair, then leaves or moss. Its eyes—sometimes they're human, sometimes they look like empty sky, or flowing water. He—It took a bath."

"Tyler doesn't?"

"A bubble bath. It came out to help me carry groceries. And it cleaned Tyler's room."

A corner of his mouth curled up. "Have you thought about keeping it around?"

"But, Leith, what happened to my real cousin? Owen said that Tyler and the Coyle girl had overturned his boat in the middle of his pond in the middle of the night. I saw it floating upside down in the water. I think Tyler was taken then. How much—how close to them are you? How much do you Rowans know? Can you help me get Tyler back?"

He was silent, pondering a moment. Then he touched my wrist lightly. "Let's sit down."

He led me around the mill wall to the water's edge; we sat in a little grassy clearing on the bank. The brook ran deeper there, its voice less quick and frothy. It curled around boulders instead of pebbles. Still, the sound carried our words in the right direction, away from the boundary tree, the pathless wood.

Leith said, surprising me again, "I know about Owen. I've seen them in the woods together."

I sucked in breath. "Really? What—what is she like?"

He smiled a little. "Pretty much what you'd expect."

"How dangerous is she? Can she—take him, too, the way Tyler was taken?"

He scratched his brow, gazing at the water, where a

dragonfly the color of turquoise and as long as my thumb hovered, a dazzle of blue, then skimmed away. "I've just seen them. I don't watch them. It's private. Mostly they were just talking. I saw him laugh. Another time, I heard her laugh. It sounded like—like bluebells ringing. Or a wind chime made of water. I only saw them once as lovers. And then—only because I have these eyes. It was as if she'd covered him with light. Anyone with normal eyes would never have noticed."

I blinked, my eyes dry, but burning oddly. "You make it sound beautiful."

"Well, how else would it be, for them to draw us to them like that?" He paused, flicked a pebble into the brook. "Maybe Iris is right. Maybe they are terrible and dangerous. Maybe Owen is risking life as he knows it, loving one of them. But that's how it looks to me, when I see them together. Just two people who love each other and are trying to keep it secret to protect themselves."

"Dorian doesn't see it that way."

"I know."

"She thinks you don't see it at all."

His mouth curled again. "I know. She just thinks I'm a hardheaded mountain man with a shy heart. I can gut a fish and skin a deer, sneak up on a rabbit, catch a trout with my hands, and run with the coyotes. And run like a wild thing at the threat of a suit or an office job."

"What about Owen?" I asked hollowly. "Can he see what you are? Part human and part fay?"

Leith hesitated. "I don't know. He's good at hiding things. It's hard to tell what he thinks. I wouldn't bet on anything.

Except," he added steadily, "that if he recognizes what I am, he can probably see the same thing in you."

I was silent. Owen had given me the warning about Tyler; he had seen that coming. I wondered if he might know what to do about it. "Do you have any ideas?" I asked Leith. "About what to do if you find a changeling child under your roof?"

He ran a hand through his hair, red brows quirked. "Don't they have stories about that? You're the one with the bookstore."

I hadn't thought of that. Bookshelves were littered with changelings; the tales seemed to end well, the true child properly restored, but I couldn't for the life of me remember how. Whoever had sent the startlingly tidy and polite impostor into Gram's house had done it for a reason. To talk? "Maybe we bargain," I guessed. "Or maybe not. Maybe they just wanted to find out who could recognize it. Three with eyes to see . . ."

"What?"

"It's from a rhyme Gram taught me. It never had any meaning before. But how can I tell Gram what it is without telling her that?" I asked uneasily. "That I can see better than she can?"

"Ask Owen to tell her about Tyler," Leith suggested. "He must be used to juggling truths and half-truths with Iris."

His voice sounded dry. I looked at him. Owen and Leith juggled half-truths around each other all the time, I realized. "You don't trust him," I guessed.

"It's more that he doesn't trust me. And I don't know if it's because I'm a Rowan and might take his daughter away to wear skins and live in a cave. Or if it's because he thinks I might take her farther away than that."

"They're both afraid for each other, Owen and Dorian."

He nodded, blinking, his eyes suddenly shadowed. "I love her. She's good-hearted and beautiful and she belongs in these mountains; she never wants to leave them."

"She never has."

"Neither do I. We don't have to explain what we love to each other. It's all around us; it's the history in these old mountains. And it's the way history never really changes them. I think of that, and I think everything between us is safe and uncomplicated. And then I remember." He threw another pebble into the water with more force. "And I re-member what else I am."

"How did it happen?"

"Who knows? There's stories. Who can tell if they're true or not? Rowans keep things close . . . My grandmother told me a story when I was little, about a man who shot a deer and it ran off, wounded. He followed it, to kill it, because you don't just leave matters like that, you don't let animals suffer needlessly. He didn't see the deer again. But he found a young woman with a bullet in her shoulder. She had hair as red as fire and skin soft and white as apple blossoms. So of course he took her home and married her. She had some kind of speech impediment—didn't use words much—but they got along fine until a year and a day after her red-haired child was born. Then she turned back into a deer, and that was the last the hunter saw of her. Took me a few years before I realized my grandmother was telling me about my mother. By then, I had another mother, and I could only barely remember a time—more like a dream—when there might have been someone else, and then for a while maybe no one . . . I asked my grandmother about it, but she just said it was a story, maybe it had happened to some Rowan, way back, or maybe not, but nobody knew for certain."

I was silent, my own mother's face suddenly vivid in my head. Her tale had died with her, it seemed; not even Gram could guess at it. Who had she loved? For how long? An afternoon? A decade? Did she even know what power had possessed her? Or had it seemed just some sweet-faced stranger with whom she had spent an idle summer's hour, and forgotten by twilight, except to remember that she hadn't even asked his name? Had it been that innocent? Or had she been truly possessed, taken, ravished—any of all those storybook words—by some darker mischief in the wood, and left to explain the inexplicable? Raped by a fairy, she might have thought, but never said, not knowing that Gram of all people would have believed her.

Leith was looking at me questioningly. I shook my head. "Not a clue . . . Gram asked my mother on her deathbed, for my sake, she said, but even then my mother wouldn't say."

He grunted softly. "Maybe she didn't want Iris to know."

"Maybe . . . She was pretty hardheaded, too." I stirred restively, then, remembered that I'd left Gram in the attic while I ran after a Rowan. "I've got to get Tyler back before Gram recognizes the changeling—it might threaten her, or something. I've got to find out who sent it. Leith, do you know anyone who might know how to get the attention of the wood-folk?"

"Rowan, you mean?" He shook his head. "There are others like me scattered through the mountains. We recognize each other when we meet. But no one talks about it. The others tend to be even shyer than I am; they live on the edges of our world, as close to the wood as animals—or the wood-folk themselves. They aren't seen often, and they don't encourage visitors." He hesitated, looking at me, then added slowly, "There is a place I know . . . Deeper in the woods, past the fallen tree where the road ends, there's a circle of trees. Even when I'm hunting, and not paying attention, when I walk into the circle, something changes. Time slows. Stops, maybe. I can almost understand the wind. Color seems richer there, as if you finally see it for the first time, recognize the treasure that it is. Sometimes, when I stand and listen, I can almost hear voices . . . it seems that someone just beyond eyesight looks at me . . . But as many times as I've waited, no one has ever come. If you want to talk to one of them, and they want to talk to you, maybe you can find each other there. Do you want me to show you? It may not be worth the walk. But maybe . . ."

Maybe, maybe not. But maybe.

"Yes," I said recklessly, and he rose. I followed him to the end of the road, past the boundary tree and beyond all the warning signs I recognized from the tales you never take seriously until you're lost in one and have long forgotten how it ends.

· 13 ·

Tyler

I was in the most beautiful and the most horrible place I'd ever been in my life. I couldn't remember how I'd gotten dumped out of a boat on a pond into what looked like a room in somebody's palace. I was crouched on a soft white sheepskin laid on a floor of flagstones and gold. Windows were open all around me; curtains so fine you could see through them, and glinting with tiny jewels and beads, drifted in the breeze like ghosts. I smelled flowers beyond the windows, and something else, something spicy that you might want to eat if you could remember what it was. There were soft chairs, cushions, even a bed under a green velvet canopy. Everything seemed touched with gold: chair legs dipped in it, the canopy edged with gold ribbons, gold thread in the cushions, a tabletop etched with it, and the tray and cups and the bowls on it all made of solid gold. I could have eaten golden pears and nuts and candied fruits, drunk out of a gold cup, then crawled behind the canopy to fall asleep on a blanket that looked woven out of spiderweb and cloud. And gold.

I didn't want any of it. I didn't want to move. I was damp and slick, sweating pond water it felt like, and I smelled like an old fish tank. I kept feeling the dark water flow past me as I fell into it, deeper and deeper. It dragged things loose in my head; nothing was secret anymore; nothing was safe. The water seemed to turn into memories, and all of them were of my dad. Me teaching him a game on the computer. Looking up from my homework and finding him watching me with a funny smile on his face. His hand on my head. Sitting beside him on the couch, my legs just long enough to prop on the coffee table next to his. Eating chips and shouting together over a soccer match. Him hounding me outside to mow the lawn or rake the leaves; me whining to him for more allowance, a bicycle, a dog. Me falling out of a Sunfish; him diving in after me; both of us treading lake water and watching the sailboat blow over.

On and on—his floppy hair, his father's gold wristwatch ticking in my ear; his finger pointing at words as he read me a story. His gold wedding ring. The scar on his chin, the gold cap on his tooth, the little hole in his ear where sometimes he wore one of my mother's earrings. His voice. His big feet. They made me want to cry. Everything made me want to cry. But I couldn't; tears wouldn't come out. It was stuck inside me, this nasty, monsterish feeling, of something so uncomfortable I couldn't stand it, but I couldn't get rid of it, either. All I could do was hunker down around it, feeling it grow and grow as memories collected, and feeling myself turn into a troll, something surly and mean and snarling, my dank skin growing burls and warts, hoping nobody would come near me because my voice would flare out of me like a welder's fire.

That's when she came in.

I don't know who she was. She had long smooth white hair and dark blue eyes, and supermodel cheekbones. She moved like air. She picked up a gold cup with fingers so long and delicate they could have wrapped around it twice. She held it out to me. A yellow butterfly fluttered out of her mouth, making a sound like a question.

I just curled closer to myself and told her no. A frog fell out of my mouth, something left from the pond water. I watched it glumly as it hopped across the sheepskin.

She spoke a flower, still waving the cup at me. I shook my head. She insisted, with a pearl. I yelled at her then, to go away; tiny turtles and black beetles came out of my mouth. She tried the candied fruit then, cherries so bright they hurt my eyes, slices of orange and lemon with the peel still on, sugared lumps of things I couldn't identify. I turned my head away, spat a few more bugs onto the floor.

She stood staring at me; finally she said a tiny blue butterfly. Then she was gone. I stretched out a little on my island of sheepskin and wallowed back into memory as deep as I could go.

After a while somebody else came in. She looked like Undine—she was trying to, anyway. The pale curly hair was right, and so was the fishing vest. But her skin looked slick and blotchy, like a mushroom that had been in the fridge too long, and her eyes were too small, and black instead of green.

She spoke words though, instead of butterflies. "You should eat something, Tyler. You'll feel better."

"No," I said. I never wanted to eat again. Or drink or sleep or even talk. "Just leave me alone."

"Pepsi?"

I snorted. Like they had a drinks machine down the castle hallway. "Go away."

She didn't. She set the bowl of fresh fruit on the floor between us, sat down, and started nibbling on grapes. At least they looked real enough. But she ate the stems, too, as if she couldn't taste the difference. I watched her a moment, then pushed my eyes against my arm, blocking out the light.

"Don't you want to know where you are?" she asked.

"No."

"Why you're here?"

"No."

"You're in the queen's palace of perpetual summer—"

"No, I'm not."

"Yes."

"No. I'm at the bottom of the pond. Down in the muck and fish droppings, the slimy roots of water reeds and dead frogs. And I'm staying here. The dead don't eat, and they don't drink, and they don't breathe, and they don't talk except in worms."

I clamped my mouth shut. She talked for a while about bright days and warm nights, and breezes scented with newly blooming flowers, as though we were at some tropical resort. I let her voice fade away. I watched my dad in his bathrobe pour his first cup of morning coffee, his hair standing straight up, just like mine did. I watched him tie my shoelaces. Watched him watching me tie my shoelaces. Yell when I cut current events for homework out of the newspaper before he had a chance to read it. His face when I gave him a matte-board frame I'd made in school decorated with tinfoil stars and pieces of painted macaroni. That frame with a picture of me in it, hanging next to his computer.

On and on. Teaching me to ride a bicycle, yelling when I forgot to feed my fish for a week and they went belly-up in the tank. Helping me bury them under a rosebush. Asleep on the couch until I stuck a feather up his nose. Me stumbling down a dark hall in the night to tell him there was a bear in the house, then hearing the bear-noises turn into his snores. Him floating on a blowup mattress in a pool with his eyes closed while I careened toward him in a cannonball dive. Him lying in a strange place with his eyes closed, in a suit and a tie, just like Grandpa Liam. Sleeping, people around me kept saying. He looks just like he's sleeping.

Well, so was I, and I wasn't going to wake up until he did.

The other one—the substitute—the changeling. Patrick. He smiled a lot, but his eyes were hidden. Like a house with an open door and a welcome mat, and all the window blinds shut. You couldn't see in; he couldn't see out. He'd come into my room while I was at the computer, rubbing his hands and talking like a Scout leader about sports. Didn't I think I should: a) Get out in the fresh air, b) Get some exercise, c)

See what the rest of the world was up to. Wouldn't I be interested in: a) Swim team, b) Going out for track, c) Soccer, d) Basketball, e) Golf, f) The local gym, g) Anything except sitting on my butt playing computer games on such a bright sunny day. He could barbecue manly stuff, but when he tried a simple thing like waffles on the stove, he'd set the smoke alarms off. He was always asking what band I was listening to, and then asking me to turn it down. He asked once to play a game with me, and then gave up when he lost the first time. He took me running with him once, hiking once, sailing once, after he gave me the rudder and I got us stuck on a mudflat. He tried. Once. *Give him time*, my mom kept saying. *Give him a chance. He's not your dad. But he'd like to be your friend.*

Down on the pond-bottom, I didn't want anyone. I wanted to be left alone.

I smelled something. It smelled like a memory, which is why I opened my eyes. The Undine-thing was gone. I was alone except for the teasing smell, light and sweet, like grass or trees but with a few wildflowers thrown in. It meant something really good, but I couldn't remember what. It lingered under my nose, while I searched for it in my past. A girl's perfume? The smell of a store where I'd gotten a special present? Then I saw her.

She wasn't the butterfly girl, or the Undine-thing. At first I saw her sideways, the way I was lying; she stood so still she seemed unreal, not breathing, not blinking, just standing in a pool of light and watching me. I sat up on my knees to see better.

After a moment I realized my mouth was hanging open. I

closed it, still staring up at her. She looked like she was made of gold. Her skin and hair were ivory-gold, like the honeycomb Grandpa Liam had shown me in the wood. Colors seemed to flow around her, little silky drifts and ribbons of green and purple and blue, red and orange, yellow, ivory and gold, like she carried her own private breezes with her. I wanted to look at her forever. I didn't know anyone could be that beautiful and still be real.

Maybe she wasn't, I thought then, but I didn't care. Something about her felt old, like a boulder, or a tree when it's watched the sun and the moon rise for a century or two. Quiet inside, like it's got all the time in the world.

She smiled and came to me. She knelt at the edge of the sheepskin, so that she could look straight into my eyes. She lifted her hand, touched my cheek with her long, delicate finger. I smelled that light sweetness again, and I wondered dizzily if it was the scent of her I remembered, in the air on a long-ago summer day, that had made me feel something brilliant was about to happen.

"Tyler," she said.

"Hah," I said. My mouth was hanging open again. She was so close, I saw my reflection in her eyes.

"I made all this for you. So that you would be happy. You aren't happy."

"I'm—I'm—" Nothing useful would come out.

"There is rose-scented water for you to wash with, a pool full of warm, crystal water just outside if you want to bathe. The bed is for you; you don't have to cling to this little island of sheep wool. Don't be afraid. Nothing will hurt you."

"I'm not afraid," I whispered. Her eyes were green, like new spring leaves. Like Undine's, almost, but full of light. "Who are you?"

Her smile deepened. "No one ever asks. No one ever has to. You know me. And I know this all seems a little strange to you, but you need do nothing except breathe my summer air, lie in the light, eat fruits and the finest bread and savory meats and sweetmeats, drink the purest of waters. You are my guest; you may have anything in my house you desire. Anything under my sky. Come. Take off your heavy shoes, feel summer beneath your feet. Come out and hear the birds sing. Or stay here and my musicians will play music while you rest." I didn't see her reach for it, but the gold cup was in her hand, and she held it out to me. "Drink. It's just cold, fresh water, sweeter than the rarest of wines." I lifted my hand, touched the cup. She breathed, "Drink."

I smelled the water just before I took the cup. Then I felt it again: the cold, dark, swift plunge into memory, the dank heaviness seeping through me again. I slumped back on my knees, while all the color and richness around me grew suddenly meaningless, worthless, nothing anybody could really want.

"No, thanks," I mumbled, and curled up again on my damp, smelly island. I shut my eyes and made her go away. There was an odd clink, as if the gold cup had fallen, or a word coming out of her had changed into something metallic before it hit the floor. Then even her scent was gone. I dug back into my underwater murk, wrapped myself in mud and memories, and hid there.

· 14 ·
Iris

I called Owen when Sylvia followed Leith Rowan into the wood and didn't come back. They might have just walked together over to the nursery to visit with Dorian; it could be that simple. But she would have called to tell me. Other than that, I couldn't imagine. I refused to. All those broken threads in the quilt had set a chill in my heart. Doorways unguarded, windows and chimneys wide open to any passing power— and now the heir to Lynn Hall had gone out for a moment, four hours earlier, and no telling by now in what world that moment was measured.

"Owen," I said, when I heard his polite, unencouraging greeting. "Is Sylvia over there with Dorian?"

I heard his breath check. Then he grunted slightly,

acknowledging my question, without wasting time on entire words. I waited.

"She's not here," he said when he came back to the phone. "Dorian is in the nursery with customers. She hasn't seen Sylvia today. Why?"

"She followed Leith Rowan into the wood to talk to him for a moment, she said. That was four hours ago."

"I'll be there."

He hung up before I could tell him I didn't want him over here; I wanted him to go searching the hollow up Blue Bear Creek, where generations of Rowans lived farther back than anyone else went in those ancient mountains. Dorian and Leith. I'd heard their names coupled more than a few times in the past season. Owen would know by now on what lost branch of the creek, what offshoot of the twisty mountain roads Leith lived.

Tyler was drifting through the kitchen, looking wistful, though he'd eaten his way through leftover vegetable soup and a quarter of a loaf of oatmeal bread a couple of hours before.

"Sit down," I said, and gave him some milk and cherry-chocolate cookies. He started at the crack of the screen door; Owen hadn't wasted any time. Tyler started again, nearly spilling his milk, when Owen came through the door and looked at him. The boy had grown delicate overnight, it seemed, skittish as a fawn. Love, I supposed, had wrought its changes, though I'd never seen it give anyone the appetite of a young vulture before.

Owen looked a trifle stunned, at least for him: his eyes

widened and he was rendered mute by the clean, tucked-in shirt, the tied shoelaces, the slicked-down green hair.

"Hello, Mr. Avery," Tyler said politely, and offered a gift: "Would you like a cookie? They're awesome."

"Ah," Owen said. "No." He added, not to be outdone in manners, "Thank you, Tyler." He dragged his eyes off the boy finally and looked at me. Here? he asked silently. Or some place private? Tyler solved the problem, picking up his milk and cookies and taking them into the den; I heard the door close. Owen gave me an incredulous stare.

"It's all right," I told him. "He's in love."

"What?"

"That's why he's so peculiar. Judith Coyle."

Owen closed his eyes and pressed fingers against his brows, murmuring something, a habit he'd acquired to clear his thoughts.

"One thing at a time," he said, emerging again. "Sylvia. She went where?"

"We were up in the attic," I explained. "She saw Leith Rowan in my wood through Hurley's telescope, and she went down to talk to him. I have no idea why. She said she'd be back in a moment. You must know where Leith lives."

"Why would she go there?" he demanded.

It wasn't like him to ask unnecessary questions. "How would I know?" I asked him back. "I just want to know where she is."

"Why would she—" he started again, then stopped, stood thinking.

"And another thing," I told him. "That quilt I made years

ago, each pattern guarding an entry into the house—" He nodded, fixing me with one of those ponderous, inexpressive gazes. "Well, the mice got at it who knows how long ago, and if there's an unbroken pattern anywhere on it, I didn't notice."

"Are you telling me this entire house is unguarded?"

"No. I've added other guards to its passageways through the years. But those patterns guarded everything—every window and door, every flue, every water pipe, even Hurley's skylight, which I added to the quilt when he put it in. The only thing I didn't think to guard were mouseholes. Do you know where Leith lives? Can you go there and find out if Syl is with him, or if he saw her at all, or if she just—" Just walked out of the world. I shied away from saying that. "If he knows anything."

"I'll find him," Owen promised. He hesitated for some reason, finally added, "I think you should come with me."

"Why? How could I follow if you have to hike up a stream or a hillside? Anyway, what if Sylvia calls, needing me?"

He glanced at the closed door of the den, and then back at me, looking oddly uncertain. "Then why don't you call some of the guild members and have them come over and get the quilt? They can work on different patterns, get it back together as soon as possible."

"It's closing the barn door," I grumbled. But it was an idea, so I said I would. "Call me," I added. "You have one of those pocket phones, like Sylvia. She might come back here while you're out there, and I can let you know."

For some reason, that made him laugh. "Cell phone," he

said. "I'll leave you the number, but there's probably better reception on the moon than anywhere a Rowan lives."

Whatever that meant. "Just hurry," I said, and he left.

I had just lifted the phone to call Jane when Tyler opened the kitchen door again. I dialed Jane's number, watching him walk over to the cookie jar and dip into it. Jane's phone rang. Tyler's hand emerged, stuffed with cookies, I saw with the kind of ungrudging awe the aged yield to the young when they perform their careless miracles: walking barefoot across a rain forest, somersaulting on a skateboard, surfing down the Amazon, consuming an entire pepperoni pizza.

Then I saw his shadow.

His arm crossed a shaft of sunlight as he put the lid back on the cookie jar. In that trifle of time, the shadow of his skinny arm dwindled even more, grew knobby, misshapen; his fingers looked like a handful of twigs, and more than anyone human could use. Of course I stared; I couldn't control that. But he was busy wrapping the cookies in a napkin, so he didn't meet my eyes for that second: he didn't see in my expression how the sudden terror prickled painfully across my shoulders, and I could feel my hair blanch a shade whiter than it already was.

Then he raised his eyes and smiled at me, and a voice said in my ear, "Jane Sloan."

"What?" I had forgotten about her. The Tyler-thing's smile faded a little; I saw the sudden wariness in its eyes, a darker, wet-moss green spilling into them.

"You called me," Jane boomed irritably. "Who is this?"

As always, her voice stiffened my backbone, put some starch into my expression. I managed a pinched smile at the Tyler-face and a frown at the phone at the same time.

"Jane," I barked back. "It's Iris." I flapped a shooing hand at the changeling, who, reassured, began its sidle toward me and the door. I opened it, gave the passing shoulder a couple of gingerly pats, feeling for unfamiliar knots and bumps, then closed the door firmly.

"Iris!" She made an effort, considering my bereavement. "How are you? What can I do for you?"

I had a sudden vision of the strange twig-child clinging to the other side of the door like some weird insect, its ear growing hollow and crusted with bark to hear us.

I toned down my own regal register. "Jane. Can you come over?"

"What? I can hardly hear you."

"I need your opinion about a quilt. It's been up in the attic too long."

"Guilt? You have something guilty in your attic?"

"Quilt!"

"A guilty quilt? What is that? Some antique local expression I've missed? You mean as in—" I heard her suck in air with excitement. "Iris. You couldn't have—"

My voice spilled out again, probably shook the changeling off the door. "Jane, don't be ridiculous! This is about threads, not beds! Just, please, come over."

"Well, of course, I would, but Agatha isn't here to drive me."

"Call Joe Barnes. Better yet, call Penelope. Bring Miranda or Lacey if they're not busy. I need all the opinions I can get."

"Have you called Owen?" she asked practically.

"I've sent him on another errand."

She paused, finally impressed. "I'll be there as soon as I can."

I hung up, listened for a breath, then realized that my listening was probably audible, and opened the door abruptly, as though I were running errands myself. The hall was empty. But light from the open porch door showed me a pool of cookie crumbs, like fairy dust, outside the kitchen door, that continued in a line across the floor underneath the closed door of the den.

I stared at it, my mouth dry, and wished, suddenly, desperately, for Owen. Or Sylvia—she might not know what to do with a changeling, or even her unpredictable grandmother, but her instincts were sound, and there was a comfortingly fat waffle tread on the sole of her boots.

The phone rang.

I felt my old bones try to reshape themselves for a breath, before I pulled myself together and picked up the phone, hoping for Owen again.

"Yes."

"Ms. Lynn?" a man said.

I rubbed my eyes, answered impatiently, "Yes, what?"

"This is Tarrant Coyle. I was hoping I could come by and speak to you for a moment."

I hung up, which was the only thing I wanted to say to Tarrant Coyle. Then I went back up to the attic to get Hurley to help me bring the quilt down.

He'd been up there for hours, trying to get his new platform balanced properly so that it wouldn't scrape the floorboards when he turned it. I'd sent what I thought was Tyler up earlier with a sandwich for him; I wondered grimly which one of them had eaten it. There was an empty plate on the floor beside the platform, and Hurley, aiming his lens at the woods, showed no sign of falling over from hunger.

"Have you seen Sylvia?" I asked him.

"She's with Leith," he said, with such lucid idiocy that I nearly exploded.

Yes, she's with Leith! I wanted to rage at him. She's been with Leith for four hours and counting, and whatever wood she's in I would bet your addled old head that it's not the wood under your nose. And what, will somebody please explain to me, is she doing with any Rowan for four hours in any wood anywhere?

I just said tersely, as I opened the cedar chest, "Hurley, come and help me with this. I need to take it downstairs. I'll trip over it if I try to do it myself."

"Certainly, Iris," Hurley said obligingly. But I had to wait, while something in the trees distracted him. I heard footsteps on the stairs and closed my eyes tightly, hoping for Sylvia, or Owen, or even Jane, limping up without her walker.

But it was the changeling, smiling brightly as it came in.

"Gram," it said to me, and nodded to Hurley, who had absently turned the telescope to peer at it. "Grunc. I came to help."

It must have run out of cookies. "Good," I said, and piled the quilt into its arms. Hurley had completely forgotten to help; he'd even forgotten to move, just stood there watching us through the telescope.

The changeling asked, over the drooping hillock of quilt, "Where do you want it?"

"In the big room full of furniture, on a couch."

It turned, paused at the top of the stairs to look back. "Are there more cookies?"

"I'll make you more," I promised, and it disappeared down the steps. I closed the cedar chest, thinking wearily that the Tyler-thing could disappear out the back door and into the wood with that quilt for all the good those broken patterns would do any of us in either world.

Hurley was still looking at me through the telescope. He asked cautiously, "Who was that?"

"I haven't a clue." I heard a car coming down the driveway, then. Hurley, distracted again, trained the telescope on it. I asked tightly, "Who is it?"

A car door slammed. "Jane Sloan," he said tonelessly.

I sighed. "Good."

Another door slammed. "And Miranda. And Lacey." His voice brightened at the sound of the last slam. "And Penelope," he announced, emerging at last from behind his lens and smiling at the thought.

The Starr sisters wore their gold and pearls, their silk twin-sets with midcalf skirts. It was nearly check-in time at the bed-and-breakfast, I remembered, even as Penelope said, after she had shoved open the front door, "I'm just dropping everyone off; we're expecting guests any moment."

I stared at her hair. It seemed to glitter, like fairy-tale hair, with threads of white-gold in the honey-gold. She flushed a little, adding pink to the mix.

"How did you do that?"

"I streaked it this morning before breakfast. Are you all right, Iris? Is there anything I can do before I go?"

"Nothing that simple," I said tersely, and her eyes widened a little.

"Trouble?"

I nodded. But I didn't know where the changeling was, so I just said, "Lacey and Miranda can tell you later."

"Call me when you want to go home," she said to them. She kissed my cheek and went back to the car. Jane, with her nose for it, had already started down the hall toward the trouble. A piece of it, anyway. We caught up with her, paced ourselves to the walker, which she whipped along in her no-nonsense fashion quickly enough when she sensed something unsavory ahead. She came to a complete stop in the doorway of what I still thought of as Meredith's drawing room. The changeling had put the quilt where I had asked, spread out on one of the couches. We all looked at it, unable to get past Jane's walker.

"Iris," she barked. "Is that—Is that what I think—"

"Yes," I said wearily.

"Well, how in the world did you let it get into that condition?"

"Mice got after it, I suppose. I thought I'd put it in a safe place."

"Oh, my," Lacey whispered. "All of it?"

"Yes. Every single pattern."

"Jane," Miranda said briskly, "if you can bring yourself to

move a step or two, we could examine it more closely. Perhaps it's not as bad as it looks."

"It is," I assured her, as the logjam in the doorway broke and we moved in around Jane.

"Oh, my," Lacey said again, breathlessly, searching through the broken threads on a square. Her voice firmed abruptly. "Iris. Do you still have your crochet pattern designs?"

I nodded vigorously, relieved that she could see the possibilities. "Yes." I paused, cleared my throat. "Well. Here and there around the house. If I can remember where I put them . . ." They were beginning to look askance at me. So was I, at myself, at the monumental carelessness of the one who should have been guarding Lynn Hall most carefully. I touched my eyes, wishing, suddenly and irrationally, with every bone, for Liam. "I'm sorry," I said. My voice sounded harsh with failure and bitterness. "I screwed up."

"Iris!" Jane protested.

"That's how they put it now, isn't it? It's ugly, but that's what I did."

Lacey put a comforting hand on my arm. "It's easy enough to forget about an old quilt in an attic. Any of us can do that. And I think, if we all work quickly enough, we can get this back together in no time. All we need are the patterns. We'll take the quilt squares apart, match your pattern copies to the crochet designs on them, and pass them out to everyone who can crochet. I'm sure Sylvia can learn quickly enough—" She stopped, finally sensing the absence of Sylvia. "Dear. Where is Sylvia?"

"That is the problem," I told them tightly. "Isn't it? The passages are open and I don't know where she is."

They stared at me, and then at one another. Jane sat down suddenly on top of the quilt. "Iris," she whispered. I had never heard her sound so fragile.

I couldn't see the changeling, where it might be crouched and listening, but I had to tell them about it. "That's not all—"

Not even that was all.

I heard steps from the direction of the back of the house, heavy and tentative. Not Sylvia or Owen, I thought puzzledly. Not Hurley, either. A man, burly melting to lumpy, rounded the doorway facing the kitchen, and peered at us tentatively. Something reassured him, brought a smile to his face; he stepped forward.

"Iris," he said, nodding at me. "Ladies."

It was Tarrant Coyle, in ironed denim jeans and a shirt that didn't express an opinion or draw you a picture, just buttoned up and stayed mute. So did we. He took his baseball cap hastily off his head, and held it over his heart.

"I knocked at the back door. The boy let me in. Tyler." I started to speak; he held out the cap, firmly and solemnly. "Iris, believe me, I would not be here bothering you in your time of distress, unless I felt it was rock-bottom important. And before I go any further, let me say that, as regards to Liam—"

"No."

"Pardon?"

"As regards to Liam, don't say anything," I told him irritably. "Just be quiet about Liam. Tell me what you're doing here."

"Well." He cleared his throat, then took us all in again, and smiled. It was a little, suggestive smile, as though we all shared something together, and I didn't like it a bit. "I understand from my daughter Judith that you ladies belong to a secret society. She says you're all witches, and the society has been ongoing for over a hundred years. Now."

"Really, Tarrant," Miranda said with enough ice in her voice to freeze the gold in her earlobes. "If Judith is talking about the Fiber Guild, I assure you that all we do is sew."

"I know. Darn socks and swap yarns. Heh. She spies on you. And she's told me what you really do. And what I think, ladies, is what we have here is an incredible opportunity for a business partnership. Can we sit down and—"

"No," we all said together.

"Okay. Let me put my cards on the table. Iris, you sell or lease—or you persuade Sylvia to sell or lease Lynn Hall and the woods and the adjoining lands to Titus Quest Company for a major sum of money—more than enough for you and Hurley to find a cozy place to live, and to compensate Sylvia—and we'll be in business."

I closed my eyes, heard Jane demand bewilderedly, "What business, Tarrant? What are you babbling about? I've heard more sense from a hound with its tail caught in a door."

Tarrant widened his stance, solidifying his position, and continued, unfazed, "This is my vision, ladies. And it's like nothing that's been conceived or built anywhere, ever. We'd fix up the hall and make it into a kind of museum—so it'd never be full of hordes eating cotton candy—just quiet, intelligent visitors who'd like to learn a bit more—"

"About what?" Lacey asked faintly.

Tarrant took his eyes off his vision and slewed them, meaningfully, toward my wood. "About who else lives in that wood. Who uses Lynn Hall as their passage between worlds. Of course. I can offer the entire Fiber Guild consulting fees about that—for your history, anecdotes, the craftwork you do, artifacts, written tales about sightings, adventures—especially those who got taken and survived—"

Jane gave one of her fruity snorts. "Sounds like space aliens."

"Exactly," Tarrant said with enthusiasm. "That's what gave me the idea. And then, in the adjoining field, we'd put the commercial stuff. The theme rides, the vendors, the games, all that stuff. But in the wood itself—now this is really special—we'll mark the places where things might happen, for real, and make a guide-yourself-path for the really brave, who are willing to take the risk, actually make contact—"

"Tarrant." My voice hit the chandelier above our heads; I heard prisms tinkle. "Why are you still here? Why are we listening to you?"

He looked at me like the goat who's just eaten the shoe you threw at it. "I think you know why, Iris," he said evenly. "I think you'd rather do it this way than have it all over the county that all of you—including the principal's wife, the local historian, and a couple of mothers with families—belong to an ancient, secret coven of witches who corrupt the young and innocent—my daughter included—by enticing them to join."

In the silence I heard the screen door slam, saw the changeling go dancing through the roses toward the wood.

· 1 5 ·
Relyt

The Grunc Hurley saw me. But he didn't say, he didn't tell her, the witch Gram, who promised me cookies, so I was safe. Until he says: I saw it through my magic lens. I saw you. Eye saw you. Your scaly tree face, your twigs. Your shadow, that flows and flows across our night, across the secret borders of another world. Netherworld. Other.

Three witches came into the house, so I didn't stay for them to look at me. I listened, but the witch Gram didn't say Tyler. Quilt, she said, and Sylvia. And quilt again, and quilt, quilt, quilt. Never Tyler missing. Oh! Tyler lost. O! Just stitches and Sylvia until the man with the red cap came sneaking around the back and saw me see him. So he had to come in, then. He said some interesting words—cotton candy, museum, artifact, commercial—but they didn't mean anything to me.

So I left them and went into the wood to find my heart.

They have human words for her; I've heard some. Queen. Huntress. Sorceress. She. She who bids me come and go. She who must be obeyed. They give her names that come and go like leaves. Never the same one twice, and always dangerous to say. To say is to summon. They think it's that easy. If she came to me every time I said or thought her name, she'd never leave my side.

But this time she found me.

Sometimes she only sends her voice, coiling and purring like a cat into my mind. Or like a bolt of lightning, sudden, swift, and white-hot. I've seen enough of love in human fashion to know she doesn't. Love. Me, or any of us. But it doesn't stop me. Or any of us. She is our moon. Our tidal pull. She is the rich deep beneath the sea, the buried treasure, the expression in the owl's eye, the perfume in the wild rose. She is what the water says when it moves. She is what humans remember when they step into the wood: a glimpse of her, memory receding faster and faster, into sunlight and scent and shadow, of what once they saw, once they knew.

She uses me, but I don't care. For her, I sharpen my wits. I learn. If I make mistakes, I use my charms. The Grunc Hurley saw me with his lens, but not with his own true eye. So now I know. He didn't say: where is Tyler? He only said: who is that? So he doesn't know what he knows. And he gave me something to give to her that she wanted: the little gift of knowledge.

We can be seen in that lens.

I never expect her. So when I saw her, my limbs went fluid, my shadow peeled off the ground, went swooping away like a shout. She stood between worlds, in a fall of light, a blur of tree and shadow. A human, glancing at her and away, wouldn't have noticed. Unless there was that snag at the eye or the mind. That backward glance. That closer look. But only if she wanted. If she chose to be seen.

She chose my eyes. I bowed my head, a windblown shrub, twigs tangling. She smiled at me. I drank her smile like wine, like air and light. But the smile didn't reach her summer eyes, the young leaf green that inhales light and more light until it glows within.

"I have something for you," I said, to kindle that smile. "The Grunc Hurley sees us truly with his attic lens. Shall I steal it for you?"

She shook her hair, that cascade of gold that flowed into the light. "Never mind the Grunc Hurley, my sweet. I want you to do something else for me."

Anything. Anything, anything.

"The boy refuses all my gifts, my comforts. He won't eat, he won't drink, he won't even move. He barely speaks, even to me."

If I did that, what would she give me? I wondered instantly. If I spurned her and all her gifts? Her eyes flashed a laugh at me, as though she heard. Anyway, I never could. Foolish Tyler. Clever Tyler. To make her lack, want.

"This is what I want you to do . . ."

She told me. And then the light was empty. It took longer

for my eyes to see that than for her to leave me. I stood gazing at nothing, nothing, for a senseless moment until my eyes said she had gone elsewhere.

I turned away, went to look for what she wanted.

It didn't take long. Of course the Undine would come. She would want to know, to talk, after the midnight swim Tyler took through the pond water. I found her lurking at the edge of the trees, gazing up at Tyler's window. I wasn't interested—she was too young, too ignorant—but I had to pretend. So I gave her my sweetest Tyler-smile. Still her eyes grew big at me. But at what she sensed, not saw, because she only said:

"Tyler." Her voice squeaked. "Is everything all right? Did you get into trouble?"

I shook my head. "My cuz talked to Owen. And then to me. Nobody is really angry."

"You look different."

"I took a bath. Got the frogs out of my hair."

"It's not that . . ." She studied me, her face puckered. I turned away, keeping to the shadows, not knowing how close to witch she was already. I heard her sniff and looked back at her, smiling again.

"I spilled Gram's bubbles in the water."

She laughed then, a little mourning-dove coo that flew sweetly into my ear. Her skin was flower-petal new; her eyes pale green like young apples. I thought, Well, maybe . . . But I didn't let her see that, either.

"What are you doing out here?" she asked.

"Looking for you."

"Oh." She turned away then, but not before I saw her strawberry blush, her little bird-V smile. She bent down quickly, picked up a dry seedpod, and tucked it under a flap in her vest. I saw something flash in the attic then: the Grunc's telescope, the eye searching, watching. I bent down, too, picked up a hazelnut cap, flicked it away.

"We could go for a walk," I said. "I know a place where mushrooms grow as big as babies' faces."

She squinched her face at me, but it was only playing. "It's too warm and dry for mushrooms, now."

"Oh."

"Anyway, I can't." She frowned then, at the house, not at me. "I have to wait for my father. He's in there talking to Iris about some weird idea."

"Weird."

"I told him—" She stopped, began again. "You know how you say things when you're excited, thinking someone else will be as excited and as interested as you? But they see something else—they look at what you're saying all wrong—but then it's too late, you've already said it."

She expected a noise, so I made one, to whatever she said with all those words.

"It's been years since I started talking about it, and I thought he understood—he made me think he did—so I kept telling him."

"What?"

"About the Fiber Guild. How I watch them. How they're all witches, doing magical things with their threads to keep the wood-folk away. How I want to be one. I mean, I was eight or something when I first told him! And all these years later, I find out what he's really thinking about everything, all the secrets I've told him—"

"What?" It was a good word. Like a rock in a river, sticking up to let you land on it, so you could make your way across the flow. What. Watt. Wot.

"Know what he said to me while we were driving out here?"

My lips shaped "Wh—" again, but she flowed right over it.

"He said he'd been waiting for the perfect moment for years, and this was it: Liam dead, the heir to Lynn Hall living on the other side of the country, and Iris getting too tottery to keep up the place herself. With all I told him, he was going to make us rich."

Her mouth clamped shut. Mine was open, but I had trouble trying to find a word that matched whatever it was she was talking about.

"How?" I tried finally, another rock word.

"You won't believe it." The berry was under her skin again: strawberry, raspberry, staining that cream. I wanted to put my hand on her bare neck, lick her cheek. But she might not like that, and then she wouldn't trust me, and then how could I do what I had to do?

The screen door banged; her father came out on the porch, thump, thump, putting his cap on, and leaned over the railing to call "Judith!" at the trees. It startled me until I remembered that Undines have names. "Jude! I'm leaving! Let's go!"

She just stared at him, her arms folded. "So go," she muttered. "I'm not coming with you ever again. I'll live here in the woods."

I liked that. "Okay."

The Coyle man came off the porch, shambled like a bear through the rose garden, shrugging off thorns. He came to the trees, peered in. He nodded to me, and said to her, "There you are. Did you hear me call?"

"I can't believe," she said, her voice small and taut as a thread, "you did that."

"What? All I did was make a business proposition."

"You betrayed all I told you in confidence. Iris will never trust me again."

"Oh, piffle. I hardly mentioned your name. Anyway, it's to Iris's advantage. She'll stew over it for a day or two, then get to thinking seriously about it, and I'll get a call from her before the end of next week. I guarantee you. Wait and see."

"She must think you're nuts."

"Doesn't matter. She'll do it for whatever reasons."

"You're blackmailing her. Over me."

His eyes narrowed. They were some murky brown, like his hair, sticking out around the cap, but they weren't mean, just stupid. "Look," he said. "This is the idea of the century, and I didn't have to use you to make her think about it. It's good enough to stand on its own two feet. It'll be great for Iris, and for this community. I bet Tyler here'd think it's a winner. Wouldn't you, Tyler?"

I said that word again, feeling murky myself, not understanding anything.

Patricia A. McKillip

"Think of it," the Coyle said. "A three-part adventure. Did you tell him what's in these woods?"

She gave a little nod. "Some."

"Fairies, boy. Real ones. I bet half of what we think are fireflies are really Them, flying around at night like little stars. They've been here for centuries, and the Lynn family knows all about it. They probably have documents, letters, stories about sightings. The entire Fiber Guild must have stories. We'll use the house as the fairy museum, so to speak, and we'll put the rides on that field, all with a fairy theme. The Little Folk. Brownies, elves, that kind of thing. And flying— lots of flying rides. Maybe a castle. Or a witch's house— maybe we can get the Fiber Guild to do their sewing in it. Or would that be better in the museum?"

"Dad!" the Undine wailed. "They'd hate that! Anyway, it won't work unless it's secret."

"Well, it's not, is it?" he asked, eyeing her. "Secret any longer. Is it?"

"But—"

"Anyway, listen to this, Tyler. This is the best part. We'll put trails through this wood to all the places that might be openings, passageways to the Otherworld. Mushroom trails, bread crumb trails—whatever they have in fairy tales. And people can walk through the woods, and maybe, if they're quick enough, or smart enough—whatever it takes to see a fairy, we'll have to do some research on that—they can have their own personal encounter with the Otherworld. Wouldn't you be interested in that, Tyler?" He touched my shoulder. Then he looked at his fingers puzzledly, without knowing why. "Isn't that an idea whose time has come here to stay?"

I felt laughter, like little bells shaking all the way through me. "Sure," I said.

"Tyler!" the Undine breathed reproachfully.

"I mean, I'm not sure. Don't you think it might be dangerous?"

"What's dangerous? They've been around for centuries; nobody's even noticed they're here, except the Fiber Guild, who keep them all locked up so nobody else can see them. That's not fair. Do you think it is?"

"No."

"Tyler!"

"He's just being fair," the Coyle said. "He's part Lynn, and he can see it."

"You don't know what you're talking about! Either of you!" Her eyes were suddenly shiny, under water. "It's secret because they're dangerous! Not little Tinkerbells and brownies—they're powerful and nasty and the Fiber Guild keeps us safe."

"They're just shy," the Coyle argued stubbornly. "And the Fiber Guild keeps them trapped. Now come on, I don't have all day to spend here. I have work to do."

"I'm not going home."

"Well, okay, if you want to spend some time with Tyler, here."

"Ever!"

He blinked, then smiled. "Ever's a long time. You'll find your way home soon enough. Maybe Tyler can make you see what—"

She turned away from both of us and ran.

The Coyle followed a few steps, then stopped, puffing. "Tyler—"

I nodded, trying to look worried. "I'll find her."

"Try and make her see what I'm doing, will you? I've got a vision, boy, and it's a doozy. Tell her to call me when she wants to come home."

"Okay."

He went back into the yard. I followed the Undine deeper into the woods. I could hear her cracking twigs, stirring up dead leaves, running like a startled deer, with no direction but away.

"Judith," I called. "Please stop. I'm sorry. I'm just confused about all this—Please." I put some panting in my voice, then I pretended to trip over something, and yelled, "Ow!" Then I really did trip. Some tree put a gnarly root out between my feet and I went flying, just like the Coyle said we did. I landed so hard my breath went somewhere. When I caught it finally—a little snatch of air, another snatch—the wood was quiet around me.

The Undine stood in front of me. Her tears glittered on her face, in her eyes; all the beautiful color was everywhere under her skin. She was panting, too. But her wet eyes weren't angry, and when she knelt beside me, neither was her voice.

"Oh, Tyler. Are you hurt?"

"No." I made a sound like a laugh. "Just clumsy."

"Why did you—why did you encourage him like that?"

"I don't know." I pulled myself over to the tree, leaned

against it, dragging in big gulps of air, entire cauldrons. "I mean, I don't know anything about any of this. You told me some of it, but I didn't understand much then, either. How do I know what fairies do or don't do? Or what the Fiber Guild knows or does or doesn't do? I wouldn't recognize a fairy if it bit me on the nose."

"You said they might be dangerous."

"I was just saying what you told me before. I never thought about them. I don't even know where to begin. I mean, what did he mean about openings in the wood where people might see them? Are there really places like that?"

She sighed. "They're what the Fiber Guild guards. And my dad wants to—just open them all up and see what comes out. It's like opening up all the cages in a zoo and waiting to see if a hummingbird or a grizzly bear comes out."

"What kinds of places?"

"Like the pond. Hollow trees. Springs. Places where the worlds touch."

"Here?" I asked skeptically. "In my Gram's wood?"

"Oh, yeah."

"Yeah?"

"Come on." She tugged at my sleeve as she stood. "Get up. I'll show you."

"Is it far?" I asked. "I told Gram I'd be home for supper."

"Just come on, Tyler. You've never worried about time before. Anyway, it's not far at all."

But it was: she led me there, and then I led her farther than she had ever gone in her life, even in her dreams.

·16·
Owen

I went to Leith's place first. I had been there a couple of times with Dorian. That's how I knew things had gotten disturbingly serious between them, when Leith invited me to dinner. Being welcomed under a Rowan's lintel was tantamount to becoming a member of the family, after you passed the rigorous test of locating the lintel in the first place. Iris had been right not to come with me. After I drove down dirt roads that splintered off one another in maddening groups of three, none ever suggesting, by so much as a roof shingle nailed to a stump, who might live down those goat-paths, I had to park where the road ended, walk over a fallen trunk across a stream, and then down the stream bank until I came to a two-room cabin with a fire pit in front of it, and a couple of chairs made of unstripped birch on the porch.

Of course no one was there.

I stood on the porch, trying to eke a clue out of the landscape where to look next. The stream flowing lightly past me under the mossy trunk told me nothing. Neither did the pair of crows watching me from the branches of a hemlock. I heard no human voices, nor did I see any other signs of human habitation. Leith might have been the only Rowan living within that private corner of the world. Except that there was no sign of him, either.

The eerie, flickering face of the changeling eating cookies at Iris's kitchen table stole into my thoughts. Its eyes, human one moment, hard little seed pods the next, dark and empty as a hollow in a tree the moment after, had nearly caused me to jump out of my skin. Fortunately, I don't change expression easily anymore; neither Iris nor the changeling seemed to notice my shock. That I saw it so clearly could mean only one thing: it was a danger to those I was born to protect. I feared for Iris if she did recognize this imp of unpredictable power and obscure motives, and I had no time to waste before I got back to her. I would have to drive all the way to the village before I could call her on my cell phone, and even then I could tell her nothing that wouldn't add to her worries. I could only hope she had followed my advice and summoned a few seasoned veterans of the Fiber Guild, armed with needles and pins, to stay with her.

The thought that Sylvia herself might have been taken,

lured away into twilight realms, gave me a moment of blank, unreasoning panic. I had no idea where else to look for her, but how could I look for her there? The world around Leith's tiny porch, trees edged close to his cabin, boughs brushing tenderly against his windows, birds flitting through the long, dusty-gold, late-afternoon light, a squirrel scolding my intrusion, the ceaselessly chattering water, seemed at once mysterious and utterly prosaic. It did not admit to any possibilities except its own lovely and intractable habits. I couldn't see within the wind; I couldn't understand the language of water.

But, I remembered with relief, I knew someone who might.

I didn't know where to find Rue, either, but I knew a place to start looking. I managed to make my way out of Rowan territory with the dumb luck of desperation; all the roads I chose led me out, rather than in tangles. I made a quick trip back to my house to call Iris before I continued the search.

"Owen," I said when she answered. "Is she back yet?"

"No." She bit the word off explosively, sounding exasperated in the extreme. "And there's more trouble."

"Tyler?" I suggested obliquely, in case she hadn't noticed the changeling.

"You noticed," she answered bitterly.

"Yes."

"Well, even that's not everything."

"What—"

"The rest can wait—just find Sylvia. Did you see Leith?"

"No."

She spat a word I didn't know she knew into the phone

and slammed it down. I turned, trying to think through the echo in my ear, and found Dorian watching me. I hadn't heard her come into the house, but I was relieved to see her.

"At least you haven't vanished. Are there any customers in the nursery?"

She shook her head, frowning. "No. I was about to close the shop. Who's missing?"

"Sylvia, apparently. Iris hasn't seen her for hours. Would you go over there when you're finished? She could use some help."

Dorian nodded vigorously, holding my eyes in that way she had when she knew she hadn't heard everything. "What's wrong? I mean, Syl's a big girl; she might just be out shopping or visiting or something—"

"When last seen, she had followed Leith into the wood behind Lynn Hall to talk to him for a moment. According to what Iris told me, that was over five hours ago."

Dorian's eyes grew wide; her fingers, kneading the crooks of her elbows, had slackened. "Leith?"

"You haven't seen him this afternoon, have you?"

"No." She paused, added slowly, "He usually comes by on Saturdays to help me in the nursery. He calls when he can't make it."

"Did he call?"

"No." Her fingers got busy again, untied her work apron. "I'll find him. He might be at the cabin. Or Dr. Caddis might have had an emergency somewhere."

"I stopped by his cabin. He isn't there. I doubt that he's been with Sylvia all this time; I just wanted to ask him if he knows where she might have gone. We don't need Leith, and

I really wish you would go to Iris." Her eyes were on my face again, the flecks of color vivid in them. I nodded. "There's trouble. Iris will explain."

She swallowed. Then she said tightly, pulling her apron off, "I'll lock up the cash box and go over."

"If I run across Leith, I'll send him to Lynn Hall."

"Do you know where you're going?"

"Yes."

Her mouth tightened; she breathed, before she turned, "Be careful."

I waited until I saw her pickup heading toward the hall. Then I drove half a mile back down the road, parked, and began to hike down the old mill road, while all around me the dazzling light, the deeper shadows, the serene stillness of the wood warned me of that gray old man Dusk walking the path through the wood behind me.

I remembered the place where I had first seen Rue as vividly as if I'd been there yesterday. I walked a double path toward it: the one under my feet, the one through memory. One imposed itself upon the other; the leaves crowding around me pushed into my thoughts. At the road's end, where it dwindled away beside the mill wall, I clambered over the ancient, fallen oak into the pathless trees. Mossy stones marked the flow of underground water; I followed that. Rowans hunted all year in these woods; because of their poverty and sheer stubbornness, local law looked the other way. More than one indignant hiker had been hastened out by random bullets careening off the trees; the hunters were never caught and rarely seen. Leith had told me that they only discouraged strangers that way; they were careful around the rest of us.

The underground stream led to a grove of birch growing in a circle. The first time I found it, I'd been following a path of gigantic pastel mushrooms growing along the stream, under the hemlock. It had been spring, then; the birch had put out young leaves of such sweet, fiery green that seeing them in a shaft of light had taken my breath away, for all the many springs I'd seen. Within the shaft of light, within the circle of slender trees, something moved. Someone. I had stopped, transfixed, watching a slender figure emerge out of leaf and light, and look my way.

This time, as I reached the circle, I saw the last shaft of daylight vanish into dusk, and the face that looked my way was Leith's.

I stopped, trying to put this and that together and growing profoundly uneasy. Leith wore an expression I'd never seen on him before, and wished I hadn't then: he looked uncertain, grim, and vaguely guilty of something.

"Owen," he said, nodding briefly, without surprise.

"What are you doing here?" I asked incredulously, wondering for an instant if he, too, had a lover among the wood-folk.

"I'm—I brought Syl here."

Astonished, I joined him within the trees. In the dusk, the birch leaves hung so still they might have been the jeweled leaves of fairy tale. "Well, where is she?"

"She went looking for Tyler."

"Tyler. Tyler's at—" I stopped. Tyler wasn't at Lynn Hall. And Leith knew it, and so, apparently, did Sylvia. I heard my voice rumble out of me, like a roar from a provoked bear. "Where is Sylvia?"

"She went—she went—" The unflappable Leith grew incoherent; he waved a hand at the trees around us, and finished unhappily, "She found a way in."

"In."

"She's part—" He drew breath, held it, while I stared at him. "I know you understand," he said finally. "I've seen you with—with the woman you love. I can see you because a part of me is—is fay. And so is Syl. We saw it in each other when we were schoolkids. That's why she moved so far away, so no one else would see it. That's why I'm drawn to this place. This doorway. I brought Syl here to see if someone would come to her, and tell her why they took Tyler. But she—she found a way in, herself. She walked into the light, and after a while— she wasn't there. I've been waiting for her."

I was staring at him again. "Sylvia?" I heard myself say from a distance. The heir to Lynn Hall had just walked out of the world into fairyland. The heir to Lynn Hall, born to guard, and watch, and keep all passageways locked against the wood-folk, was one of Them herself. And one of us.

And so was the young man who had stolen my daughter's heart.

I wanted badly to sit down. I wanted badly to bellow at Leith until his hair streamed in the wind of my wrath, and his face turned the color of water. But when the shouting was done, the facts would still be there. I wasn't fay; I was Avery, born to use whatever magic that name had given me against the Otherworld. But I had never recognized anything Other, any danger in either Leith or Sylvia. And I had crossed a boundary, too, loving whom I loved. Like Sylvia, I had lied to Iris.

I leaned against one of the birch trees in lieu of sitting and tried to put my wits in order. First things first. "We'll get into this later. Right now, I need you to go to Lynn Hall and—"

"I don't want to go anywhere near Lynn Hall," he protested. "I can't tell Iris I know where Syl is and not tell her where. I'll wait here for Syl. You go."

"Dorian is there."

He regarded me silently for a breath. "You don't care? About what I am?"

"Of course I care. But she loves you, and I think you love her, and considering whom I love, I can't put up a case for the deceit and treachery and lovelessness of the entire folk of the wood."

"What will she think?" he murmured uneasily.

"I have no idea. You'd better ask her."

He didn't answer. He was looking over my shoulder, past the ring of trees; the gentle wonder on his face made me turn abruptly.

Rue stepped into the circle beside me. In the dusk, her smooth hair glowed an eerie, buttercup gold; her dark eyes warned of night. As always, she left me mute in that first moment I saw her: something of the wood that had taken a human form, yet could not disguise its own wild beauty, its Otherness. She stepped to my side, laid her hand on my shoulder.

"I heard you call me," she said softly. "You should not have come looking for me."

"I had to."

"I know." Her eyes went to Leith. "Red cap. A Rowan."

He smiled a little, said breathlessly, "Yes."

"I've seen you."

"I'm Leith."

"And you've seen me. More than Leith, I think. More than human." Her fingers tightened a little on my shoulder. "You must leave these woods. It isn't safe here tonight."

I didn't dare touch her; I would have lingered there all night, just to feel the pulse in the crook of her elbow against my lips, just to hold her long, light bones. "I'm looking for Sylvia," I told her. "Leith saw her disappear into your world. She's searching for Tyler."

Rue shook her head, her brows tilted with a very human worry. "I haven't seen your Tyler. If one of you has been taken, you must deal with the one who has taken. That is no simple matter."

"Can you take me where Sylvia has gone?"

She shook her head again. "I have brought you as close to our world as I dared, so close our boundaries have blurred . . ."

"Yes," I breathed.

"I dare not bring you closer. We have been one another's forbidden secrets. I could not bring you into our world without revealing that."

"Sylvia—"

"She found her own way in; she left nothing for us to follow. It's a journey out of time, into an ancient, complex realm. Humans who stray into it sometimes never find their way back."

"I'll risk it," I told her recklessly. "Why would anyone

have taken Tyler? Only because he's a Lynn? Or does your queen want to use him as a bargaining chip? Would she keep Sylvia instead?"

Rue's hand covered my mouth, swift and moth-light. "Don't," she pleaded. "Don't keep saying names. Don't keep thinking, wanting. Just go, now, quickly."

I couldn't help it; I took her hand, to feel her long, delicate fingers within mine. "Come with me. Or come to me later—"

She said something, made some small sound. Her face turned away from me; she was staring over my shoulder. So was Leith, I realized belatedly. Then a sound thundered out of the woods around us, unfamiliar and overwhelming. It sounded like a crazed human shout, its echoes overlapping but increasing in force instead of fading. My bones froze. Rue wavered in the sound like smoke shredded by wind. Leith gave a hoarse, shocked shout back at it. But he didn't run; maybe, like me, he couldn't move. I could only turn my head slowly, reluctantly, afraid to see, but unable not to look.

I saw them at the edge of the trees across the little clearing: a dark line against the twilight wood. I couldn't see their faces, or their mounts clearly, yet they were more than shadows. The Wild Hunt, I thought instantly, and knew we couldn't outrun that. The figure in the center was crowned; I saw the watery ripple of silver as some fay light struck it. Here and there a piece of harness glinted, a tiny bell shook, a black ribbon took to the wind, a bird riding a shoulder or the antlers on a helm, caught that stray glittering in its unblinking eye.

"It's the wrong time of the year," I heard the prosaic woodsman whisper.

"You Rowans hunt in any season," I said unsteadily, as Rue's fingers, still human in my hand, trembled, cold as ice. "Why shouldn't they?"

The wood spoke a word again, this time with a little less thunder. Rue's hand slipped out of mine. She began to drift away from me. I caught at her; I might as well have tried to grasp my own shadow. She pulled at my heart; she winched it out of me with each flickering, dissipating movement; she seemed to melt away as I watched.

"Rue . . ." I whispered, and tasted the bitter word, felt it burn my throat.

One final word flew out of the trees, this like a swift, hard blow, as though invisible lightning had cracked through the air between us. I flinched, and felt the pain a moment later. It was, I realized, exactly as if I had been struck by something heavy, weighted with metal, and obscurely familiar.

Then the magic was gone; there was only the wood in the twilight, growing dim and cool. The pain I had felt as Rue left me had only just begun: already my skin longed for her, my eyes, my stunned heart, my numb and remorseful brain.

"Now what?" Leith demanded.

I had no idea. "We wait," I suggested wearily, "until we find something better to do."

He stared at me as I sat down within the ring. "Your face . . . It looks like something hit you."

"That last word."

"What?"

"I think she flung a gauntlet at me. We've been challenged."

· 17 ·
Tyler

For a long time nobody came. I think I fell asleep, curled up on the sheepskin; even in my sleep I tried not to let myself touch anything but that. Like I was floating in dangerous waters, full of hungry sharks, killer whales, gigantic squid, and if I let a hand or a foot drift off my life raft, they would bite it off. They would get me, then. Whoever they were.

My waking thoughts ran into my dreams; they were all about my father. Jumbled memories, maybe not all of them true, since I was dreaming; some of them were probably wishes. Like learning to ski, which he'd always promised we would do together someday. In my dreams, he finally took me to the slopes, where we didn't even need lessons. We were all geared up, bright clothes and caps, and flying down a trail together, ski poles tucked under our arms, snow fanning out behind us, while we laughed and shouted, and a misty-blue world of distant mountains and forests spread out everywhere around us. We were brilliant. Awesome. My dad was so fast he disappeared inside his own private snow cloud. I was trying to keep up, and cheering him on, when I started feeling funny. I couldn't see him anymore, inside the blur of snow. He had somehow skied even faster than the snow he kicked up, like sound traveling so fast it can't be heard until it catches up with itself. He had traveled so fast that all that was left of him was a memory of motion.

I woke up, feeling so alone that I didn't know how I could keep living inside myself.

The Undine-thing was back, sitting on the floor with its back against the bed. I glanced at it, and groaned, and closed my eyes again, just wanting to burrow somewhere lightless and dank and silent, where I didn't have to think.

It poked me, and whispered, "Tyler."

There was something funny about its voice. It leaned over me then, put its lips very close to my ear. "Tyler." The word fluttered in my ear like a tiny hummingbird. My eyes opened really wide. I smelled a mix of sweet berry shampoo, grass, dirt, sweat. My head came up then, and I saw her own true eyes.

"Judith?" My voice squeaked. I was never so happy to see anyone in my entire life.

She put her finger to her lips. She didn't look very happy. Her face was dirty; her hair was tangled, with little bits caught in it of leaf and crumbled wood, lichens, spiderweb, and even a dead roly-poly bug. She looked like she'd crawled through a hollowed-out log. "Where are we?"

"You don't have to whisper. It's not like they don't know we're here. How did you get here, anyway?"

She scowled. "That thing brought me. That Tyler-thing."

"What Ty—?" I stopped. I sat up all the way, then, remembering for the first time that there was still a normal world out there, with Gram, and Grunc, and Syl in it, and they'd be wondering where I'd gone. Or maybe not. "There's something wearing my face around Lynn Hall?"

"I thought it was you. It tricked me into going into one of the passageways between worlds, so here I am."

My mouth was hanging. "It's that much like me?"

"Well." Her face got a little less pinched for a moment. "Almost. It took a bubble bath."

I snorted a laugh. "And they still think it's me? Why did it take you?"

"I don't know. It didn't say. But we have to get back there and warn people before it steals somebody else."

She got to her feet restlessly, moved around a little, looking at things. She made a face at the bowl of candied fruit, then picked up a mirror framed in gold and made another face at herself. She rubbed a streak of dirt off her cheek, picked the bug and a few twigs out of her hair.

I made a brilliant deduction. "You didn't come through water."

"No. I took the Tyler-thing to a big old hollow tree. It said it didn't understand how I could possibly see that as a passageway to anywhere. So I finally stepped inside the tree, which I've done at least a couple dozen times before, trying to see if it would really work. This time, it did."

"What happened?"

"It was like there was no inside . . . I just fell into the ground. I rattled down through tree roots and dirt and bracken, and finally slid out here. And there you were, snoring on the sheepskin, with dried pond scum in your hair. So I knew it was really you. But where are we? Whose house is this?"

I shrugged. "I don't know. People came in a while ago; they kept trying to get me to eat." I paused, remembering. "One was so beautiful. Not like superstar beautiful. Like something ageless and changeless, that everyone still keeps falling in love with. Like the moon. I think she is the queen of everything. She said she made this place for me. She wanted me to eat and drink. Sleep in the bed, wash in the pool . . . Before her, another one came that they tried to make like you. But its eyes were all wrong. It kept trying to get me to eat, too. I don't know why."

Judith's eyes were narrowed, looking at something far, far away. "That sounds familiar . . . Why does that sound familiar? Did you eat or drink anything?"

"No. I almost took a gold cup full of water from the queen. She made it sound so good. And then I remembered the water I'd fallen through, fish-tank water, turtle-pond water, and it didn't sound so good anymore."

"Glamour . . ."

"What?"

"That's what it's called. Fairy magic. When they make

something, like these hangings on the bed, look like they're woven out of gold and silk, but really they're just made of cobweb and straw. Or when you trick a fairy by moonlight out of its pot of gold, and in the morning all you have is a tin bucket with some dead leaves in it."

I thought about that. "So she's not really that beautiful?"

That made Judith grin for some reason. "She might be. She always is in stories. I'm just saying that's how they work their spells over humans, sometimes. They make us think we see what we want to see. Maybe they trick us so that we can never see them clearly, never come too close, never learn too much about them."

She was wandering around while she talked, picking things up, opening little drawers in tables, lifting the corners of rugs with her foot. She went to a window, raised a curtain an inch, and peeked out.

"What's out there?" I asked.

"Trees, flowers, a pool . . . it's pretty. You haven't looked?"

"I haven't moved off this sheepskin."

"Really?" She came back to me, then, knelt in front of me. "Why not? Weren't you curious?"

"No."

"Were you scared?"

I thought. "No. I was mostly just—I wanted everyone to stay away and leave me alone. I just wanted to think about my dad." She didn't say anything. I went on after a moment. "They kept saying eat, and drink, and sleep in the soft bed, come swim in the nice pool. But none of it made any sense to me. No one told me why I'm here; they just dropped me in the middle of this fancy resort and told me to have fun. Like I wanted to be here."

"Nobody ever said they understood humans very well."

"I kept thinking and thinking about my dad. All these memories came back . . . Maybe part of it was going to Grandpa Liam's funeral. It reminded me of my father's. And my mom getting married again, and suddenly having a different—whatever he is. I didn't think about Syl or Gram wondering where I was, not even about anybody coming for me, or how I'd get out of here. I just started remembering, and I didn't want to stop. And then you came."

"Do you want me to leave you alone, too?"

"No." I shook my head, hard. "No." I reached out, and suddenly her hand was in mine, and I wasn't embarrassed, and I didn't want to let go. "I didn't know how much I wanted to see you until I saw you."

She smiled, her face turning pink, and I realized, like something smacked me in the forehead, that she liked me, too. Me. Green hair, geeky glasses, grungy clothes, and I hadn't taken a bubble bath since I was two.

"I can't believe that other Tyler fooled me," she sighed.

"You haven't known me very long. And the last thing you expected was a fake me."

"He was too clean. And he tucked in his shirt, and combed his hair, and he smiled so much."

I thought then that maybe I should give the bubble-bath idea some attention. "I think I'm hungry now," I said, surprised again.

"Don't eat," she warned. "Or drink. I can't remember why. If it's something they want you to do, you probably shouldn't do it."

"Well, what should we do?"

"You could get off the sheepskin."

I was still sitting on it. For a moment, my fingers tightened on the wool. I wondered if she was trying to trick me, too, into leaving my damp and smelly island where I could be safely miserable. She just held my hand and waited, without laughing at me, or getting impatient. I remembered how happy I'd been to see her, deep in me, beyond the murk and memories. How I said her true name instead of her fairy-tale name, because I knew who she was.

So I let go of her and stood up and walked off the sheepskin. Just like that. She smiled a little, crooked smile, and got up, too.

"Now what?" I asked.

She scratched her head, dislodging a scrap of bark. "I guess we can try to find a passageway back. If we got in, we should be able to get out. If we can find some path that Iris hasn't guarded."

"There should be at least two. Owen's pond and your hollow tree."

"Unless she's sewn them back up again."

"You mean we could be stuck here?" I demanded.

"Well, that's what the Fiber Guild is for."

That's when I started to be afraid.

Judith went to the door and opened it, a simple thing that

never crossed my mind to do. She peered out. I looked over her shoulder. The long hallway lined with closed doors, the flagstones and chandeliers, made me blink.

"It looks like Lynn Hall."

Except that the chandeliers were made of gold and had candles in them instead of bulbs. And there were carpets on the flagstones, weavings of white and gold and green that looked like they'd just been made that morning. There wasn't a smudge or a fleck of dirt on them, not even a stray grass blade.

Judith breathed into my ear, "Let's go."

The hallway we walked down seemed endless, maybe because I kept expecting one of the doors to pop open, someone to leap out at us, yelling, "Gotcha!" Finally, we saw a little door in the far wall that was different from all the others. It wasn't painted; it was carved all over with fruit and flowers and vines. The handle was the prong from a deer's antlers.

"Weird," Judith muttered, and played with it carefully until the door opened. We went through it into a little courtyard. Vines and flowers grew up everywhere along the stone walls. Fieldstone, just like Lynn Hall was made of, though I'd never seen a garden in it like that. Stone paths wound under little trees, plots of flowers. In the middle of the courtyard was a fountain. When I heard the water splashing, my mouth remembered that it hadn't tasted water since I got dumped into the pond. The statue of a woman stood in the center of the fountain. Water poured out of the urn she tilted on her shoulder, and splashed down into the bowl. The statue was barefoot and smiling; she pointed with her free hand at the water, as though she were inviting us to come and drink.

The water looked clear and fresh as rain. Staring at it, I could almost taste how cold it might be, how sweet, coming from that cheerful statue's urn. I heard Judith swallow. But as I stepped toward it, she caught my arm.

"Are you sure?" I asked her helplessly. "Maybe it's only food we should stay away from. Or everything but water."

Her face squinched; I knew she couldn't really remember. But she only whispered nervously, "I don't think so. Let's get out of here. It's creepy that there's no one around but this statue."

It was hard to turn my back on that water. But I did, and saw another door. This one was more like a gate, made of small birch trunks linked together with rings of gold. It reminded me of old chairs in Grandpa Liam's study, made of sapling branches, he told me, so supple they could be curved and tied together with strips of bark. The gate didn't have a latch. I pushed it, wanting to get away from the noisy reminder of water behind me, and it swung open.

We walked into what looked like a picnic in Gram's rose garden.

Every rose tree and bush was in full bloom. Tables spread with lace and gold cloth stood around the grass; all of them held gold and silver platters of huge slabs of meat, whole fish, mounds of fruit so high you could get killed if the pile toppled when you pulled out a pear, great wedges of cheese, bowls of salads, stews, so many kinds of vegetables I didn't recognize half of them, breads and cakes and pies and roasted nuts. I could smell everything very clearly, not a gross tangle of smells, but little individual breezes blowing under my nose: hot salty beef, then crusty bread pulled straight out of the oven, then garlic, or pepper, or orange when you first break into the peel and the juices spray, and then some kind of intense dessert, a serious chocolate felony, not just a wimpy misdemeanor. And silver pitchers stood everywhere among the food, some beaded with water from the icy liquid inside.

My stomach felt like it was about to float away. My knees went wobbly. I would have crawled over to that garden of smells and fallen facedown into whatever I reached first, as soon as I'd drained one of the frosty pitchers dry.

But Judith was pulling at me, and saying my name over and over until it finally made sense. "Tyler." She was still whispering for some reason. "Tyler. We have to go now."

Just one bite of that roast chicken, I wanted to moan. Just one gulp of water.

But she tugged, and I stumbled after her, not knowing where we were going until all the smells were behind me, and I could see again.

Trees bordered the rose garden, just like at Lynn Hall. Only these made a thick, dense wood you couldn't see far into. All the trees looked alike, slender as birch, with a greeny bark and long, pale leaves. They were crowded so close that I didn't think we'd be able to move through them. But Judith, running now, plunged into them, and so I followed.

I nearly bumped into her a moment later. She had stopped dead among the trees and she was staring up at them. She took a sudden step back into me, and groped for my hand, making a little whine in her throat.

I looked up. Leaves and bark were somehow turning into faces, hair, hands, clothes, all around us. Some of the faces were still streaked with the smooth, green-brown bark; if you blinked, they seemed to turn to tree again. Blink again and there was a face, a shadowy arm, a green skirt. The faces were just human enough to show what they were thinking, and it wasn't very friendly.

One spoke, and I recognized her somehow, in spite of the tendrils of her hair that curved into leaves, and the strange color of her skin. She was still beautiful, the way a mountain is, or a starry night, something like nothing else you've ever known, that you'll never really understand, and that will never ever notice you. But you don't care; you want to take it away with you in your heart.

"You haven't shared our feast," she said to me softly. "You have refused all my gifts." Her eyes turned to Judith, whose eyes were so wide I could see the white all around them. "I brought you here hoping that in the company of another human, he might take some interest in what I've made for him. But you rejected all my harmless pleasures. You made him run from them."

"We don't—" Judith's voice still came out in a whisper; she cleared her throat, started again. "We don't know what you want from us."

"Don't you? I've seen you peering into windows at the witches. I've watched you in the wood, looking at this and that, studying, learning. I've watched you stand at the borders between our worlds, wanting to come in. Now you're here, and all you can do is run. Have you learned all you wanted from us so quickly? You have come to my great banquet and eaten nothing. You've heard the pure water singing in my fountain, and drunk nothing. Is that how you learn as well? Peering in and never entering? Never taking a chance? Always hungry, never eating, thirsty and never daring to take one sip—"

I was ready. I would have marched back into the rose garden and clambered into the middle of one of her tables and started laying waste. Judith, her eyes narrowed now, the skin of her face as white as ice, answered abruptly, "Gingerbread. The witch's house. Eat and you get eaten. And the nasty goblins, trapping the sister who eats their fruit, and pinching the one who tries to rescue her. And that other story—the woman who gets snatched out of her world and has to spend half her life in the underworld because she eats six little seeds from a fruit. Fairy tales are full of food and most of the time if you eat, you're toast."

The queen stared down at her, her own eyes wide and unblinking, like a tiger's before it pounces. Then she spat a word that came out as a hazelnut, and in the next moment there was nothing around us but trees. Everywhere. We walked and walked, but we were in a prison of trees. An entire world of trees. We might have just been going around in circles, but when we couldn't find any other way out, we fell over, exhausted, among all the trees that ever were, and went to eat and drink in our dreams instead.

· 18 ·

Iris

When nobody came back by nightfall—not Syl, nor Tyler, not even Owen—I went to war. Those I loved were disappearing around me, and I could feel the thunderheads building in my heart. Bad enough that Liam had left me; at least I knew where the body was. The Starr sisters and Jane had stayed with me throughout the long afternoon; Dorian had joined us later, to tell us that her father was still searching. Another five hours had passed; the full moon was rising to stare into our world. *Where is she?* I wanted to ask it. *You can see.* Dorian's face had grown pale and set. Once or twice she opened her mouth to tell me something, then changed her mind. I waited, but whatever it was stayed unsaid. I sent her into Liam's study finally to make the calls for the gathering, and I went into the kitchen to work a little common household magic.

Hurley and the Tyler-thing were safely in the den; I could hear their voices as I passed, laughing at something on TV. The changeling had kept out of my eyesight most of the day since I recognized it, though it didn't give me any reason to suspect it knew I knew. But I knew exactly where I wanted it now, and I knew how to get it there.

I heard the click-step of Jane and her walker while I was measuring flour.

"Genevieve can't leave the bar," she announced, muting her customary foghorn because we didn't know who might be listening. "Penelope has to mind the bed-and-breakfast; Bet and Jenny are at a Rotary Club dinner. Hillary, Charlotte, and Agatha are all on their way. What in Blueberry Hill are you cooking at a time like this? It's an emergency meeting, not a social event."

"They aren't for you," I said shortly. "And keep your voice down."

She frowned at me. "What is it, Iris? What haven't you told us?"

"Later," I breathed. "Just send Dorian to me, will you? I need her to do something for me."

She did, without comment, though she followed Dorian back in, probably breaking the legal speed limit for walkers so she could listen.

"I want the chairs in a circle," I told Dorian, who was the

only one of us present who had any muscles. "And I want you to go to the end of the driveway and tell everyone to park on the road and walk in. Take the flashlight in Liam's study."

Dorian, her eyes wide, just nodded. She'd been phoning here and there, I knew, trying to find Leith; he seemed to have vanished along with everyone else. Jane's eyes were narrowed, trying to drill their way into my thoughts.

She whispered, which I didn't know she remembered as an option, "Iris, what are you doing?"

"You'll see," I promised, and shoved the bowl under the beaters. "Mix this, please, while I chop. I'm in a hurry, and I can't talk about it now."

I heard the den door open when Jane turned on the mixer. The Tyler-thing poked its head in the kitchen door a moment later, smiling.

"Cookies?" it said to us. I saw Jane's sour lemon-drop mouth sweetening a little at its puppy-dog friendliness. She almost cracked a smile in my kitchen, which would no doubt have caused the decorative plates to leap off the wall.

"Cookies," I agreed. "What are you and Hurley watching?"

"Funny family pet videos."

"Ah. Well, I'll let you know when they're done."

"Thank you, Gram."

"Such a well-mannered boy," Jane said after his head disappeared. "A shame about the ring in his eyebrow and the green hair, but really what could you expect with Kathryn marrying so soon after dear Ned was killed?"

"Exactly what I told myself," I said, turning the mixer off

and scraping the nuts into the bowl. "When Ned died, I just knew that boy would get his eyebrow pierced and there'd be no stopping him."

"You know what I mean, Iris."

I went after the dried cherries and the chunks of dark chocolate with my chopper. "Of course."

"Of course a growing boy needs a father figure, but where on earth did she find Patrick? He looks like an ad for some kind of tooth-whitening product."

"I can't imagine."

"Do you know?"

"What?"

"Where—How—What she sees in him?"

"Haven't a clue."

She gave up picking at me, since I was just using her fuel to stoke a deeper fury. I threw the last ingredients into the bowl, and stirred them unmercifully. "Jane, do something useful and turn on the oven on your way out the door?"

She sniffed, but I was rattling pans too noisily to hear her, so she just did what I asked. I threw spoonfuls of dough on a cookie sheet, and heard the sticky front door creak open. I froze, unreasonably hoping. But I heard a soft laugh, a gentle phrase upended into a question: women's voices.

I slid the cookies into the oven and went to meet them.

Genevieve was among them, which delighted me.

"The guy who takes my days off happened to be at the bar," she said, kissing my cheek. "So he's subbing for me. Dorian said you have a quilt emergency."

"We have several," I said. She was dressed in a pair of

pencil-thin jeans and a black sweater with a deep V-neck, a lovely setting for her long blond hair. Her lipstick was the color of the jewel in her navel, the color of the cherries in my cookies, and the sight of her took an edge of worry off my mind. I turned to greet Agatha, saw Charlotte and Hillary coming up the drive with Dorian. "Good," I said tightly to no one, and took them all to show them the moldering threads overlaying the quilt still spread over the couch. Miranda and Lacey passed out crochet hooks and hastily sketched patterns and threads of any color I'd been able to find. Dorian had pulled the chairs into a circle with some thought to our frailties; there was enough room to walk between them.

I waited until everyone was seated. There were nine of us, which seemed to me a satisfying number. I took them through the first emergency: the quilt, and its urgent need for repair. Dorian stared at me incredulously when I asked Jane to teach her how to crochet. Obviously she was wondering how I could rattle on about such mundane matters when her father and her lover and her best friend all seemed to have dissolved into moonlight. But she knew me. She swallowed her doubts and tried to pay attention to Jane. Agatha was teaching Hillary, who was looking with disbelief at the elaborate patterns on the quilt squares and the simple chain stitch running off her hook.

"How in hell—" I heard her murmur, and Agatha pinched her lips around a smile, glancing at her mother.

I smelled the cookies.

The changeling poked its head in wistfully just as I opened the oven door.

"Not yet," I lied hastily. "Give them a couple more minutes. They're too soft."

It closed the kitchen door again. I listened for the den door, heard it close, too. Then, as quietly as I could, I took the pan out of the oven and slid the cookies onto a plate. I left the oven door open, the empty pan on the table, and took the cookies into the next room. I put the plate on Genevieve's lap.

"Just hold them," I told her tersely. "And keep your stitches going, ladies. We have another emergency to trap in our threads. Genevieve, I want you to smile your best when it comes in, and offer it cookies. Talk to it, while we weave the net."

I heard little shreds of words starting and fraying around the circle. But nobody questioned. This was why we had gathered for over a century, and for those who'd been paying lip service all those years, now was the time for a leap of faith.

The changeling, sniffing like a dog, came into the room.

It hesitated when it saw the circle. I saw it shift one foot backward, as though not even my cookies were enough to lure it among us. Then Genevieve, facing it, gave it her warm, cherry-red smile, and lifted the plate.

"We couldn't wait," she said. "They smelled so good. Come and take some before we eat them all."

None of us was eating any, I realized then. But Agatha smoothed over the mistake, reaching for one and biting into it. The Tyler-thing, its eyes on Genevieve's smooth golden hair, and the creamy V of skin within her black top, brightened. It stepped into our circle, went over to her, and took a handful of cookies.

Genevieve was used to chattering amiably to customers through difficult situations, and the changeling looked so much like Tyler that she didn't seem struck by anything amiss, except for whatever was amiss with me. I doubt that anyone else noticed much beyond my own relentlessness: I chained faster than I thought my fingers could move. But no one questioned my eyesight or my sanity; everyone just crocheted quietly along with me. Our chains grew quietly as the changeling talked about funny pet videos and scattered crumbs on the floor, and Genevieve kept its attention, chatting and working her own chain as she balanced the plate on her lap. Slowly our silence and the rhythm of our hooks worked their own magic: our minds began to touch, seep together, link themselves around the changeling. Stitch by stitch, thought by thought, we cast our chains, circling and circling, until it finally realized it stood alone among us, while we circled it with our eyes, our hooks, our chains.

It made a little sound, spraying crumbs. Then it froze, only its eyes roving, trying to see our faces, or a gap in our web, a place to escape. In its sudden fear, it lost control: thumbs turned visibly into twigs; a cheekbone hardened into bark; its nose flattened, grew knobbed like a burl. Lacey's face turned so pearly I thought she might faint. Jane, whose eyes were starting out of her head, muttered something to Lacey that caused her spine to snap straight. Hillary, staring at the changeling, looked, with her spiky hair and elfin bones, as though she were turning into one herself. Genevieve, her marvelous social abilities floundering at last, stuffed a cookie into her own mouth, squeaking a little as she bit.

I said to it, "Tell us who sent you. And why. And what you have done to Tyler."

"Witches," it hissed, spraying crumbs. It spat a few more out, as though tasting poison. "Magic. Wicked magic."

"Chain stitch," I told it. "Elementary. Did you also take Syl?"

"Syl."

"And Owen?"

"Leith," Dorian added faintly. It was trembling, shifting, tugging at air, or invisible bonds.

"I go where I'm sent," it answered. "Do what I'm told."

"Who sends you? Who commands you?"

It flopped on its knees, looking so like Tyler for an instant that I nearly dropped my hook. Then its hair turned into brambles, and I breathed again. I saw its eyes grow white and luminous as moons, as though they reflected some distant light.

"She. She commands my heart."

"Did she also command you to take Syl?" Jane asked, sensing, as she did sometimes, that I could use somebody's strength. I flung her a grateful look, and worked my chain, picking up speed again.

Its face puckered into an unexpectedly human expression. "The cuz Syl? No."

"What about Leith?" Dorian asked again. "And Owen?"

"Not Owen. I don't know Leith. She didn't say them."

It tugged an arm, an ankle, testing our invisible threads. Apparently they held; it grimaced, making the distorted face that peers at you out of tree bark. "She'll come for me," it warned suddenly, loudly. "She'll take me back."

"We might bargain," I said tersely. "If we choose. We might keep you, trapped here forever in our stitches. Or we'll unravel you, bramble and twig and leaf, and stitch you into a pattern that not even your queen will recognize."

"She'll see me," it insisted. But its voice quavered. "She will come."

"Easier for you if she gives us back our Tyler. And anyone else she has taken who belongs to us. Then we will give you back to the wood. And then we will find every path and passage, every door between our worlds and stitch them so tightly closed that you'll forget our world exists."

"Whoa," it said faintly, or maybe, "Woe."

And then it shouted, or cried, or wailed, made a sound that blasted through the room, and flung open doors to fill the house. It could have stopped hearts, that sound; it certainly stopped our hands. But it only made us clutch our hooks instead of dropping them, and it failed to break our chains. Then it curled up around itself and turned into what looked like a small tree stump in the middle of my carpet, shooting a few upright leafing twigs out of itself, maybe to signal that it was still alive.

We sat stunned in the aftermath, staring at it, and waiting for the echo to die down. In its fading, I heard a heavy panting coming from beyond the circle. I jumped, fear skittering on its spider-feet across my neck and down my arms. We all turned, slowly and apprehensively, to see what the changeling's shout had summoned from the wood.

It had called up Tarrant Coyle, I saw with amazement. He stood in the hall doorway, hand to his heart, catching his breath and staring at the tree stump.

"What," he demanded weakly, "in heck-fire kind of demon was that you ladies conjured up?"

Miranda answered pointedly, which was fine with me; I couldn't find a word in my head. "That wasn't a demon, Tarrant. It was a changeling. You spoke to him, I believe, earlier today. Tyler."

His eyes bulged. "That's Tyler? What'd you do to him?"

"Tarrant!" Jane snapped. "Pay attention! That's the kind of magic you think you want to be dealing with in Iris's wood."

"Changeling," Lacey supplied faintly. "A fairy substitute for a human child."

"Looks like a stump," he muttered, wheezing at it. "Or a weird kind of altar. You sacrificing things now?"

"We just got rid of Hurley," I told him irritably. "He knew too much."

"Iris," Charlotte said reprovingly. "Don't confuse Tarrant; it doesn't take much, apparently."

"I'd like to know what Tarrant is doing here, sneaking around my place as though he thinks he already owns it."

"I wasn't sneaking! I was just walking down the hall—the front door was open—when there was this bloodcurdling yell, and I saw that—that—come to think of it, it did look a bit like Tyler, just before it changed. That green hair . . ."

"Tarrant!" I wanted to throw my hook at him. "Just tell us why you're here?"

"I can't find my daughter," he said fretfully. "I saw the cars parked on the highway, and I hoped she was still here with you." He crossed the room, flicked a curtain open. "Or spying on you, anyway."

"Still here? When was she here before?"

"She was with me this afternoon, when I came to talk to you. She didn't want to come home with me. She was mad at me. So I left her—" He paused. His eyes widened, moved reluctantly to the twiggy thing in the middle of the floor. "I left her in the wood," he said to it dazedly. "With Tyler."

The phone rang.

I nearly leaped out of my chair, remembered in the nick of time what I was holding. I handed my hook and chain carefully to Miranda, who knew enough not to set it down, to keep it suspended between worlds.

"It has to be Owen or Syl," I told them tightly, and banged the kitchen door open so hard it hit the cookie sheet on the stove and sent it clattering to the floor. I snatched up the receiver, gripping it so tightly it was a wonder it could speak at all, and demanded, "Yes?"

A man's voice asked hesitantly, "Is this Iris?"

"Yes!" I bellowed.

"Wow," he said, awed. "My name is Madison. I'm a friend of Syl's—well, more than a friend. Between you and me, I'm

Patricia A. McKillip

trying to persuade her to marry me—and I'd really like to talk to her. If that's possible?"

I tried to say something civilized, gave up finally, and told him the truth. "I have absolutely no idea."

I hung up and crept back to my chair to anchor my wobbly knees before I sat down on the floor.

234

·19·

Syl

Leith led me along an invisible path, an underground stream, through the wood to a circle of birch trees. I don't know how long we waited. Standing there, listening to the lightly chattering leaves, feeling the sunlight inch across my hair, my hands, I felt all sense of time drift out of me. There seemed so much else to consider besides my fears. The stunning threads of gold in Leith's red hair; the wedges of flame on his cheeks as he lowered his eyelids: butterfly wings of fire. He leaned against one tree, arm around its trunk, cheek against its milky bark, such a still, intimate pose that it made me wonder how well he knew that tree, if their silence was another form of language. Once he glanced at me: the deep flash of blue in his dark eyes made my breath stop. He gave me a little, crooked smile. The trees swayed and breathed around us, though I hadn't noticed any wind at all before. In our private wood, our little endless moment, such things didn't matter. Nothing mattered, not Gram, or Lynn Hall, or Tyler, just the sunlight moving slowly across my eyes, into my heart.

I stood in a dream of light. It was so lovely, this warm cascade, that I wanted to slip out of my body, become an indistinguishable part of it. Now and then, like bits of another dream, I glimpsed Leith, sitting among the tree roots, his face upturned to watch me; I saw the green wood, oddly shadowy now, beyond the ring of white birch. Once I heard him say a word. See, it sounded like. Or Sigh. Syl. I didn't know what he was trying to say. I didn't care.

Then I dissolved into the light. I felt it transform my bones, fill my head until there was no more room for thought, pool in my eyes until I could see nothing but that gentle, dazzling stream of gold.

My heart spoke one last word, an astonished, expanding O! before it burst into light.

I stood in front of Lynn Hall.

As I recognized it, I recognized myself again: my mortal body, all my human fears for other mortals, the part of me that could never live in such beauty. I had glimpsed what I could not have, and I felt a terrible grief at the loss. Light had spilled me out of itself onto this ragged lawn, among those straggly roses with their speckled leaves and their buds withering before they could open. The pear tree, under which Grandpa Liam had breathed his last, held only a few leaves and tiny, blackened swellings of new pears. Beyond the dying garden, the wood was so overgrown with vine and bramble that I would have needed a scythe to enter it.

I looked at the hall, which seemed entirely overgrown with ivy; tendrils drifted up from the chimney pots like smoke. The back screen door was sagging off its hinges. The inner door was open. I had come for Tyler, I remembered grimly; he couldn't stay here, either. I shook away the lingering, timeless light in my head, the lovely memories of enchantment, and went to find him.

I entered the hall cautiously, but I didn't hear anyone, or see so much as a shadow move. I could only find a couple of rooms open. The kitchen held little more than an open fireplace, a battered table, and a sink with a few tin pots in it. A doorway with a faded tapestry hung across it to separate it from the kitchen led me into another room. This held a bed cobbled out of stripped saplings, a thin, lumpy mattress, a sheepskin, none too clean, on the flagstones, and a clay bowl on a rickety table with a withered apple and a couple of walnuts in it.

A movement on the sheepskin caught my eye. I looked more closely, and found a little toad making its way clumsily across the wool. I picked it up and opened a window, which whined and splintered paint on the way up. I had let the toad fall into the cool shadow of the hall before the fairy-tale implications reverberated through my thoughts: all those damp, unlovely, imperiled creatures belonging both to air and water, in need and rescued by good-hearted strangers passing by. I tried to go farther into the hall; other doors were nailed shut.

That, too, reverberated uncomfortably: it seemed one reincarnation of the hall in my great-great-great-grandmother's manuscript. I didn't want to think about it. I just wanted to find Tyler and get back to the Lynn Hall we both knew. I went outside again, walked around to the front of the hall to look out over the neglected field. Weeds had grown so high they blocked my view of anything that, in my own world, I might have recognized. I was not surprised.

This didn't look like any fairy world I would have imagined. It looked more like Lynn Hall under a curse. I went up the low slate steps leading to the front door and turned the doorknob. As I expected, the door was swollen shut, and couldn't even rattle in its frame. I kicked at it a couple of times with my bootheel, then gave up. I sat down on the bottom step, dropped my chin in my hands, and brooded at the baffling scene.

Tyler's voice, somewhere near my right foot, said, "Thanks."

I stared down, saw the little toad making its way along the wall.

"Tyler?" I asked incredulously. It didn't say anything else; it disappeared into a hole under the steps.

But it had spoken a word in Tyler's voice. So he had been here, in this place, maybe in that drab bedroom before he found his own way out.

Three with eyes to see . . .

I had no idea why that little scrap of nursery rhyme flitted through my head. But it made me remember that I did have eyes to see; I was part wood-folk myself, and maybe this bleak house, this unkempt, parched landscape were only a memory of truth. I had taken a magical path to get there; surely not all the magic lay in the journey. Where was the enchantment here? The poetry? The beauty that lured mortals into the land beyond time?

"Where indeed?" a breeze whispered in my ear. I started. Then I stood up, searching through narrowed eyes, trying to see into thin air.

"Tyler!" I shouted abruptly. "Tyler!"

Not even a bird answered.

The whole landscape was a riddle, I thought bemusedly. A puzzle. A trick. Hiding something, maybe, or trying to reveal something; I hadn't a clue which. What could a weedy field or a dying rose tree say? Or a great house with all the life in it forced into two mean rooms? What had happened to all its grace and loveliness, all its tales and memories?

The wood, great swathes of ivy and brambles hanging from the trees, looked no more inviting and far less accessible than the weed-choked field. But things happen in a wood. Children get lost and found; princesses are abandoned and rescued there; lovers meet, get separated, meet again. All I had found and rescued in the house was a toad that hadn't hung around to chat.

I went across the stiff, brown grass to the edge of the wood. The brambles clinging to the trees sent tendrils snaking into other trees, making a wall of thorn and flowers—little wild roses, blackberry and raspberry blossoms—between me and whatever was hidden inside. I found a dead branch and beat at them, feeling like the prince in the fairy tale on a rescue mission. How had he gotten in? He had gotten lucky, I remembered. Other princes had failed and died, impaled on thorns; he had come, through no virtue or skill or worth of his own, on the right day. The briars parted, and he strolled in.

Evidently today was not the right day for me, but I wasn't going to wait a hundred years. I battled with the brambles until I was breathless and sweating, but it was like poking at a snail. They drew thicker and tighter, the more I smacked them. I flung down my weapon finally and yelled at whoever had stolen Tyler and shown me the ruins of Lynn Hall.

"What do you want? What is it you want from me? I've come to take Tyler home, and I'm not leaving without him!"

"What makes you think you can find your way back?" someone asked behind me.

I whirled. The voice was a woman's, but I couldn't see anyone among the ragged rose trees. Not even anything, like the toad, that in a fairy tale might have spoken. It was a good question, I admitted. But I decided not to think about it yet.

Kitchens, was what I did think, then. Kitchens are full of sharp implements. Even the poorest kitchen had a knife to skin the stolen hare with. Or to cut the brambles in your path. I went back into the hall, rummaged through the rickety drawers, one after the other, and found nothing but useless oddments: a mousetrap without a spring, a spoon without a handle, a fork with two tines bent one way, the middle tine bent the other, one blade of a very dull pair of scissors, a tarnished silver candle-snuffer. I reached for the last unopened drawer with exasperation, and realized, as my fingers closed around the drawer pull, that my mother had put it on.

Frozen, I stared at the drawers. All of them had the same drawer pulls my mother had chosen to replace the broken wooden knobs in Gram's kitchen drawers. They were small, round glass prisms of different colors; multifaceted, they caught light from every direction and refracted it back in every hue of the rainbow, casting little streaks of color unexpectedly throughout the kitchen. They had seemed to me an extravagant choice for my mother, who preferred things functional and elegantly simple. But, in the end, scant weeks before she had died, she had filled Gram's kitchen with these butterfly lights.

I couldn't move. I didn't know where I was anymore, what I was seeing around me, whose house this really was. I opened my fingers, looked at the pale green prism on my palm, and it blurred and swam in the sudden, burning tears that welled and overflowed and fell, for the first time in my life. I caught them in my fingers, stared at them, astonished that I had to come all the way to fairyland to learn how to cry.

"I never knew what happened to her."

I whirled, the tears shaken down my face. A man watched me from the kitchen doorway. A rainbow from one of the knobs quivered on his cheekbone. His hair was dark and curly, his eyes golden brown as hazelnuts. He stood there quietly as I stared at him, wondering why that coloring, that tapered jaw, those dark brows, peaked with a touch of uncertainty, looked in any way familiar.

Then I swallowed, and pushed back hard against the cupboard so that my knees wouldn't give way and drop me on the floor.

I forced myself to answer. He had a right to know. "She died some years ago. Mortal years." My voice hurt, coming out. "Did you—did you love her?"

He nodded. "She didn't believe me, though," he said softly. "She didn't trust me. She said—my kind don't love. Our blood runs cold; our hearts are empty. We trick mortals into loving and then abandon them." He let one hand rest on the cupboard beside him, his fingers open to catch the rainbow there. "So she abandoned me."

I blinked away tears again. "She was just—She was taught that."

"I know. We know."

"Is it true?"

He shrugged a little, his face calm, thoughtful. He looked scarcely older than I, but in another world, he might have been as old as the flagstones under our feet. "Sometimes. Not always. As it is in your world."

"Yes." I took a breath, my mother's face vivid in my head, lovely and fierce and desperate. "She loved me so much," I whispered, "that I don't see how she could not have loved you."

He bowed his head, hiding his eyes; his hand closed around the rainbow, but it eluded him, dancing on his fingers. "I always hoped to see her again. But she never called to me."

"She was afraid," I guessed. "Maybe of you, maybe of Gram . . . Who knows? Maybe she knew she didn't have the time, or the strength to fight for you, if Gram found out."

He raised his eyes again—my eyes—and I saw the question in them: Do you?

Maybe, I thought. You could be a trick, and your whole world a beautiful, empty lie, as Gram believes. But if you are a heartless illusion of love and beauty, come to trick me into challenging the entire Fiber Guild because I am your child as well as Morgana's, then I have to believe that I am a heartless illusion of a human, incapable of loving, too, and if that's true, then what am I doing here in the first place?

"Maybe," I breathed. "Maybe not. But maybe. Where is Tyler?"

"In the wood."

"How do I get in there? The thorns won't let me in."

He gave me a look of very human surprise. "We thought you would know. They're your threads."

I felt my blood run cold then, as cold as fairy blood. "Oh, no," I whispered through my fingers. "Oh. No." Then I shouted wildly, "Gram!" as though she were in the next room. "Whose house is this, anyway?" I asked him raggedly. "In what world did Lynn Hall ever look like this?"

"It is what Iris sees when she envisions us reclaiming Lynn Hall, using it for our door between worlds."

I looked around me, shivering, stunned. "Gram thinks we're so terrible?"

"We," he answered pointedly. "Not you."

"Not yet." I pushed cold hands against my forehead, trying to think. "I can't lie to her forever. Threads. A thread has a beginning and an end; people follow them through labyrinths and dark forests."

"Here they lead nowhere," he said a trifle bitterly. "Except to the knot at either end."

"Threads can be cut. Stitches can be undone."

"There's great power in her threads. A magic born of fear and hatred as old as this house seeped into the wood and field and water around it. How can we fight such power except with the same ancient forces?"

"I don't know," I told him breathlessly. "Nobody ever asked me that. Nobody ever came to me to say the things you're saying to me."

"You belong to both worlds; you are one of them and one of us. You must pass back and forth between your worlds with every thought, every breath. How do you reconcile them?"

"I never have."

"Try," my father pleaded. "For all of us."

I nodded, gazing at his so familiar, unfamiliar face that my mother must have loved so much she ran, terrified, from love. "I don't even know how to get back to Gram to tell her what she's done," I told him ruefully. "I came through a dream, I think. Gram hasn't been able to shut the passage through light."

He smiled a little, a rainbow trembling at the corner of his mouth. "You came that way? That's the oldest, and simplest, and most difficult way . . ."

"She'd need to thread her needle with the sun." I turned restlessly, wondering if I could travel a rainbow's arch between worlds. "Up the chimney?" I guessed, looking dubiously at the blackened hearth. "Magic goes up and down chimneys in tales. Or maybe I can find a passage in the attic, if I can get the hall door open."

He nodded toward my ankle at the drawer behind it. "There's the one you haven't opened."

"There's nothing in those drawers."

"There's everything before they are opened: gold, hope, a good knife blade . . ."

I bent to open the drawer with the green prism pull. It had already given me so much, I realized, and I'd barely touched it. At first glance the drawer looked as though I'd emptied it.

"What's in it?" my father asked.

"Nothing." Then I looked closer. "A bit of thread."

"Three with eyes to see," he said, and at the third glance I recognized it: the way out.

I picked up the inch or two of thread that was caught between cracks in the wood, as though someone, reaching for something, had snagged a sleeve and pulled a thread loose.

It kept coming. I pulled out a foot or more, and then I pulled the drawer out, and saw where the thread went: under the cupboard, out the back, and underneath the tapestry hung between the rooms.

I turned to my father before I followed the thread into the next room; he smiled at me, a rainbow in one golden eye. I walked behind the ancient, faded hanging

and into the circle of the Fiber Guild.

·20·
Iris

That was the loveliest thing I ever saw.

Before I recognized her, before my eyes finished seeing what they saw, and my head put a name to it, that's what my heart thought. A slender, golden-haired woman stepped out of air into light and shadow, one of our threads arching gracefully from her fingers to the end of my hook. She had unraveled my chain, I realized, and wonder changed to mortal terror, just that fast. Then I knew her and, for the third or fourth time that evening, I nearly jumped out of my chair.

"Sylvia!" My voice croaked like an old raven with shock. Tarrant, sitting apart from us, gave a brief bark of astonishment. Nobody else said anything, or moved. Mouths hung open all around the circle; no words came; nobody could even blink. For that moment, she held them all spellbound.

Then I heard a throat-clearing rumble from Jane, and her support hose snag together as she shifted. Miranda's teeth clicked together as she closed her mouth; she murmured succinctly between them, "Shit."

"Is that you?" Dorian asked faintly, her voice trembling. "Or another changeling?"

Sylvia looked at her. "Me. I just met my father." She turned to me again, her eyes wide, distant, a stranger's regard, which at that moment she pretty much was. "That's who I look like."

"Oh, my," Lacey whispered.

I tried to summon up something more coherent. "Is that where you've been?" was all I could manage.

She nodded. "I went looking for Tyler. Leith took me to a place in the woods. A passageway he knew."

"Leith," Dorian said, straightening abruptly in her chair as though she'd sat on a pin. "He doesn't know—Syl, what are you saying?"

"Ask him."

"Where is he?" Dorian pleaded. "Where's my father?"

"I'm not sure . . . Leith watched me when I crossed into the Otherworld, but I don't know if he came, too. I never saw Owen."

Dorian put her hands over her mouth, said through them, "What are you saying, Syl? About Leith?"

"He's part fay," Sylvia said simply. "Like me. We've known

that about each other since we were kids. That's why I left these mountains as soon as I could." She gave me that stranger's glance again, the one that told me that I couldn't hurt her, or that she was afraid I could. "I didn't want you to find out that I'm what you all fear most."

Well, there she gave it to me in a nutshell: the tangled mystery of Morgana's love, the knot of all my loves and hates. What, her cool eyes asked me, are you going to do with me?

I felt old suddenly, a hundred years older than I'd been five minutes before, and frail, and useless, and completely confused. Something hung by a thread between us: from the beginning stitch still looped around my crochet hook to the end of the strand between her fingers. Love, I guessed it was, or life, maybe just truth at last, considering where she had found the end of my thread to follow it.

"What am I supposed to do?" I demanded of her, of everybody silently listening. "Stop loving you? Just like that? When did you stop loving me?"

I saw her swallow; the thread trembled between us.

"Oh, Gram," she whispered. "Never."

"Then why should I be the one to stop?"

"I thought—you've always hated—"

"Well, nobody—not a Lynn or an Avery, not even Morgana, and certainly none of the wood-folk—ever gave me a reason not to. Is that why she never told me? Because she was afraid I would have hated you?"

"I think—I think probably, Gram. She never told me, either."

I pulled my crochet hook through the thread and threw it on the floor. It hit the little tree stump; a twiglet rustled. Sylvia seemed to notice it finally; she looked down, and her brows went up.

"It's the Tyler-thing," I said impatiently, before she could ask.

"So I see. You scared it."

"It scared me."

"How did you recognize it?" she asked hopefully.

"Not with your eyes," I told her bluntly. "I saw its shadow. Where is Tyler? You didn't bring him back with you."

She shook her head. "I tried. Gram, he's trapped in your wood behind your stitches. You will have to let him out."

I was the only one speechless, then; everyone else found something to say about that, including Tarrant.

"You mean your sewing circle really works?" I heard him exclaim, and then Jane's bullhorn overrode the clamor.

"We didn't steal him away," she protested to Sylvia. "We didn't send a changeling to take his place. Whoever wants it back, let them bring Tyler to us."

"And Judith," Tarrant added heavily.

"Judith?" Sylvia repeated, her brows going up again. "Your daughter? How—"

"We think the thing there took her, too. I left her with it. Looked just like Tyler, anyway. You didn't see her there?"

"No. I didn't see either of them. I couldn't get into the wood to find them. Those stitches are like a wall of brambles around the trees."

"How do we know that, Sylvia?" Charlotte asked practically. "That the brambles weren't put there to trick you, and force us to destroy our work?"

"I agree," Miranda said gently, but implacably. "There's no telling what would come out of that wood if we take out the stitches around it."

"Whose pattern is that?" Agatha asked at a tangent. "We need to know where the stitches are if we decide to take them out."

"It's one of mine," Lacy answered. "I gave it to Iris years ago: a long linen runner crocheted all around the sides."

"I remember," I told her, which was a minor miracle. "It's in my bedroom, on the dresser."

"We're not," Jane boomed adamantly, "cutting a single stitch. There must be another way to rescue the children. Sylvia could go back and try again."

"Absolutely not," I snapped. "They might decide to keep her, too."

"Or she might decide to stay?" Charlotte said coolly, always the one to pinpoint the unpleasant angle.

"Thank you, Charlotte, for bringing that out into the open."

"I think it's obvious. Half the one, half the other, and heir to Lynn Hall, the most powerful passageway in these mountains. She's kept that from us, all these years. So how do we know what else she's keeping from us? How do we know if anything she tells us is true?" She looked around the circle as we gazed at her silently, and added, without a blink, "Someone had to say it. It's there."

Hillary said in her blunt little voice, startling us, "It's there, if you look at it through the Fiber Guild's suspicious eyes. Maybe Syl has a different way of looking at it."

"I think—" Sylvia said.

"What other way is there of looking at it?" Charlotte asked reasonably. "We've all read Rois Melior's manuscript. She had the clearest view of things. They're a cold, loveless, dangerous people; they steal humans, trick them, even kill them. What clearer record do we have of them than hers?"

"Then why," Dorian said sharply, color running all through her face, "has my father found one worth loving for over a dozen years?"

You could have heard a pin drop. Leaves, like little ears, were trembling all over the changeling-stump. I could hear my heart beat, like a drip of water into an empty bucket. Time slowed for a little, or I just stopped thinking about things, went somewhere else that was peaceful and simple.

Then I blinked, and found Sylvia crouched beside me, holding my hand. "Gram," she whispered, looking up into my face. "Are you all right?"

I touched her face, with all its fay and human beauty. "Yes. I'm still breathing. Owen in love, all these years . . ." Around us the circle was silent again; everyone might have vanished, for all I knew. "Do you know what, Sylvia?"

"What?"

"It would be such a relief not to have to carry all this secrecy, this fear, these rules, these worries, all these threads and patterns around all the time. Especially at my age." Owen's dark, brooding face came into my head then. The one I trusted more than anyone except Liam had lied to me, too, all these years. "Like Morgana," I murmured. "Like you . . . concealing, not daring to tell me . . . Was it love, too, with Morgana?"

"I think so. He loved her."

"Really?" I said, surprised. "All these years . . . Maybe we were wrong?"

"Maybe. Maybe not. But maybe."

I smiled, brushed her cheek again. "Where is Owen?"

"I don't know, Gram."

"He went looking for Leith," Dorian said, breaking the hush around us, the little bubble of timelessness. "He said he knew where he was going."

"I want to talk to him."

"So do I," Jane muttered. "I'd like to know what he thinks he's been doing, an Avery hiding something like that from a Lynn all those years."

I ignored her. "What should we do?" I asked Sylvia. "What do we need to do to get Tyler and Judith back?"

"I don't know."

But she did know; I saw it in her steady, conjecturing gaze. Was I strong enough? Wise enough? Brave enough to do the obvious? I wasn't certain either. It went against centuries of common lore, local history, family tradition. And at my age . . .

"All right," I told her grimly, as the faceless, ancient figure took shape in my imagination, her spiky crown spearing moonlight on its way through the trees. "How do I find her?"

Of course that caused explosions around the circle, from

Jane and Charlotte especially. After an extraordinary glimpse of Lacey shaking her crochet hook in Charlotte's face, I got up, breaking the circle, which was an unprecedented thing to do in the middle of a spell. I went to my bedroom, found the runner under the jewel box on my dresser. It was a long oblong of white linen, with a delicate scattering of embroidered violets at either end; its sides were completely hedged in with some seriously intricate crocheted spirals and chains.

I took my nail scissors to it.

Then, because the front door was still open, and I didn't want to go back into the storm, I walked out into the night instead. I thought of all the times Liam had done just that: stepped out of the door into that glittering swarm of stars and fireflies, leaving all the noise and artificial brightness behind him, along with his wife, who was busy making her complex patterns out of the fields and trees he wandered through. I went around the house to the back, where trees caught stars in their leaves, and the fireflies flashed their tiny, fairy lights in the shadows.

I dropped my handful of shredded threads at the edge of the wood and waited.

· 21 ·

Owen

We waited interminably, decades and centuries, it seemed, for Sylvia to return to the circle of trees. Time flowed oddly, shifting in huge, unpredictable segments. Now the air was smoky with dusk. Now it was black, brilliant with the brief, impassioned language of fireflies. Now, in a swift jump forward, the full moon hung overhead in a sky so laden with stars they seemed about to fall to earth like ripe fruit. The taciturn Leith, inspired by moonlight, told me stories of his childhood: how no Rowan's door was ever locked, in case someone needed to borrow something, how he knew every tangled road and who lived on it, as well as the denizens, two-legged and four, along every branch and brook and stream in

Rowan territory. He told me how he had raised a fawn that had gotten separated from its mother when he was little older than the fawn. That had led to helping other creatures: an owl with a missing claw, a crippled rabbit he refused to yield to the stewpot, even a lost bear cub he had tracked through a fall of late-spring snow.

He even told me the truth about the scar under his cheekbone.

"I slipped on ice one winter morning and banged my face on the corner of the outhouse. I didn't want to talk about it. All the other kids had indoor plumbing." He paused. "Now you'll have to become part of the family. You know my secret."

"You mean besides the secret that you're part fay?"

"Naw. You can't blackmail me with that one. I know your secret."

I was silent, wishing beyond hope that it were still true. My ears caught every rustle in the dark. But it was never Rue, and, anyway, she didn't rustle; she came to me as silently as starlight.

"I wish . . ."

"Anything could happen," Leith reminded me. "Maybe Syl will—"

"Sylvia can't rescue us all. If she brings herself and Tyler out safely, I'll be content."

"No, you won't."

"I'll have to be."

Sometime later, flicking away a stone my tailbone found, I had an idea. "I have a flashlight at one end of a ballpoint pen in my pocket. You could find your way out with that. Tell Dorian you're safe and and see if Sylvia has returned."

"I already told you: I'm not going anywhere near Lynn Hall tonight. Anyway, I'm a Rowan; I don't need a flashlight. I could smell my way back to the mill road. You go."

"To face Iris and tell her that the heir to Lynn Hall found her way into fairyland without a map? No, thank you."

Later, I talked about my wife. I couldn't see Leith's face; we both seemed caught in some endless, enchanted night within the circle; it seemed safe to talk about anything there.

"Her name was Frederica. She'd been called Fred all her life, and she made me promise, before she would agree to marry me, that I would never shorten her name. Sometimes I wonder if that's why she left me. I got careless and accidentally called her by the name she hated. It seems as likely as any other reason I can come up with, why she ran away from me."

"She didn't leave a note?"

"Not a word, not a note . . ." I slid down the tree roots, stared back at the moon above our heads. It seemed very close; it could have seen through my skin, into the memories and the pain of being abandoned, which had been dead embers, I thought, until Rue was taken from me. "I thought she was happy. She started the nursery; she loved to garden. Dorian and I adored her. We played music together, cooked together. Dorian looks like her: that curly hair, cinnamon, nutmeg, strands of pepper and cardamom, those eyes . . ."

"River eyes," Leith murmured. "Speckled like a trout."

"Frederica's were more amber, with flecks of gold and gray in them."

"Maybe she was fay. She had to leave her mortal shape after three years and three days or something. When did you meet her?"

"When we were two."

"Oh."

"Her father was a friend of my uncle's, from the city. He and his wife came to visit; they fell in love with the mountains and decided to live here. Maybe that was the mistake we made. She'd lived here all her life, married a man she grew up with; she wanted change. Adventure."

"Could be," Leith said. I couldn't see him anymore; I only heard his slow, thoughtful voice. "Things like that happen. Or maybe it's not so simple at all . . . Maybe she went for a walk in the wood and found this place. This circle of trees. She fell asleep here, and woke up in a different world entirely. She'll come back someday, thinking she's only been gone an afternoon, and find that a hundred years have passed in the world she accidentally left."

"She'll find my grave and drop a tear on it," I said dryly.

"She'll see Dorian's children's children, and recognize them by their speckled eyes."

I was silent again, oddly comforted by that tale. Frederica hadn't meant to leave us. She had fallen into an enchanted sleep, during which she had some lovely and unusual dreams . . . She woke to see the sun setting, the woods growing shadowy around her. She stepped out of the circle and found, as she walked home, that during her dreams her world had changed beyond imagination . . .

"Maybe."

"Listen," Leith said abruptly, urgently, and I did. At first I heard nothing, but I didn't have his Rowan ears, which must have heard the trees sough on the other side of the hill.

All around us the birch began to chatter. Wind out of nowhere flowed over us like a tidal wave. As quickly as we could push to our feet against it, it ebbed; the wood was suddenly, utterly still. The fireflies had gone, probably blown clear into the next hollow.

"What is it?" Leith breathed, still clinging for balance and trying to see into the dark.

"I don't know, but I don't like it."

I took the penlight out of my pocket but didn't turn it on. There was another strange sigh of wind through the trees around the circle; twigs, dry leaves, needles crackled and snapped, as though something enormous, dark, and swift traveled through the bracken. More quickly than I could blink, a puff of red glowed among the trees, a little ball of fire that was gone the moment I saw it.

"I really don't like this . . ."

I heard Leith shift, but he didn't answer. Then we heard what sounded like the high, light ring of a thousand tiny bells.

And then a horn's clear, sweet call swept from ridge to ridge across the valleys, echoes overlapping endlessly without losing their purity. We listened for a long time, it seemed, before they began to fade.

"The Wild Hunt," Leith said dreamily. For an instant, in our enchanted circle, he seemed about to answer its summons.

Then he stiffened, and I flicked the penlight on. We stared at one another. Then we both began to run.

It wasn't easy, floundering over rocks and tree roots at that hour of night. But the direction of the wind and the flow of riders through the trees had been toward Lynn Hall; we had no time to think. Leith, ahead of me, followed the meager, dancing pinpoint of light I trained ahead of him. I followed his steps, trying to keep up, and listening, my nape-hairs prickling, for hooves and bells and wicked laughter at our backs.

We had no hope of getting to Lynn Hall before them, but just getting there, as fast as possible, seemed imperative.

"What's Iris been up to tonight?" Leith wondered raggedly, as we finally reached the fallen boundary tree and flung ourselves over it.

"No idea," I managed. I hadn't run so far so fast in years, and we still had the mill road to travel before we reached my car. A sudden gust of wind behind us, strong enough to set the old hemlocks creaking, made me find my second wind. The rugged road, with its dips and ruts and sections worn down to bare root and stone, was difficult enough to walk in daylight. By night, even under that moon, it was treacherous. But a moment's glimpse, across the brook, of a horse whose breath seemed a cloud of mist and white fire, a rider wearing what looked like horns the color of bleached bone, inspired me to a mindless burst of strength and energy that lasted until we reached the end of the mill road and my car.

The keys were still in my pocket, and the car hadn't morphed into a pile of rust during our sojourn in the circle of trees. We tumbled into it; I peeled away to take the turn down the long road between the Trasks' pasture and Iris's hayfield.

We saw them clearly then: riders streaming out of trees, down roads and ridges, even following the path of water, some with owls on their heads, or great racks of burning horns, horses breathing fire or stars, all of them headed toward and vanishing into the wood behind Lynn Hall. I heard Leith's incredulous gasp. I floored the gas pedal, careened around the turn into the highway so fast I felt the back end still trying to go straight. Other cars were parked near Iris's driveway. I didn't wonder why they were out along the road; I was just relieved that she wasn't alone. I sprayed gravel turning into the drive, and again when I braked, opening my door at the same time.

The front door was open. Lights were on in the living room and the kitchen. There was a tree stump on Iris's carpet. No one was in the house. So I thought, anyway, until I bumped into Hurley in the kitchen.

"Owen," he said. He seemed shaken, his face slack, his eyebrows working. "There is something happening in the wood. I was watching it through my telescope. So I came down to tell Iris, and I saw it out the window with my own two eyes. I've never seen it with my eyes before."

"I haven't, either."

"Are you going out there?"

"Yes," I said, moving fast out the other kitchen door toward the back porch.

"Then I'll come with you."

I went out onto the porch and stopped dead. Most of the Fiber Guild, including my daughter, stood scattered among the roses. For some peculiar reason, Tarrant Coyle was among them. Under the bright moonlight, I could see Iris at the boundary between lawn and wood. There was a taller, slender figure beside her; light cast by the windows burnished her sleek hair the same elusive cobweb shade as Iris's.

"That's Syl," Leith breathed. "How did she get here?"

Her head lifted slightly as though she had heard her name, but she didn't turn. Facing them both, ranged among the trees, was the mass of riders we had seen coming. Some looked nearly human; others began with a semblance of normality that trailed off into leafy branches or flowering wood. Faces in the shadows were amorphous, indecipherable. Moonlight glinted off metal and jewel, odd bits of harness. Small bells sang. A horse's eye, predawn black, reflected a tiny, cold moon the perfect circle of the moon above the wood.

The rider directly in front of Iris wore a crown of what looked like silver and moonlight. Tall and graceful, she at least assumed a human shape; her long pale hair flowed like a cloak over the dark, shimmering robes she wore. Fireflies, flickering constantly around her, blurred her and her dark mount; a human eye, casting a casual glance into the shadow, would not have recognized what it saw.

She and Iris seemed to take the measure of one another silently: two ancient warrior-queens, guarding their boundaries.

The woodland queen spoke finally. "You called me."

"It's her," Hurley said surprisedly. "The one in my tele-scope."

I don't know which surprised me more: Hurley's seeing eye, or the implication that Iris herself had flung open the door between worlds and roused this army massed against her.

"You have some children of ours," Iris answered.

I blinked. That would explain Tarrant's presence, I realized.

"And you have one who is mine."

She had a lovely, fluting voice; it could have blended eas-ily into the light rill of branch water, or a dove's coo. Iris's voice held all the untuned, timeworn notes of her mortality. But it held steady; I heard no fear in it, just her usual, reas-suring brusqueness.

"What do you want," she asked the queen, "in return for my grandson and his friend?"

"What will you give me?"

"The one who is yours," Iris answered.

"And what else?"

Iris hesitated. In the exacting world of fairy tale, that seemed fair: Iris was getting two for one. But she seemed un-certain, and made what sounded like a terribly reckless bid. "What more do you want?" she asked the fairy queen. "What do you want that I can give you?"

The woodland queen didn't answer immediately. She dis-mounted, causing a minor galaxy of glittering fires to move across her from crown to foot. She took a step closer to Iris, where the shelter of trees ended and the lawn began. Iris didn't step back, but she did grasp Sylvia's arm, maybe to stop herself.

"You turn back our paths of flowing water," the queen said. "You block our passageways through tree and well and pond; you thread your thorns and weedy vines between our worlds as though you own them both. As you close our paths, you close your minds to us. In your thoughts you keep us trapped in some bleak place that you must never enter, no matter how our ancient wonders call to you across the boundaries. We are the word you must not say, the food you must not eat, the wine you must not drink, the forbidden love, the dangerous wood, that which tempts and lures and always, always destroys. Is that all we are to you?"

"Yes," Iris said. Her changeling granddaughter's face turned toward her then, and Iris cleared her throat. "Until tonight. Until now. That is what we have always been taught."

"Then this is what I want," the woodland queen said, taking another step, and then another, toward her. It was as though we watched a river spilling over its banks, and if Iris did not move back she might be swept away and drowned. She stayed stubbornly rooted, though behind her, a few of the guild members in the rose garden eased toward the house.

"What?" she asked, her voice sounding harsh, and I realized that even she was a bit unnerved. So was I, by then. Two women, one frail with age, the other young, and inexperienced, and possessing a conflicted heritage, were all that stood between our tranquil world and that fay, glittering horde.

The queen stepped out of the wood. "To give you a different tale."

In the wash of light from the windows, we saw her face clearly, not the cold-eyed winter queen of Rois Melior's manuscript, but the golden queen of summer, with her corn-leaf eyes, and her bewitching smile, and her bare feet scarcely bending a blade of Iris's grass.

She gave a soft call then. I tensed, preparing for the storm that Leith and I had glimpsed. The screen door banged behind us; we both jumped. A creature smelling of earth and leaf mold and vanilla musk shambled down the steps and through the roses, inspiring some colorful exclamations from the guild. Its odd, tree-imp face turned toward Iris before it passed into the wood.

"Awesome cookies, Gram," it said. "Thanks."

I could see the human faces then, emerging from the trees, tired, dirty, and about to puddle into tears of relief. They flung their arms around Iris and Sylvia, and then Judith saw her father and ran to him. The voices among the roses had risen to a piercing tumult; Iris flung her own voice into it.

"Hush!"

Everyone did, including a couple of mounts nervously shaking their harness bells behind the queen.

"I took your children and sent you one of ours just for this," the queen told her. "Not to harm you, but in hope that you might find a reason to talk to me. Our world is very old; yours is very powerful. Tales make us seem fearsome, and so we can well be. But not always. And your stitches may bind us in our world, but they also bind the beauty and the wonder in it, which so many of you, wandering in and out of our world, bring back with them to tell about."

"Including my granddaughter," Iris said simply, touching Sylvia's hair. "She turned my thoughts around, in the end."

"Yes," the queen said softly. "She was very brave to come freely into our world."

"You saw me?" Sylvia asked.

"Of course, I did. I made everything you saw."

"How did you—how did you know about the drawer pulls?"

"I didn't. It was you who picked them out of my random magic. You gave them significance. You found the thread. You found your own way home."

"Oh," she whispered, a sound so faint it might have been lost, except that everyone else on both sides of the border seemed spellbound.

"It will be hard," Iris admitted, "to change the habits of centuries. Ways of looking at the world get ingrained and tenacious after so long a time. Even now, it's hard for me to trust you."

The queen nodded. "I know. And I wonder when you'll all decide you have been dreaming, and go back behind your doors to resume your stitchery, and lock yourselves away again from the world you enter, time after time, in your stories. But perhaps, if the three of us think hard enough, we will find ways to live more peacefully with one another."

"Maybe," Iris answered slowly. "Maybe not. But maybe."

A breeze, very light and faint, stirred through the woods. I was looking, I realized finally, at an empty, dwindling cloud of fireflies. Voices were rising again; women moved, hesitantly, out of the garden toward the trees.

Except for Dorian, who took the porch in a single bound and had her arms around Leith before he could take a step. "It's about time!" she said fiercely, patting my arm in greeting when she could spare a hand.

Tarrant, his arm tight around his daughter, brushed past us without a backward glance. "For my money, you can keep Lynn Hall," he told me with mystifying intensity. "Stitch up everything in sight. Did you see those fire-breathing horses? And that huge guy with the horns coming out of his head?"

Even Jane had made it across the lawn, gripping Agatha with one hand and her walker with the other, to peer into the wood.

She barked, "Did I just see what I think I saw?"

"I thought it was beautiful," Lacey said gently, as I passed her to join Iris. "All the fireflies and those strange, lovely faces in the moonlight . . ."

"Owen!" Iris exclaimed. "Where on earth have you been?"

"Waiting for Sylvia in the wrong wood," I told her, and asked Sylvia, "How did you find your way back? "

She shook her head slightly; her face, all its reserve melted away, looked a trifle dazed, and oddly peaceful. "I found one end of Gram's thread in a drawer and followed it back to a Fiber Guild meeting," she answered vaguely.

The humorless Charlotte drifted past us to put an arm around a tree and stare wordlessly into the wood.

"Charlotte?" Iris said. "Are you all right? Charlotte?"

"I had no idea . . ." she whispered.

"What?"

She looked briefly at us, an expression on her face it probably hadn't worn in twenty years. Then she wandered into the woods, in the wake of some vision. Sylvia smiled; Iris sighed.

"I hope I did the right thing," she said, rubbing her eyes tiredly.

"You were magnificent," I told her.

"Was I? Are you sure, Owen?"

"Yes," Sylvia and I said together.

"Where did Tyler go?" she asked fretfully. "He just got back, and now he's gone again—"

Sylvia put an arm around her, turned her toward the house. "He's in the kitchen, Gram. He said Judith wouldn't let him eat or drink there."

"That was my fault. So many things are my fault . . . Morgana's secrets, you running away from home—"

"Gram, let's go in; we're all tired."

"Even Owen afraid to tell me things—"

"How did you know?" I asked her, stunned.

"Dorian announced your love affair to the Fiber Guild. Come in with us? I'd like to hear more about it."

"Yes. In a moment."

I waited more than a moment, until all the women had gone, and even Charlotte had come back from her private dream. Until even the fireflies had gone elsewhere. But no kindly gesture from the woodland queen granted me my wish, and I could only rue the bygone day.

· 2 2 ·

Syl

I left Lynn Hall a few days later, flew back home to put my store in order, and find someone to do my job for the rest of the summer. Madison met me at the airport. I think I fell in love again at the sight of him: his big-boned, easy grace, his long black hair, most of all the smile that flashed out of all of him when he saw me. I could love him, I thought dazedly. I didn't have to be afraid.

Later, we curled up in my bed, eating Chinese food out of boxes and talking. I had the soy sauce and fortune cookies on my side of the bed; he had the wine and most of the napkins. We reached across heedlessly when we needed something, endangering each other with waving chopsticks. I dropped rice on his pillowcase; he spilled soy sauce on my silk pajamas.

"Never mind," I said, and took them off, and tossed them over the end of the bed. Madison stared at me.

"What's happened to you? You just—you just threw your clothes on the floor. You didn't get out of bed and put them neatly into the hamper."

"I know," I said, hardly believing myself. "Life's messy?"

"You learned that in a week? At a funeral?"

"Sort of."

Someday I'd tell him, I thought. Or he would guess. Or not. It didn't matter yet, and when it did, I would find a way.

"Your grandmother is fierce," he commented, refilling our glasses. I started, shaking wine onto the sheets.

"You talked to her?" My voice squeaked. "She didn't tell me."

"Well, I'd hardly call it a conversation. I told her who I was—and that I wanted to marry you, so she'd take me seriously—and asked if I could possibly talk to you. She said she had no idea and then there was this bang in my ear."

"She has an old-fashioned dial phone."

"A what?"

"What day was that?"

"Ah—Saturday night, it would have been."

The shortest night in the year, the longest night of my life . . .

"She really didn't know where I was then," I told him. "She was worried."

"Where were you?"

I floundered. "Out. Looking for Tyler. He went missing, too."

Madison gave me a long, clear-eyed look, as though he glimpsed the tale that thereby hung. But he shelved that for now, to my relief, and took another bite of mandarin beef. "I almost flew out then and there," he said calmly. "That message you left had me a bit worried. You changed your mind so fast about needing me."

"I did," I sighed, remembering the call under the hydrangea bush. Already it seemed a decade ago. "That was when Gram told me that I'd inherited Lynn Hall. It scared me. What she might want from me."

"So what does she want?"

"Nothing much now," I said contentedly, stretching like a cat, my chopsticks probably decorating the wall behind me with sauce. "Just to spend a month or two with her this summer, helping her fix the hall up. She and Hurley will stay there for as long as they want. When it's empty, I'll decide then what to do with it."

"I'm coming out there," Madison warned me, "when my summer class ends. So don't go falling in love with anybody else."

"Don't you, either."

He looked at me, surprised. "Really?"

"Really," I said soberly. "Really, truly."

He gave me a winey, mandarin kiss, and then looked at me again, silently, steadily. "Okay, then," he said softly, and put his arms around me, spilling my wine again on both of us, like some ancient ritual blessing.

Tyler spent a good part of the summer at Lynn Hall, too, helping us now and then as we painted, chose wallpapers and linoleum, replaced curtains, dealt with the formidable clutter in the attic. He and Hurley went fishing together; Hurley taught him to use his drill and lathe, which Tyler managed without losing fingers. He talked about his father, thoughts and memories spilling out at random. Once, while we were in the attic, packing Gram's discards in boxes for the local thrift shop, he talked about what happened in the wood.

"It hardly seems real now," he told me. "More like a dream. Is it that way for you?" I shook my head. "Oh. Well, mostly I was curled up in a ball on a sheepskin, thinking about my dad. Or I was following Judith around. She and I only have each other to talk about that part. She says I should keep it secret. That no one will believe me. Do you think that's true?"

"Not entirely. You'll meet a few people around here, I think, who will believe you. Just be patient. You'll learn to recognize them."

He was silent a moment, rolling old juice glasses in newspaper. "I understand what the queen was trying to do," he said finally. "Why she did what she did. But mostly, I felt like she just brought me to a place in a fairy tale where I needed to be most. Where I didn't have to do anything but think about my dad. And be miserable. As sad and angry and hopeless as I wanted to be."

I swallowed, remembering the place where she had brought me. "She has a gift for that."

"And then Judith came, and helped me." He smiled. "Just what I needed. You look at the queen of the wood one way, and she's beyond wicked. Stealing children, making humans get lost in her world. Look at her another way—and there's a different story."

"Maybe, maybe not," I murmured. "That's what all those old tales say. Maybe this is what happened, maybe that. Something happened, that's what we know for sure. The story changes every time you take another look at it. It changes into what you need most at the moment you choose to look at it."

Tyler was silent again, maybe swallowing that, maybe not. He only said, "Nothing really changed. My dad is still dead. Grandpa Liam is still dead. My mom is still married to Patrick. What's different is that I can see things a little more clearly. Like when I get a new pair of glasses. I see what I've been missing."

"I know that feeling."

"Really? I thought you already had everything figured out."

"I only thought I did."

"Well, how can you tell the difference between thinking you do and really doing it?"

"You can't. You can't see what you can't see until you can see it."

"Well, how do you—" He gave up, smiling. "Never mind. I guess you have to be there."

"You will," I promised him. "You'll outgrow Patrick so fast he'll be missing that green-haired boy before he realizes he never knew you."

Tyler grunted. "I'm thinking of bleaching it. Judith said that'd look cool with my black eyebrows."

"There. You see?"

"See what?"

Judith, I thought. Fashion. Passion. "You're already on your way beyond Patrick."

Gram didn't call a guild meeting the next month. She needed to think, she said. She needed some peace and quiet, is what she told the incredulous members who called to remonstrate. They were the ones who hadn't seen Gram's confrontation with the wood. All they knew was that for the first time in a hundred years, there was no monthly meeting. It was, Jane told Gram, as if the moon had decided not to rise on that night. But it was a comment, not a criticism; she understood as well as Gram that they needed to rethink their stitches. Gradually the story of that night made its rounds, over cups of coffee, in the supermarket parking lot, at the Village Grill, where Genevieve passed what she had seen to discerning customers, along with mugs of beer and burger baskets.

"I'm glad Iris is thinking about it," she told me when I stopped in one slow evening and we had the bar to ourselves. "I wouldn't want to make that decision. I mean, that Tyler-clone turned into a tree stump right in front of me. I don't know how far we can trust them. But if I never had to crochet another baby bootie, I'd be beyond ecstatic."

Gram finally talked about it with me, when we sat out on the porch one tranquil night, smelling the roses and watching the coracle moon sail above the pear tree.

"I can understand it better now," she said abruptly, out of nowhere, I thought, but I was wrong.

"What, Gram?"

"Why Liam loved to ramble. He was never afraid. The wood was never something to be kept tied up in stitches. Water was just water; it didn't have to be guarded, feared for, mistrusted. It was just something lovely going its own way under the stars. I could never see those fireflies without wondering what they were hiding. Or pass a hollow tree without trying to remember whose stitches were guarding it. I still do. But now I find myself looking at it the way Liam might have. Wondering, if I stepped inside the hollow, what I'd feel, or smell, or hear. If for an instant, I'd think like that tree."

I smiled at the thought of Gram inside a tree. "Did he really do that?"

"Owen said he did. He'd walk in drifts of autumn leaves. He'd skip stones on water, walk on fallen trunks. He'd play in the woods like a child. All the while I fretted and counted stitches and tried to sew the world into order."

"What will you do, Gram?"

"About the Fiber Guild?" She was silent a little, gazing into the dark, listening, maybe, as I was, for the faint jingle of harness bells, for a distant voice that was neither human nor animal. "It's very old, and could be very powerful, if we need it to be. And it creates, as well as binds. I won't disband it. But maybe, for a while, we could just sew. Concentrate on what we make instead of what we control. See what happens."

"Are you going to undo all the old bindings?"

She shook her head. "There's enough wide open now. The old spells will fall apart eventually with time, if we don't need them." She paused again. "We'll see. At least, I will as long as my old threads hold together. After that, you'll have to make decisions."

"I will," I promised her. "But don't be in any hurry to leave me. You know I can barely thread a needle."

The Fiber Guild met again the following month, on the night Madison was flying in to visit us. His class had ended; he was bringing his fishing pole, he said, his camera, his binoculars and bird books, and an assortment of instruments, including a fiddle, spoons, and a nose harp.

"Might learn a few old tunes in those mountains," he told me with enthusiasm. It occurred to me to wonder then which of us might have to drag the other away.

"Madison."

"Yes, my darling, my dear."

"Oh, never mind," I said helplessly. If he fell in love with the mountains and Lynn Hall, time would figure that one out, too. "I'll see you at the airport."

Dorian was coming with me, out of curiosity and to keep me company. Neither of us would make the guild meeting; we would pick Madison up and have dinner afterward in the city, which was a respectable way of getting out of sitting around for several hours and poking holes in a cloth with a needle. I drove over to pick Dorian up, found her and Owen both in the nursery. It was Saturday, and there were still customers, buying late-blooming mums, and bulbs, and whatever produce had ripened in the nursery's vegetable garden.

Dorian combed her hair with her fingers, took off her

apron, and passed it to her father. "If Leith comes by after work, tell him I'll be home before midnight," she said, and kissed her father's cheek.

"Be careful," he told us, his eyes losing their absent look for a second. "Watch out for deer."

"Always. Do you want us to pick up anything for you?"

He shook his head. He'd always been somber, but there had been a dark energy about him that I missed. Gram had noticed it, too: he had lost interest in his life. Losing Liam and then his fay love, almost at the same time, had taken the heart out of him, she guessed.

"Are you sure?" Dorian asked, fretting over him. He patted her shoulder.

"I'll make myself some supper, play a little music . . . You have fun."

The greenhouse door opened; another customer entered, stopped immediately, as they all did, to stare at the great cascades of fuchsias in their hanging pots, trailing blossoms to the ground in one last, magnificent display before winter killed them.

But this customer wasn't looking at the fuchsias. She was gazing at Owen, who was pulling out the green beans and cherry tomatoes Dorian had picked and then forgotten in her apron pockets.

Dorian passed her with a smile, not noticing anything. But I couldn't move, watching, wondering, recognizing something in her, though she looked like one of us, any of us, in her thin silk shirt and long, faded skirt. Her feet were bare, I noticed; she limped a little, taking a tentative step toward Owen. Her face had once been beautiful; now, aged a bit maybe in her translation into human, she still looked striking, with her slanted eyes as dark as autumn berries, and her hair, long and petal-smooth, streaked buttercup and ivory.

Owen saw her.

He closed his eyes. I saw him take one long breath and loose it, before he began to smile, and I went out quickly, turning the OPEN sign around as I closed the door softly behind me.

A year and a day, they had together, maybe, before she turned back into fairy. Or maybe a decade and a day. Who knew? But he would have forever the gift she gave him: she had found her way back.

And so had I.